Love Finds You

in

Miracle

KENTUCKY

Love Finds You
in
Miracle
KENTUCKY

BY ANDREA BOESHAAR

summerside
PRESS

Love Finds You in Miracle, Kentucky
© 2008 by Andrea Boeshaar

ISBN-13: 978-1-61664-076-7

All scripture quotations are taken from the King James Version of the Bible.

The town depicted in this book is a real place, but all characters are fictional.
Any resemblances to actual people or events are purely coincidental.

Cover and Interior Design by Müllerhaus Publishing Group,
www.mullerhaus.net

Published by Summerside Press, Inc., 11024 Quebec Circle, Bloomington,
Minnesota 55438

Fall in love with Summerside.

Printed in the USA.

To Heather

....

May you look over your shoulder and find

Love standing there

Where He's been all along.

IN 1777 A VIRGINIAN NAMED COLONEL BENJAMIN LOGAN came through the mountains with Daniel Boone seeking fortune. While Boone went north to found Boonesboro on the Kentucky River, Logan's trail led to the banks of a creek where he built a fort that later became Stanford, Kentucky. Around 1865, the railroad became a major part of Stanford and provided a much-needed railhead for southern Kentucky. The depot that served this railroad still stands, having been restored to its original splendor. Located just north of Main Street in Stanford, it inspired the name of The Depot Restaurant, where Meg first meets Vance. Miracle is a small rural area located outside of Stanford that was named for a prominent family in the area. Bill Miracle, a member of this family, is the mayor of Stanford. Locals pronounce the name "merkle" rather than "miracle." Though small, Miracle is a friendly Kentucky town populated by honest, hard-working people.

Andrea Boeshaar

Chapter One

....

Meghan Jorgenson's heart banged an erratic beat against her ribcage as she rushed out of the apartment that she had once considered her home. The last of her belongings filled her arms, and an unpredictable man followed on her heels. Dillon had never harmed her physically before, but Meg wasn't taking any chances.

In a word, she didn't trust him.

"Hey, where do you think you're going?"

Dillon's voice echoed in the dim hallway, but Meg didn't reply as she ran down the wide apartment stairwell. She had tried not to wake him, but she needed to retrieve her clothes from the bedroom closet—and it was ten o'clock in the morning, for pity's sake. Every normal human being Meg knew was up well before ten on a weekday morning. But not Dillon, the loser-poet, who had stayed up all night, pacing the apartment and agonizing over a simple line of prose. "My heart is a stone. My heart is a stone. My heart is a stone. . ."

Finally, Meg had replied, "And your mind is on loan—as in get out of here, Brainless, and let me get some sleep!"

Dillon had several choice expletives for her. "You're the reason I can't write. I can totally feel negative energy everywhere."

"Then go write somewhere else."

"But this is my crib, my creating space."

"*Whatever.*" Meg had turned over on the couch and pulled the blanket up over her head, relishing the thought that the apartment she shared with Dillon McDade for more than a year wouldn't be her "crib" in another twenty-four hours.

And now it was the time to get out.

"Meg, stop. Talk to me, will you?"

"Nothing to talk about." She reached her car and walked around to the driver's side. Juggling her load, she managed to open the back door. She tossed in her clothes and a small cardboard box.

"How can you up and leave? Aren't you even going to say good-bye?"

"I said good-bye to you months ago, when you brought home that sleazy waitress." She glared at Dillon, who stood in the doorway of the 1940s brick apartment building. She noted his navy gym shorts and a white T-shirt. His streaky blondish-brown hair, which he usually pulled back in a ponytail, was parted in the middle and hung to his shoulders. He looked unappealingly disheveled. What had she ever seen in this guy? How had she ever found him charming, his words stirring? Without the clouds in her eyes now, Meg saw him for what he was: a two-timing hack poet who desperately needed a day job.

"I told you that tumble meant nothing," Dillon shouted from the doorway.

"Yeah, well, it meant a lot to me. It meant our relationship was over. O. V. E. R."

He raised his hands in a helpless gesture. "Why didn't you say so?"

"You're kidding, right?" She sent him a wide-eyed stare. "I made it clear months ago that it was over between us."

"No, you didn't."

"I've been sleeping on that lumpy, sorry excuse for a couch all summer." She cocked her head. "Or has your bed been so occupied that you didn't bother to notice I wasn't in it?"

"That's a cheap shot, Meg."

"You deserve a lot worse."

A man walking by realized he'd wandered into a war zone and quickened his strides.

"Look, Meg, this is crazy. Let's not fight. I thought all was forgiven and forgotten. I swear I didn't know you felt this way."

Meg looked at him in disbelief. He didn't know? How could he have forgotten all the times she'd begged him to move out, only to have him refuse, stating that his name was on the lease along with hers and that he had his rights? So she decided she'd be the one to leave, but, unfortunately, she didn't have the immediate funds necessary and hadn't been sure of where to go. Mom said she could move in, but Meg didn't think her mother's situation was any better than the one in Chicago with Dillon. She'd begun to feel trapped. Everything in her life had seemed so hopeless.

But not anymore.

With her financial commitments fulfilled, various other obligations met, and a small sum in her purse, she was free to leave. She had a plan and a place to stay. She'd no longer be stuck in a dead-end tutoring job, hoping in vain to get into the state's public school system, and she'd no longer be Dillon's meal ticket.

The weight of the world seemed lifted from Meg's shoulders.

"No more talking. I'm outta here."

"Hey, what about the rent? It's due on the first."

"Good luck."

Dillon's face turned specter-white. "But—"

"I worked it out with the landlord. My name's off the lease."

His dark eyes now sparked with fury as he stepped from the building. He cursed her up and down while another passerby gawked at him.

Meg slipped behind the wheel of her black Honda Civic and started the engine. As she stepped on the accelerator, she glanced in the rearview mirror and saw Dillon standing on the sidewalk, bellowing obscenities at her taillights.

She grinned. Not only did he look like a raving maniac, but when the heavy glass front door had slammed shut, he'd locked himself out of the apartment building.

Maybe there's a God after all, she mused, making her way to the interstate. Once on the ever-congested tollway, she weaved through traffic. Her nerves were taut, her muscles tense. Turning on the radio, she willed herself to relax, to let the music emotionally distract her. But the intenseness of the situation she'd just left behind troubled her all the way through Indiana.

Meg recalled the day she'd been given a way out of her situation in Chicago. Grams had called from her home in Miracle, Kentucky, to inform Meg that a charter school for gifted kids in nearby Stanford was in need of a new third-grade teacher.

Meg had decided to go for it. She was both qualified and familiar with the area from visiting over the years. Grams had always been good to her, and Meg had no qualms about moving in with her until she could find a place of her own.

So she applied for the job, managed to scrape together enough money to drive to Kentucky for the interview at Fairview Academy, and wished upon every nighttime star that she'd get the job.

She did.

And now, as she drove across the bridge that spanned the wide Ohio River and spotted the blue WELCOME TO KENTUCKY sign, something soared deep inside of her. It was really happening! She'd made the break. A new life awaited her.

* * * * *

"You expectin' company, Retta?"

Squinting against the brilliant sunshine, made even brighter by the linens she pulled off the clothesline, Loretta Jorgenson saw her neighbor traipsing through the yard.

She smiled. "Well, good mornin', Tom. And yes, I am expecting company. Don't tell me you forgot. Today's the day Meggie moves in."

"That's right. Guess she won't be company for long, then, eh?" Wearing blue jeans, a white T-shirt, and a lopsided grin, Tom lowered his lanky frame onto one of the wooden benches at the picnic table.

Loretta regarded the man who'd lived next door for the past thirty years. His bristly hair had gone from blond to white over time, and a scant few wrinkles had been added to his crinkly face. Through thick and thin, he'd been a true friend to Loretta and her late husband, Jeb. But for the last couple of years, since Jeb's passing, Tom had become as much of a necessary fixture around her place as the clothesline in her backyard.

"After I make up Meggie's bed, I'm fixing me a cup of coffee. Want some?" Loretta lifted the brown wicker laundry basket and tossed a smile at Tom.

"You know I do."

"All righty, then. I'll be back in some minutes with a couple of mugs full."

Tom's grin remained plastered on his weathered face as he retrieved the pouch of tobacco from his T-shirt's breast pocket. His black pipe, with its worn brown trim, already lay on the picnic table. "I'll be here waitin'."

Loretta entered the house, the linens draped over one arm. The fresh scent of sun-dried bedding made its way to her nose. She longed to bury her face in the sheets and inhale their crisp, clean smell. When her youngest son, John Edward, was a boy, he used to insist he'd have "good dreams" whenever Loretta changed his bedding.

The remembrance made her smile and prompted her to hum "You Are My Sunshine" as she marched up the creaking staircase to the second floor. Down the narrow hallway, she turned into the bedroom on her left. Gone were the scuffed bunk beds and banged-up dressers. In their places stood a double bed, a polished oak chest of drawers, a desk, and a matching wooden chair.

How did I ever fit three boys in this house? Loretta wondered as she made up the bed for her granddaughter. It'd be nice to have somebody else in this place again. Young blood. Fresh ideas.

Loretta couldn't tamp down her anticipation.

The bed neatly made, she peeked into the much smaller room across the hall. It had once been hailed as "the single room," and each son had taken a turn occupying it. These days, the space served as Loretta's sewing room. She loved to create colorful and meaningful quilts and looked forward to making one for Meggie. Each of her seven grandchildren owned a "Queenie Quilt," or a "Queenie" for short. The quilts earned their title from an old nickname Loretta received after her third boy was born. Friends had dubbed her "queen of the house," and some still called her Queenie to this day.

Loretta smiled at the memory. Those sure were the days. Lots of hard work, but happy times just the same. Now life had slowed—so much so that Loretta had time for quilting.

Well, Meggie might be the eldest grandchild, but she'd be the last one to receive a Queenie. The quilt would have to wait until Loretta learned more about her granddaughter's hobbies and habits, likes and dislikes. They knew so little about each other, really.

Such a pity. All those wasted years.

After the divorce more than two decades ago, Meggie's mother, Tricia, moved to Louisville. From there she took off for San Diego with a military man she'd met in a local tavern. When that relationship failed, just like all the rest of them did, she moved from city to city, state to state, finally landing in Illinois long enough for Meggie to graduate from high

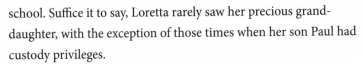

school. Suffice it to say, Loretta rarely saw her precious grand-daughter, with the exception of those times when her son Paul had custody privileges.

Even so, Loretta did her best to stay in contact.

Over the years, she had sent Meggie birthday gifts and Christmas presents, and when Meggie was awarded a scholarship at Northwestern University, Loretta often mailed her small-summed checks so she could buy a little something special for herself. Meggie always expressed her gratitude, whether it came in the form of a quick note. . .or a phone call.

But such nominal contact had never been enough for Loretta. She longed to have a close relationship with her oldest granddaughter, just like the closeness she once shared with her boys and now shared with her other seven grandchildren. She hoped her prayers would at long last be answered now that Meggie was moving in—at least temporarily.

Praise God for Fairview Academy's growth and the fact it needed more teachers. It'd been a fluke that Loretta even heard about it. She'd been getting a haircut at the same time that the principal's wife, Julia Sutterman, was getting a manicure. They began a conversation, and when Loretta learned the news, she thought of Meggie right away. Why, Meg had earned her degree in elementary education at Northwestern University—a girl had to be pretty smart to graduate among the top of her class from that place.

Julia was impressed enough to share the particulars of the job with Loretta, who was quick to tell her granddaughter about the opening. Loretta had sensed that life in Chicago didn't turn out quite the way Meggie had planned. During their occasional phone calls, Meggie had sounded so down and depressed.

But now she'd be living here, and Loretta could finally get to know her. Still, she had prepared herself in the event things didn't work out. After all, a young, independent woman might want her own apartment and more privacy than this quaint, three-bedroom, one-bathroom home afforded. But at least Meggie would have the upstairs to herself and some semblance of privacy.

She'll be here soon.

Loretta's fingers trembled with anticipation as she closed the door to her sewing room and made her way back downstairs. In the kitchen, she pulled out two mugs and poured coffee for herself and Tom. She carried the mugs outside, where Tom still sat at the picnic table, smoking his pipe.

"You know, Retta," he drawled as she set the coffee in front of him, "I think that flashin' around the chimney came loose again. I'll have to fix it before it gets cold."

"Oh, no! You're not climbing around on my roof at your age." She seated herself opposite him. "I'll hire someone."

"Won't do as good a job as me."

Tom sipped from a blue and gray mug on which the words I'D RATHER BE FISHING were boldly printed. Loretta realized that one of her boys must have left it behind, because she couldn't fathom where the thing came from.

"And I don't cost you anythin'," Tom added, "'cept maybe a home-cooked meal now and then."

Loretta grinned at her neighbor, half teasing. "What would I do if you fell off the roof?"

He shrugged. "Call 911."

"Oh, please." She sent him a glance filled with feigned exasperation. "You think the Stanford Fire Department wants to come all the way out here and waste the taxpayers' money just to save the likes of your old hide—a man who should've known better than to be climbing around on a rooftop in the first place?"

"Stop your cluckin'."

"I'll cluck if I have a mind to."

The sound of crunching gravel caused Loretta to swallow further retorts and sit up a little straighter. Seconds later her granddaughter's black compact car pulled into view and parked on the driveway.

Loretta sucked in a breath of anticipation and placed her palm over Tom's gnarled hand. "She's here."

* * * * *

Meg crawled out of her car and stretched, pulling her arms up over her head. Next she inhaled deeply of the clean country air. Almost at once, her gaze fell on Grams and an older gentleman sitting at the picnic table. Meg didn't remember the guy's name, but she did recall meeting him a couple of months ago when she'd visited and interviewed at Fairview Academy. If her memory served her right, the older man lived in the somewhat dilapidated home on the next property.

"Meggie! I'm so glad you arrived safely!"

Grams crossed the yard in seconds flat and pulled Meg into a snug embrace. The welcome brought tears to Meg's eyes. How refreshing to arrive in fresh air and a loving hug after she'd left smoggy Chicago and a nasty scream fest with Dillon.

"How was the drive?" Grams wanted to know. She stepped back but continued to hold Meg by the shoulders.

"Most of it was intense. I'm glad I stayed overnight in Louisville." Meg could have made the trip in eight or nine hours. Sooner if she hadn't gotten caught up in construction along the way. But around five o'clock the previous afternoon, hunger and exhaustion got the best of her and she stopped for the night. Besides, maneuvering the steep, winding road leading into Miracle after dark wasn't something Meg relished. "The drive from Louisville this morning wasn't bad at all."

"Good."

"Kentucky is beautiful in August. It's so vibrant and so—" She glanced around, noting the tree-covered hills looming beyond Grams' farm. "—spacious."

"We're country folk out here, but it's only about a five-mile drive into town."

"Seems longer than that."

"Only because 698 snakes up and down and all around. A body could walk to Stanford if it was a straight shot."

"No kidding about the up and down business. My ears actually popped on the way down. And I almost ran over a wild turkey."

"Welcome to the foothills of the Appalachians." Grams smiled. "I do so hope you'll be happy here."

"It can't be worse than what I left behind. Trust me."

"Oh, you poor thing."

Meg stiffened. She didn't want anyone's pity. But in the next instant she set aside her defenses and returned her grandmother's embrace. She'd lived with her guard up for so long she almost didn't know how to react to genuine caring and affection. "Thanks. That's exactly what I need."

After receiving another firm hug, Meg pushed out a smile. Grams reminded her of a slimmer version of the Southern culinary expert Paula Dean, with perceptive yet gentle blue eyes, platinum hair, and wide, happy smile.

"Can I help you carry anything into the house?"

"Um—" Meg thought of everything she owned, crammed into her trunk and back seat. She didn't feel like facing it all at the moment. "No, I'll unload later."

"You sure? Tom can help us."

Tom! That's his name! Meg grinned. "Let's put it off awhile." She spied the mugs on the picnic table. "I'd love a cup of coffee."

"Well, we got that all right. C'mon over and set yourself down." Wearing a broad smile, Grams clapped a solid, capable arm around Meg's waist and led her into the backyard. "You remember Tom, don't you?"

"Yep." She smiled a greeting at the older man.

"Good to see you again, Meggie." He inclined his head politely and puffed on his pipe.

Meg was reminded of an old cowboy as she took in the tanned complexion and the lines of time etched into Tom's face. She imagined he'd make a fitting character in an old Western movie. All he needed was a dusty trail and a sunset behind him.

Grams placed her hands on her hips. "How do you like your coffee?"

"With a little cream and sugar."

"Okay, then, I'll be right back."

Grams entered her white clapboard home while Meg ambled around the back yard to stretch her legs. The yard itself was well groomed, but the land surrounding it was overgrown with long grass, weeds, and wildflowers. When Meg was little, she recalled seeing cows grazing in what was then the pasture. There had been roosters, chickens, goats, and sundry other creatures on this farm, too.

Grams returned, coffee cup in hand, and Meg joined the older couple at the picnic table.

"Where are you from, Tom?" Meg had to admit that she hadn't given the old guy much thought before today. He'd been her grandparents' friend for as long as she could remember, but she'd had to manage so much drama in her life since she was a kid that she'd never bothered to get to know him.

"I'm from next door," he said, misinterpreting her question.

"So, Kentucky born and raised?"

"Oh, no, no, no. I grew up in the Colorado-Wyoming area. A rancher and cowhand."

Yep, he fit the part, all right. Meg smiled.

"Meggie spent a lot of her growing-up years in California," Grams offered.

"Well, then, we're practically family." Tom sent her a wink, and Meg found him rather charming for a leathery ol' cowboy.

"So how did you end up in Miracle, Kentucky?"

"That's a long story, missy. You sure you want to hear it?"

"Of course she doesn't." Grams' blue eyes twinkled with the jest. "You'll bore us to tears and we've got work to do." She leaned across the table towards Tom. "I want to help get Meggie unpacked and settled before we take her out to eat tonight."

Tom nodded without a trace of insult evident on his grinning countenance.

"We're going out to eat tonight?" Meg looked from Grams to Tom, then back to her grandmother again.

"Your gramma and I go out to eat ever' Friday evening. It's a regular habit with us."

"We're hoping you'll join us tonight." A wide smile split Grams' tanned face. "Tom and I might be old folks, but we sure know how to have a good time."

"And your coming along has nothing to do with Loretta wanting to show off her pretty granddaughter to all her friends, either," Tom added with a mischievous grin.

"Oh, you hush." Grams waved a hand at him.

Meg felt deeply flattered. "Well, sure, I'll come along."

Tom replied with a satisfied incline of his head and then puffed on his pipe.

"Come with me, hon." Grams stood. "Let's start unloading your car. As you can see, I'm anxious to get you settled in."

Meg pushed to her feet and gave Tom a parting smile.

As she trailed her grandmother to the car, she felt a sense of calm drape over her. She reveled in hearing the sounds of summer: the birds twittering in the leafy treetops and the insects buzzing in the tall grasses beyond Grams' neatly mowed yard. The azure sky seemed so close, Meg wanted to reach out and grab it. What a stark contrast to the smog and city noise she'd grown accustomed to, cars honking, people shouting.

In that moment, Meg dared to wonder if she could clamp on to this peace and make it her own.

Chapter Two

....

Meg entered her grandmother's home with her duffel bag's strap slung over her shoulder. Glancing around the sunny yellow kitchen, she wished she'd been able to spend more time here as a kid. When she had visited, it had always been during holidays, and this two-story country home with triangular twin dormers, gingerbread trim, and wrap-around porch was crammed with relatives whom Meg barely knew. Her visit two months ago had been the first time she'd been able to absorb the sights and sounds without distraction.

The clocks. Meg wasn't sure whether she should grin or grimace as she made her way up the narrow, enclosed stairwell.

When she interviewed for the teaching position at the grade school last June, Meg had stayed overnight with Grams. She'd been mesmerized by the clock collection. There were small clocks, large clocks, bird-shaped clocks, flower-shaped clocks, cuckoo clocks, and even a "music in motion" clock that played Broadway tunes. There were clown-shaped clocks, wall clocks, and mantel clocks, many of which chimed, whistled, rang, and sang. Every hour, on the hour, a bizarre cacophony filled the house. During her last visit, Meg wondered if she'd get a decent night's sleep with all the ticking and gonging going on. The next morning, however, Meg was surprised to discover she'd slept as hard as stone.

Of course, almost anything was better than that lumpy sofa in her apartment and the noise from the busy street below.

Make that her *former* apartment.

Meg walked into the bedroom that would be hers for the next ten months and set down her heavy duffel on the hardwood floor. Grams said this was the very room in which Meg's dad had fallen asleep, night after night, as a boy. A wave of melancholy enveloped her, just as it had the last time she'd been here. She wished she knew her father better. He'd remarried long ago, and he and his wife, Donna, had two kids, Kelly and Ryan. Meg had never felt truly welcome in her dad's home, and her half siblings had always seemed to regard her as an oddity. But as much as it hurt, Meg couldn't blame them. Two weeks a year just hadn't been enough time to really find out what made her father and his family *tick*.

Meg smiled at her private quip and glanced at the portrait clock on the bedside table. The framed picture, hinged to the clock, depicted all three Jorgenson boys. Meg lifted the cherry-wood keepsake for closer inspection. Dad, the oldest, must be a teenager in this picture, but he looked much the same as he did the last time Meg saw him: short, rust-colored hair, freckled face, a tall, brawny frame.

"I hope you'll be comfortable up here."

Meg set down the portrait clock and turned to face her grandmother. "I'm sure I'll be fine."

Grams lowered the square box she carried from Meg's car to the floor and glanced at the picture of her sons. "I was just thinking before you arrived how amazing it is that your grampa and I raised three boys in this house. These bedrooms seem barely large enough for one person, let alone three husky fellows. Why, your uncle John and aunt Carley have a house three times this size and only two children—and one of them's in college!"

"I think life, in general, has gotten bigger." A rueful grin tugged at the corners of Meg's mouth. "But bigger isn't better. I'll bet Laura Ingalls Wilder got a better education in her one-room schoolhouse than most kids get in their giant, brick, public schools." She sighed. "And please don't get me wrong. I'm not blaming the teachers. Most are devoted to helping their students learn."

Grams appeared to understand. "Sometimes big schools, like big cities—and big churches, too—lose that personal touch that's so vital."

Meg personally felt the public school system might be lacking more than the "personal touch," but she figured it was wasted energy to dwell on the subject a moment longer.

"Maybe you'll find living here and teaching at Fairview Academy more rewarding."

Meg's hope was rekindled. "I know I will. Nothing could be worse than this last year. The majority of kids I worked with were rebellious hoodlums who didn't want to learn. Most parents didn't care. The teachers were powerless—" Meg bit off the rest of her sentence. "Sorry, Grams, I didn't mean to drone on like that."

"Hon, it's all right. I sensed your frustration last spring when we talked about it on the phone." Grams regarded Meg askance. "And speaking of last spring, what's going on with that boyfriend of yours?"

"Dillon?" Meg wagged her head. "It's completely over between us. I'm disappointed with the way things turned out, but I know I made the right decision to leave him."

"Good for you." A wry grin curved Grams' pink lips. "You're better than the likes of that boy. If he really loved you, he'd have married you."

"Or at least been faithful and committed to our relationship."

"Well, yes—"

A heavy sadness settled over Meg. "I wanted to forgive him, Grams, but he wasn't sorry for hurting me so there was no guarantee it wouldn't happen again. I guess I just want more than Dillon could offer."

"Are you still hurt, hon?"

"A little, but I'm more relieved that I'm away from him and my former job. I'm glad to be out of that apartment, and—" She took a deep breath. "—and I'm glad to be here."

"I'm glad, too."

Meg regarded her grandmother and a swell of gratefulness rose inside. Last spring she'd told Grams about catching Dillon with that cheap trick he'd brought home from the coffee shop. At first Meg wondered if her grandmother would think badly of her for living with a guy when they weren't married. She knew Grams was a deeply religious person. But to Meg's surprise, her grandmother had lent a compassionate ear—and a sturdy shoulder on which Meg cried her heart out.

"Okay, where do y'all want this stuff?" Tom entered the room with two more boxes and several garments on hangers draped over the tops of them.

"Set them down anywhere. I'll unpack later." Meg smiled at the wrinkly faced man. She sensed he had a heart as wide as the Grand Canyon. "Thanks."

"You betcha." Tom lowered the cardboard boxes onto the polished floor with scarcely a *thud*. "I think that's all of it."

Meg stared at her belongings. "My entire life packed up into four boxes, a duffel bag, and about a dozen hangers." She shook her head. "Pathetic to think this pile is all I have to show for my twenty-six years on this planet."

"Oh, now, Meggie, you're startin' over here," Grams said, a worried little frown creasing her forehead, but then a slow smile crept across her face. "Just think of how much room you'll have in your closet for all the new things you're going to buy."

Meg had to smile also. "Always looking on the positive side. I need that. I need to turn around my thinking."

"Then you've come to the right place." Tom leaned against the white door frame and folded his arms.

"Yes, I believe I have." Meg smiled at Tom, then at her grandmother. At that moment, she realized how desperately she needed their encouragement.

"Well, we'll leave you to unpack," Grams said. "Tom and I like to go to dinner about five, so that gives you all afternoon to get settled."

"Okay." Meg eyed the soft-looking double bed, thinking maybe a short nap was in her future. After months of sleeping on the couch, she was in a state of physical and emotional exhaustion.

Grams stepped forward and wrapped Meg in another maternal embrace.

Affection—Meg decided she could use a good dose of that, too.

* * * * *

"Daddy, I want macaroni and cheese for dinner."

Cammy Bayer put her hands over the rubber-covered wheels of her chair and propelled herself out of the kitchen and down the bare floor of the hallway. She rolled past the portrait of her mother, hanging on the wall. Everybody said she looked like Mommy. Same wavy black hair and blue eyes. Cammy liked to stare at Mommy's picture and remember things, like Mommy singing in the choir at church or reading a bedtime story. Sometimes, if Cammy closed her eyes really tight and tried really hard, she could still hear the sound of Mommy's voice, telling her to come in from playing outside and wash up for supper. But it was getting harder and harder to remember.

Maneuvering her chair into the living room, Cammy halted several feet inside the doorway. Daddy sat on the sofa doing nothing. Just sitting there with his legs crossed so one ankle rested on the opposite knee. He looked sad, like he was trying to remember Mommy too, and Cammy wished she could say something to make him happy again.

"Daddy?"

"What?" His gaze slid over to her.

"What's the matter, Daddy? Is your shoulder sore from lifting stuff? I can give you a shoulder rub."

"No, punkin, my shoulder is fine." He expelled a long sigh, stood, and stretched out his tall frame. "I'm just tired."

Cammy tipped her head and gave her dad a once-over. She loved and felt proud of her father. He was the most handsome man in all of Kentucky, tall and strong, with hair the color of walnuts. He had a mustache and a beard that didn't cover his whole face, just grew around his mouth. His whiskers tickled her, too, whenever Daddy kissed her cheeks and neck.

But Daddy wasn't playing today. Since coming home from his job this afternoon, he had taken a shower and put on clean clothes. Maybe company was coming. Cammy only hoped it wasn't Mrs. Foster.

Cammy mimicked her dad's sigh, deciding she, too, felt tired—but not like Daddy. Cammy felt tired from doing nothing all day. While he worked, she had to stay with Aunt Debbie, and it was boring, boring, boring! All Aunt Debbie liked to do was watch TV and play her music so loud that Cammy had to cover her ears. Cammy felt disappointed that she didn't get to play outside today. Aunt Debbie said there was nothing a girl like Cammy could do outdoors, except she was wrong, wrong, wrong. Daddy sometimes took her to the park, the way he used to before the accident, and lifted her into one of the swings. That was fun, but Cammy supposed Aunt Debbie wasn't as strong as Daddy. Besides, Aunt Debbie had Tyler, who was five years old and as bad as any boy could be. This afternoon he snuck into the garage and dumped out some old paint. Aunt Debbie yelled for a long time, and Cammy wished Daddy would hurry up and come to get her.

She felt only too glad that twice a week she went to camp, where she got to do all kinds of fun stuff. It was a camp for kids like her—kids with disabilities. Last week they went swimming in the lake and roasted marshmallows around a campfire. Cammy liked her counselor. Her name was Ruthanne.

"Since you're tired, Daddy, I'll make dinner tonight. I know how."

"I know you do." His mustache wiggled when he smiled. "But I'm

thinking we should head over to the Depot Restaurant for supper tonight. What do you say? We'll have a daddy and daughter date. Just you and me."

"Okay!" Cammy liked to go anywhere with Daddy, and since she'd been cooped up all day, she was ready for anything. "Is it payday today?"

"No, payday is next Friday." Daddy's smile grew wider. "But I think I can scrounge up a few bucks for dinner."

"Yippee!" Cammy raised her hands like she'd seen some high school cheerleaders do whenever their team scored a touchdown.

Daddy stepped forward and knelt in front of her wheelchair. "Let's get you ready and in the van. I'm starved."

Cammy smiled. "Me, too."

* * * * *

Meg awoke to Grams' gentle shake and sweet-sounding voice. She'd slept so hard that she felt disoriented until she realized where she was.

Her new home in Kentucky.

"It's four o'clock, Meggie."

Her head in a fog, Meg felt like telling her grandmother to go eat with Tom and leave her here in bed, but she didn't want to seem impolite.

"How long do you think you'll need to get ready?"

Meg focused on Grams, noticing the lavender pantsuit she wore, and realized this wasn't a shorts and T-shirt affair. "Um, forty-five minutes should do it."

"Oh, then you've got plenty of time."

Meg forced a smile as she climbed from under the colorful patchwork quilt. Even in the warm summer air, she'd felt chilled while she slept. She smiled, thinking that in addition to love and encouragement, she needed about a month's worth of sleep.

She yawned. "Beautiful quilt, Grams. Looks like the handmade quilts the Amish sell in Ohio." Meg wondered why she hadn't noticed it back in June. Then again, she hadn't exactly been in the best frame of mind during her last visit.

"I made it." Two cherry-colored spots appeared on Grams' face.

"You made this?" Widening her eyes, Meg ran her hand over the multicolored patches of various patterns, checks, prints, and florals. "It's gorgeous."

"Well, thanks. I call it a Crazy Queenie. I used all my scraps, you know? It's a collage. Mishmash."

"Queenie?"

Grams explained how her quilts earned their name.

"You're very talented, Grams. I can sew on a button, but that's the extent of my abilities when it comes to a needle and thread."

"I do make use of my machine," Grams said with a chuckle. "Not all of it is hand-stitched. And I'm making one especially for you—a quilt, that is."

"Really?" Meg felt honored.

"Well, of course. All my grandkids have one. I'm just hoping to learn more about you before I finish yours, like your hobbies and whatnot. That way the quilt will reflect your personality."

"Oh." Meg glanced at the now-rumpled quilt on the bed. "I'd say this one suits my personality. *Crazy.*" She laughed in an attempt to cover the emotional pain she'd harbored for so long.

"Nonsense." Grams smiled and waved a hand at her. "And that ol' quilt isn't even one of my better ones. Just you wait, Meggie. The Queenie I create for you will be real special."

"Thanks." She was touched to the core. "I—I don't know what to say."

"Nothing *to* say." Grams blew her a kiss and walked to the doorway. "Hurry up and change. I'll be downstairs waiting for you."

Meg nodded as she heard her grandmother's footfalls on the creaky stairs.

Would she really make it here? This simple country living ran contrary to almost everything she'd ever known. But then, everything she'd ever known had taken her down paths that only left her feeling empty and hopeless.

Meg fought the confusion threatening to engulf her.

One day at a time, she reminded herself. The future looked a bit unsteady from her vantage point. After all, she was a city girl with a one-year contract at Fairview. Time alone would be the judge of whether the teaching position and small-town life would suit her.

Even so, the present definitely showed promise.

Chapter Three

....

Meg felt like a celebrity as Grams led her up and down the table-lined aisles of the Kentucky Depot Restaurant. The place, Meg learned, had been mentioned in such magazines as *Southern Living*, and its railroad theme made it both quaint and interesting. It was one of Grams' favorite eateries, as the owners sold her quilts among their other handmade crafts. The food wasn't bad, either. Meg had ordered the buffet and enjoyed sampling the grilled catfish, fried shrimp, turnip greens, deep-fried okra, and potato salad.

"Joanie, I want you to meet my granddaughter, Meggie." Grams' eyes sparked with pride. "She's going to be the third-grade teacher at Fairview Academy this fall."

"Well, hi, Meg, and welcome to Stanford."

"Thanks." Meg grinned at the blue-haired elderly woman with large, silver-framed glasses.

"This is my husband, Everett. . ."

Meg nodded politely as Joanie introduced him and the other couple seated at their table.

"I'm bad with names," Meg stated lamely. She'd long-since given up trying to keep everyone straight. "It'll take me awhile to remember. Please don't be offended."

"Oh, that's all right." Joanie smiled. "We don't offend that easy. We'll remind you."

"Good." Meg smiled her gratitude.

Grams tugged on Meg's elbow and introduced her to yet more people.

At long last, they made it back to their table. Tom sipped his coffee and grinned when they returned.

"I think you hit everyone in here," he told Grams. "And just in time. Dessert's on the table."

Meg stared at the slice of pecan pie *a la mode* and didn't think she could digest one more bite of food.

"Oh, look! There's Vance and little Cammy." Grams set her hand on Meg's forearm. "You absolutely must meet the Bayers. Cammy attends Fairview Academy."

"Sure." She glanced at Tom, who winked as if to say he appreciated her being a good sport.

Meg stood and followed her grandmother to a back table where a man and a wheelchair-bound little girl sat, eating their supper.

"Hello, Vance." Grams smiled at him and then at the child. "Hi, Cammy. I'd like y'all to meet my granddaughter." She pulled Meg in beside her. "This is Meghan Jorgenson, Meg for short. She's the new teacher at Fairview."

Vance stood and extended his right hand. "Good to meet you."

"Same here." Meg slipped her palm into his as her gaze took in the man's short brown hair and neatly trimmed mustache and beard. He reminded her of country singer Tim McGraw. Moving downward, she couldn't help noticing broad shoulders that shifted beneath the blue-green polo shirt he wore.

"Are you the new third-grade teacher?" the girl in the wheelchair asked.

"This is my daughter, Cammy," Vance interjected.

Meg smiled at the girl. "Third-grade teacher? Yep. That'd be me."

Cammy gasped and a look of delight spread across her face. "Then I'll be in your class! Are you a Mrs. Jorgenson or a Miss Jorgenson?"

"Miss."

"Oh, good. That means I won't get you mixed up with the *real* Mrs. Jorgenson."

Grams laughed. "I'm the real one, all right."

Meg grinned, but in spite of the easy banter, weighty questions flittered through her mind. She didn't have much experience teaching physically challenged children like Cammy Bayer. But perhaps Fairview Academy had a special needs program, and Cammy would be in her class for only one or two subjects.

Regardless, Meg couldn't help feeling flattered by the child's wide-eyed, excited stare.

She hunkered down beside the wheelchair. "How old are you, Cammy?"

"Eight."

Meg thought the girl's bright blue eyes were a stark contrast to her short, curly ebony hair. "Do you have any brothers or sisters?"

"Nope. Just me."

"Oh."

More questions swirled around Meg's head. Where was Cammy's mom? Were her parents divorced? Who took care of her? What was the nature of her disability?

Meg shook off the possible scenarios and assumptions that flew at her like mosquitoes at dusk. A moment later, she detected that certain spark of intelligence in Cammy's eyes that teachers yearn to see.

"I'll bet you're a good student."

"Uh-huh." The girl bobbed her head in a vigorous nod. "I got all As on my last report card."

"Good for you." Meg smiled. "What's your favorite subject?"

"Umm. . ." Cammy pursed her pink mouth as she thought it over. "Reading—and recess!"

Meg chuckled, but she wondered what Cammy did during recess. How did she play, and was she accepted by the other kids? Perhaps there were other disabled children at the school. It would have been nice if

Earl Sutterman, the principal, had mentioned the fact to Meg during their interview; she would have known how to better prepare for the upcoming school year.

"I like reading the best," Cammy prattled on. "I read lots of books, 'specially in the summer."

"What books have you read lately?"

"Hannah Montana books." Cammy's pale, heart-shaped face lit up. "And I read *Cold Dark Waters* and *Wild Mountain Rescue*—those two books are about the Chamberlain twins, Royce and Rebecca."

Meg stood and looked across the table at Vance. "I'm not familiar with those titles."

"Cammy gets some of her books through our church library," he explained before taking a sip of what appeared to be cola.

"Oh, I see. Are they religious books, then?"

"Christian fiction."

"Hmm." Meg gave several small nods in reply. She supposed a religious genre was appropriate for girls Cammy's age. Meg might not know where she herself stood with God—or if she even believed in God—but instilling moral values in kids today couldn't hurt, that's for sure. In fact, she wished some of her former students in Chicago would take up reading Christian fiction.

"I'll bring you one of my books so you can see it," Cammy said.

"Please do. I'll enjoy looking it over." Meg gave the girl an encouraging grin. "And I'll especially enjoy having you in my class this year."

Cammy beamed.

A woman who appeared to be several years older than Meg suddenly appeared next to Vance. Meg watched as she set her hand on his shoulder. She supposed the woman was attractive enough, but in an outdated, country-western sort of way. Big hair in various shades of blonde hung to her shoulders. Her faded jeans were snug on her hips and seemed a

mismatch for her conservative apricot blouse with embroidered trim.

"I thought you were going to call me when you got home from work today, Vance."

"My apologies." His expression changed to one of discomfort. "I decided Cammy and I needed some time together."

"You might have said so instead of keeping me waitin'." The irritation in the blonde's tone was obvious. Then she cast a glance at Meg before turning to Grams. "Well, Mrs. Jorgenson, how're you?"

"Just fine." Grams hooked her hand around Meg's elbow. "Nicole, I want to you meet my granddaughter. And, Meggie, this is Nicole Foster. She works at the PBK."

"PBK?" Meg raised her brows, curious. "Is that like the KFC?" She had noticed the different franchises when she drove into town and figured Kentucky Fried Chicken had been one of them.

Vance chuckled.

Grams grinned.

"Peoples Bank of Kentucky." Nicole brushed a few strands of hair off her forehead. She looked insulted.

"Oh, my bad." Meg hadn't meant any offense. "Obviously I have yet to learn my way around town."

Grams wisely changed the subject. "Nicole's got kids at Fairview Academy, too. How old, Nicole? I forget."

"Seven and twelve."

"Of course. I had them both in Sunday school." Grams smiled. "Well-behaved children."

"Thanks."

"It's nice to meet you," Meg said at last.

"Likewise, I'm sure."

Meg felt the chill in the other woman's reply but didn't take offense. She'd made the blunder, after all. Besides, Mom had warned her that small town folks were often wary of strangers. And why wouldn't they be?

Nicole sent them each a brief smile before turning her attention back to Vance. "Hal has the kids this weekend. How 'bout I come over later?" She sat down and leaned against Vance's arm. "I think the two of us need some time together. Cammy sees you every day."

Meg got the hint; it was time to move on. But glimpsing the dejected look on Cammy's face kept her fixed to the carpeted floor.

Did the girl feel like a third wheel? If so, Meg could relate. As a kid, she abhorred those evenings when Mom's boyfriends came over. Meg always felt so inconvenienced, and perhaps a little envious, too.

Meg hunkered down beside Cammy once more. She longed to say something cheery. "I'll be sure to plan fun things into our lessons this year, okay?"

The child's countenance brightened just a little. "Okay."

"Do you have a favorite game?"

Cammy nodded. "Clue Junior: The Case of the Missing Chocolate Cake. Daddy and I play that together sometimes." She whipped a glance across the table at him, and Meg didn't miss the scowl on Cammy's face when her gaze settled on Nicole Foster.

"Well," Grams said, "I think our *a la mode* has *a la melted* by now."

Meg pushed to her feet and laughed. "I think you're right." She smiled at Cammy again. "See you later."

"Bye, Miss Jorgenson."

After a parting grin, Meg followed her grandmother back through the comfortably crowded restaurant. They sat down at their table just as Tom took the last bite of pie.

He'd eaten all three slices!

* * * * *

Cammy thought the stars looked sparkly tonight as Daddy drove home after dinner.

"Too bad we didn't take your Sport Trac, Daddy." It was a neato blue with black trim and looked half like a truck and half like a car. And it was fast, fast, fast! "I like riding shotgun."

Daddy chuckled. "Maybe we'll take the Trac next time we go out."

"Okay."

"Did you have fun tonight?"

"No." Cammy pushed out her lower lip.

"Why not?"

"Cuz." She had wanted to go home a long time ago, but Daddy decided to stay at the Depot Restaurant and talk with Mrs. Foster. Cammy hated the way that lady leaned against Daddy and laughed, as if the two of them had a secret. Telling secrets in front of someone was rude, and if Cammy tried to get a word in edgewise, Mrs. Foster interrupted. It happened all the time. "She's not coming over later, is she?"

"What? Who are you talking about, Cammy?"

She saw Daddy glance at her through the mirror on the windshield.

"Mrs. Foster. She's not coming over, is she?"

"Not tonight."

"Good."

Daddy didn't say anything for a long while. Finally, he cleared his throat the way he always did when he had something important to say. "You know, Cammy, someday I'd like to remarry."

"You mean—Mrs. Foster?!" Cammy shrieked. She jerked forward, causing her seat belt to tighten across her chest.

"Settle down. I'm not referring to Mrs. Foster, per se. I just mean—well, I might like to get married again, that's all."

"I know, Daddy." They'd talked about this before. Aunt Debbie said Daddy needed a lady in his life, and even Grandma Liz talked about

Daddy getting married again someday. Besides, Emma Jo Hogkins down the block had two mothers, her real one and the one her daddy just married. That one was called a stepmother, except Cammy couldn't figure out why steps were involved.

"You need to accept the fact that one day there'll probably be another woman in our house." Daddy paused. "I think Mommy would want us both to be happy, and she'd want you to have a new mommy. Not to replace her. Not ever like that. Just someone to love and take care of you. The way she would have done if—"

Daddy sounded sad, and that made Cammy sad. "It's okay, Daddy. I won't mind a new mommy. Honest. As long as she's not Mrs. Foster." An idea hit. "Hey, what about Miss Jorgenson? She's not married cuz she's a 'miss,' and did you see her shoes, Daddy? They were red high heels with bows across the tops. And her dress—did you see it had strawberries on it?"

"No, I—I didn't see her shoes. Listen, Cammy, we know nothing about Miss Jorgenson, so get any notions about her and me out of your head. Besides, we're discussing Mrs. Foster right now."

Cammy scrunched up her face and stuck out her tongue.

"I can see you, young lady, and that's not nice. Now tell me why you don't like her. You've been acting up every time I go out with her."

"Mrs. Foster is rude." Cammy folded her arms.

"Rude?"

"Yeah, she acts like I'm not even there. She doesn't talk to me. She just. . .points at me cuz I'm different from her kids."

"Punkin, I think Mrs. Foster is still adjusting to you being, well, in a wheelchair." Daddy's voice turned soft and gentle. "She's not sure how to act around you because you're not like most kids." He smiled at her in the mirror. "You're a lot smarter."

Cammy smiled back. "I still don't like her."

"I know you don't and I've been thinking about things all

afternoon—about how you and Nicole can't seem to be friends."

"I tried, Daddy. It's not my fault."

"I know that, punkin, and I'm not blaming you. Not one bit. So don't ever think it, okay?"

"Okay."

Daddy let out a breath that made Cammy think he was even more tired now than before they went out to eat.

She stared at the back of his head, feeling a little bad now. "Do you like Mrs. Foster a lot?"

"Sure. What's not to like? She's pretty. She's a Christian. She's a mother, so she knows how to take care of children."

"Except for children like me."

Daddy didn't answer.

"I bet Miss Jorgenson knows how to take care of kids like me."

"We're not talking about Miss Jorgenson, Cammy. We're talking about Mrs. Foster."

"Do you love her, Daddy? Mrs. Foster, I mean."

He paused, like he had to think about it for a moment. Finally, he said, "No, I don't love her."

"Whew, that's good." Cammy's shoulders sagged with relief. If he did, she thought she might have to be like the Chamberlain twins and run away. They tried to locate their grandparents so they didn't have to live with their mean uncle anymore.

But Daddy wasn't ever mean. Mrs. Foster, on the other hand—now, *she* was mean! Cammy could tell. Once she stared at Cammy really hard after Daddy said he had to drive her to camp and pick her up again so he couldn't go to a party the bank was having. Mrs. Foster didn't like that; she wanted Daddy to go to the party with her.

"Cammy, I don't think I'll ever really love another woman, not the way I loved Mommy. I guess that's the real reason I don't see myself with

Nicole. It's got nothing to do with you."

What Daddy said somehow made her feel both happy and sad.

"I don't want you to worry. I won't even see Nicole anymore if it bothers you."

"It bothers me."

Daddy chuckled. "Did you have to think about that?"

"No."

He laughed again.

Cammy frowned. She wasn't sure what was so funny.

"Listen, Cammy, you're my daughter and you're the most important person in my life, next to God. I love you very much. I've prayed that you and Nicole would be friends, just like I've prayed that I'd fall in love with her. But it's just not happening."

"Good."

"Cam-my—"

She heard the ring of warning in her father's voice. "I don't hate her, Daddy," she quickly amended. "I know hating somebody is a sin. I just don't like her very much."

"I get the message."

Cammy worked her lower lip between her teeth while thinking over everything her father said. "So Mrs. Foster isn't going to be your girlfriend anymore?"

"No. Not anymore."

"You mean you're not going to take *forever* when you go to the bank to cash your paycheck now?"

"No, I'm not going to take 'forever' in the bank anymore."

"I heard Aunt Debbie say she's got direct deposit. Maybe you could get it, too, and then you'd never have to even say 'hi' to Mrs. Foster except if you saw her at church."

"Listen here, missy, I'll handle the banking any way I see fit. Got it?"

"Got it." Cammy knew she'd crossed the line. She gulped down the rest of her great ideas.

Daddy turned the van to the right. They were almost home. He drove up the hill on their street and turned into the driveway.

Coming to a stop, Daddy pushed the button on the remote above his head and the garage door opened. He pulled the van in and parked.

Cammy waited as he climbed out and slid open her door. Next, he pulled down the metal ramp while she did her job of unfastening her wheelchair and pulling back its brakes. Then Daddy eased her down the ramp, and, taking hold of the handles in back of her wheelchair, he pushed her into the house.

All the while Cammy cheered in silence. *Daddy isn't going to date Mrs. Foster anymore. Yay! Yay! Yay!*

Chapter Four

....

Shadows danced across the living room as Vance lowered his weary body into the equally worn armchair. He relished these precious few moments of quiet and solitude. His muscles began to unwind from the day's tension.

Sometimes his life felt like a carnival ride, going round and round, spinning faster and faster. His job as a small engine repairman kept him plenty busy by day, and Cammy consumed the rest of his time. Seeing to her basic needs was a full-time job in itself, and getting her to bed each night was no simple feat, either. Between her disability and her continual chatter, Vance was exhausted by the time he kissed her good night and turned out the light. And as he closed his daughter's bedroom door, he often paused in front of the portrait of Angie that hung in the hallway, wondering why God took her home. He missed his wife, and Cammy needed her mother. He often felt so inadequate as a single parent, as Cammy's sole caregiver.

Of course, there were days when Vance wasn't sure who took care of whom, because Cammy was more capable than many eight-year-olds who weren't confined to wheelchairs. She folded the clean laundry, washed dishes, and made macaroni and cheese right out of the box better than anybody he knew. She was smart. Brilliant, in fact. And sweet. She cared about others—everyone except for Nicole Foster anyway.

He couldn't help the grin twitching his lips as he added "opinionated" to the list of his little girl's attributes.

Vance sank his body deeper into the armchair that once belonged to his father. Sometimes it helped to sit here and wonder how Dad would have handled any given situation if he were still alive.

The wisdom chair.

The year after losing Angie, he lost his parents—Dad to prostate cancer and, a few months later, Mama to a massive heart attack. Some folks at church said Mama really died of a broken heart after watching Dad suffer with an illness he'd battled a decade before. He'd been cancer-free for years, until one day it was back and suddenly Dad was dying. Mama and Dad loved each other. Completely. The way Vance loved Angie. Theirs was the kind of *made-for-each-other* that only happened once in a lifetime.

He pondered his relationship with Nicole. They'd been seeing each other on and off all summer long.

His mind backtracked further and he recalled what a scandal it had been years ago when her husband ran off with her sister, leaving Nicole to support their two kids. Some of the older church members didn't want to speak to her; it was as if they'd branded her with the scarlet letter D for Divorcee. Other folks pitied her, and still others offered their assistance.

At the time of her divorce, Vance had been too wrapped up in his own hectic life, working and caring for his injured and disabled daughter. That time was a black hole in his life, it seemed.

But then, on this past Easter Sunday, Nicole sat down beside him, looking prettier than the lilies on the altar. It was only then that Vance remembered she was a single parent, too. He wasn't really up on the whole dating scene; he'd been a married man for most of the last nine years. The very idea of dating felt awkward. Vance felt unsure of himself. It took him awhile, but he finally found the gumption to give Nicole a call and ask her out to dinner and a movie. She accepted.

Ever since, Vance entertained the thought that they were suited for each other, two hard-working people who survived the loss of a loved one, be it through death or divorce. Although Nicole made for good company—she liked to talk and Vance was a pretty good listener—she'd never captured his heart. His interest, yes. But not his heart.

He'd been hoping that, in time, he'd come to love Nicole. Sure, he had Jesus in his heart and Cammy filled a great deal of his life, but Vance knew firsthand the completeness to be found in marriage, and he longed to experience it again. Sometimes it hurt to be around his buddies and their wives, particularly if he happened to glimpse a couple sharing a kiss or holding hands. At least a steady girlfriend made those moments tolerable.

However, Cammy had strong feelings the other way, and no matter what Vance did or said, she didn't warm up to Nicole. His little girl hardly "ruled the roost" as Nicole once suggested; rather, his daughter's happiness was more important to Vance than his own. Cammy had gone through enough trials and tribulations at her young age.

Looked like he and Nicole were history.

History. The word conjured up the idea of school, and a vision of Fairview Academy's new third-grade teacher entered his mind. Meghan Jorgenson was easy on the eye, that's for sure, with her honey-blond hair and trim but generous figure. She'd turned quite a few heads at the Depot tonight. And her little black dress, dotted with strawberries, had elicited a number of complimentary remarks from several men in the place.

Nicole, on the other hand, had nothing good to say about her. "I didn't vote for her, but obviously some of the parents in our school did. I heard she's just like her mother," she'd whispered to Vance. "No morals whatsoever."

Vance raised the point that she'd passed interviews and background checks. If she had a blemished past, she wouldn't have gotten the teaching job. He added the fact that everyone knew Loretta Jorgenson was a sweet, Christian lady who wouldn't allow Meghan to live with her if she wasn't a decent person. Meghan's dad, Paul Jorgenson, and his family were good folks, too.

But Nicole didn't want to hear it. She stood her ground. And Vance let the matter go because he didn't feel like arguing.

Nicole. Vance squeezed his eyes closed. *Lord, what do I do about this woman?*

He could tell that she felt more serious about their relationship than he did, and although he knew he'd never love another woman again as he had loved his first wife, he had been willing to settle for a comfortable marriage so Cammy would have a mother. But it was obvious that Nicole would never fill that role in his daughter's life.

Still, he didn't want to break the woman's heart.

Vance recalled a line of scripture that his dad was fond of spouting: "A just man follows in integrity and his children are blessed." Dad usually meant it as a reminder to Vance and his sister that they ought to be grateful. But somehow it helped bring Vance's priorities back into focus now.

Cammy's emotional well-being came before Nicole's feelings.

Sitting forward, he stood and stretched. Then he strode across the room and turned out the light. As he picked his way through the dark, silent house, he was reminded of a passage from the book of Psalms: "Thy word is a lamp unto my feet. . ."

Suddenly, his footsteps were sure and his spirit a little lighter. In that moment, he knew he'd made the right decision.

* * * * *

"Meggie? Meggie, wake up."

The sound of Grams' voice and the persistent, gentle shaking of her shoulder dragged Meg from a sound sleep. She rolled over and peered up into her grandmother's hovering face.

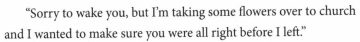

"Sorry to wake you, but I'm taking some flowers over to church and I wanted to make sure you were all right before I left."

Meg stretched, feeling confused. "All right? Of course I'm all right."

Grams smiled and straightened. "Well, honey, it is two o'clock in the afternoon."

"What?" Meg bolted upright. "Oh, wow, I didn't mean to sleep that long."

Grams patted her shoulder. "You obviously needed your rest."

Meg couldn't argue. These last months with Dillon had taken their toll on her, emotionally and physically.

"I have a little surprise." Grams lowered herself onto the edge of the bed. "Your dad, Donna, Ryan, and Kelly are coming for dinner. Your dad said they'd be here about four o'clock, but he's usually late."

"They're coming here?" Meg didn't know if she felt up to the visit from her father and his "other family."

"They're anxious to see you again."

"Anxious, huh?" She nodded. "Yeah, I can believe that."

Grams smiled and patted her hand. "Anxious as in they can't wait. Your dad wants to welcome his oldest daughter to Miracle."

Meg had her doubts. He never seemed all that welcoming before.

"Your father said they'll be here right after Kelly and Ryan are done giving their riding lessons. Teaching must run in the family. The kids teach riding to younger children every Saturday."

"Riding?" A moment later Meg remembered. "Oh, right. They're into horses, aren't they?"

Grams chuckled softly. "This is Kentucky, my dear."

"As in 'The Run for the Roses.' I got it." Meg grinned.

Grams smiled, too, as she stood and smoothed the crinkles from her soft, chambray capri pants. "Well, I'd best be going. Tom's driving me to church so I can decorate the altar for tomorrow's service. Some of us ladies take turns showing off our late summer blooms. But I'll be home in time to make supper."

Meg's stomach rumbled at the mention of food, and that, combined with the delicious aroma wafting upstairs from the kitchen, made her mouth water.

As if divining her thoughts, Grams said, "There's a pan of cinnamon buns downstairs and some coffee, too."

"I'm starved. You're fabulous, Grams."

"Why, thank you."

Meg glimpsed her grandmother's pleased expression at the simple compliment, and for some odd reason, it made her feel happy.

She tossed the covers aside and climbed out of bed. Padding to the windows, she pushed open the frilly curtains and pulled up the room-darkening shades. Sunshine poured into the room. After a moment to focus, a sapphire sky met her gaze, birds twittered in the fragrant magnolia tree in Grams' front yard, and Meg thought that if there was ever an idyllic and picturesque moment in time, this had to be it. Such a pity she'd slept away most of this incredible summer day.

Moving away from the windows, she made her way downstairs. After a quick shower, she went back upstairs to dress and then descended the creaky staircase once more. She entered the kitchen, poured herself a cup of hot coffee, and judged by its fresh aroma that Grams had prepared it right before coming to awaken her.

Meg sipped the hot, strong brew and decided she didn't mind her grandmother's maternal ways a single bit. It was actually refreshing. Mom didn't have a motherly bone in her body. Meg had been the responsible one ever since she could remember.

Mom, the quintessential party girl. For whatever reason, that lifestyle had never appealed to Meg. She'd always had the ability to look ahead, and she knew the party was going to end someday. And then what? Mom might find herself alone with nothing when she got to be Grams' age. But Meg wanted more. Meg desired to be established somewhere, to make a contribution to this world, whether great or small, to find inner peace, and to be surrounded by people who loved her.

Was that asking too much out of life?

Meg meandered into the sunny dining room when suddenly every clock in the house began to chirp, chime, and gong. The mechanical clamor startled her, but it felt so surreal to be standing in the midst of the weird symphony and she had to laugh aloud. Talk about being surrounded!

She shook her head, smiling.

By the time the last bird cuckooed, Meg had seated herself in a comfy position on the outdated, oversized plaid couch. Setting her coffee on the oak side table, she used both hands to shake out her long hair and help it dry. Another hour and her father would arrive.

Was he really coming by to welcome her? Or did he intend to let her know that her presence wasn't appreciated? Did he think she'd try to hit him up for money or that she was sponging off of Grams? She'd been told Dad accused Mom of trying to "squeeze every dime" out of him. Did he think the same of Meg?

She couldn't guess. She hadn't seen her father in years, even though his horse farm was only about four miles away from Grams' house and right down Spice Ridge Road. When Meg was a kid, he had seemed strict, unrelenting. Mom hated Dad—perhaps because he'd remarried and found happiness while every one of Mom's relationships sooner or later fell apart. And Meg? She had always tried to stay out of their way, to avoid getting caught in the crossfire.

Meg lifted her coffee mug, took a sip, and continued contemplating. Then, ever so slowly, a book resting on the end table next to the wooden rocker came into focus. The volume's worn leather cover had caught her eye. Meg stood and walked a few paces to the table and read the book's title: *Daily Strength for Daily Needs*. Lifting it, she flipped through the pages and realized she held a collection of motivational readings. Curiosity caused her to turn to today's date. Like the horoscope in the daily newspaper.

Beloved, if our heart condemn us not, then have we confidence toward God (1 John 3:21).

Meg wasn't sure what that meant, exactly. She pondered the verse's meaning for several moments before her gaze was drawn to the poem on the preceding page.

THOU art my King—
My King henceforth alone;
And I, Thy servant, Lord, am all Thine own.
Give me Thy strength; oh! Let Thy dwelling be
In this poor heart that pants, my Lord, for Thee!
                              G. Tersteegen

The piece read like something out of a Shakespearean play. Dillon could definitely take a few lessons from this guy, Tersteegen. Dillon's poetry mirrored Mother Goose, hardly William Shakespeare. How had she ever thought Dillon's work was intellectually stimulating, soul-stirring?

Her mind whirred and the muscles in her chest constricted with memories of her painful past until a line on the page in her hands jumped out at her, capturing her attention.

Give me Thy strength. . . .

It dawned on her then that she could use a little Divine Intervention about now, and she read the words over again, voicing them out loud. "Give me Thy strength; oh! Let Thy dwelling be in this poor heart. . ."

She closed the book and replaced it on the table. Seconds later, she heard a car pulling up Grams' unpaved driveway. Making her way to the windows, she peered outside and caught sight of the silver gray Suburban. Her heart pounded with uncertainty.

Dad and his family had arrived.

Chapter Five
....

"Retta, you're acting as squirrely as I ever seen you."

"What? Why, that's not true. I'm just—well, I'm excited about Paul coming over and I'm happy about Meg staying at the house. That's all."

Tom disagreed by chortling. Loretta ignored him and concentrated on arranging the pile of begonias in two matching cut-glass vases. She decided the mix of pink and white blossoms would grace each side of Calvary Hill's altar in a way that would justify all those hours of back-straining weeding she'd done all summer.

As if divining her thoughts, Tom said, "Jenny Jenkins is gonna be right jealous when she sees those fine flowers up there."

Loretta grinned, feeling pleased. She glanced over the tops of the begonias and peered at her friend and neighbor. He sat in the front pew wearing a white ribbed A-shirt and faded denim jeans with holes worn clear-through to his skinny old knees. When Jeb was alive, Loretta would never have allowed him to leave the house looking like such a mess. But Tom wasn't her husband, and she had no right to tell him what he should and shouldn't wear. He'd been good enough to drive her over here to church; otherwise, she would've had to move Meg's car and back her own sedan out of the garage. Besides, Tom put on his good clothes every Friday night when they went to the Depot Restaurant for supper, and he always looked nice on Sunday mornings.

"You're staying to dinner tonight, aren't you?" she asked him.

"That's the third time you asked me, and all three times I told you yes." Tom sported a jovial grin, adding more lines to his already crinkled face. "If that's not squirrely, I don't know what is."

Loretta tamped down her impatience with the man and realized he might even have a point. "Maybe it's a female thing."

"Usually is," he quipped.

"Oh, stop." She cast him an annoyed glance before sticking a few more stems into one of the vases. "You know it's my prayer that Kelly and Ryan come to know and love Meg. It's only right. She's their older sister."

"Half sister."

"Sister, just the same."

Tom didn't retort.

"As for Paul, well, he's finally acknowledging what a beautiful, successful woman Meg is. I almost dropped the phone when I heard him say he's proud of her. I told him he needs to tell Meg that." Loretta paused. "You know he's always been afraid she'd end up like Tricia, moving from man to man and city to city."

"Well, now, Loretta, I don't have to tell you that some things you just can't force. Relationships is one of 'em."

"I am not forcing anything."

"Okay, you're nudging then."

She pulled back her chin as indignation pulsed through her veins. "And what's wrong with that, Tom Haynes?"

"Oh, I dunno." He lifted his tanned, bony shoulders. "Guess it all depends on where the nudging is headed. Off a cliff? Now that'd be a bad sort of nudging."

"No one is going to get hurt by my nudging if that's what you're insinuating. It's my duty as matriarch to keep my family in touch with one another."

"Matriarch, huh?" He gave a snort of amusement.

"Well, that's what I am."

He took a moment to mull it over. "S'pose you are."

A weighty silence filled the small sanctuary, and Loretta sensed Tom's opposition to her reconciliation efforts. But just like she wouldn't tell him how to dress, he wouldn't tell her how to run her family affairs. At this stage in life, they both knew better. Besides, she was doing the right thing.

She finished with the flowers and placed each vase on the altar with the utmost of care. Then she stepped back and allowed herself a few moments to admire her handiwork. Make that God's handiwork. He, of course, created those lovely begonias, so sturdy and forgiving. She had merely planted, watered, and weeded.

"All set to go home?"

Loretta turned to find Tom standing, waiting for her.

She smiled. "All set."

* * * * *

Meg watched from the window as her dad and his other family emerged from their SUV. Both his kids, teenagers actually, had reddish gold hair, and Meg remembered them being tall and skinny. Now, however, both Ryan and Kelly had filled out in the right places, Ryan with his brawny shoulders and Kelly with her trim, shapely figure. As they walked toward the house with their parents, Meg noticed that her eighteen-year-old half-brother had surpassed Dad's six-feet-plus frame.

Her gaze shifted to Dad's wife, Donna, who looked just the same as Meg remembered, average build, murky blond hair, and a stern frown pulling at the corners of her wide mouth. She hadn't ever been the proverbial wicked stepmother. In fact, Meg realized she didn't have an opinion of Donna at all.

Sliding her focus back to her father, Meg decided he hadn't changed much, either. So far, this visit wasn't shaping up to be anything extraordinary.

Meg drew in a deep, steadying breath, steeling her emotions, before making her way through the house and into the kitchen.

Dad entered through the back door first. "Well, Meggie, it's good to see you." He captured her in a brief bear hug that made her lose her balance when he released her.

"Hi, Dad."

"You're lookin' fine," he drawled. "Got a teachin' job in Stanford, I hear."

"That's right."

He gave a single nod. "Hope it works out for you."

"What makes you think that my new job here won't work out?" Meg picked up on his doubtfulness and felt her already shaky confidence wane.

A moment passed and she remembered her siblings. She peered around Dad and lifted one hand in silent greeting.

"Hi," they both muttered in unison.

Seconds later Donna strolled into the kitchen, carrying a casserole dish. Setting it on the table, she glanced at Meg. "Well, well! Look at you, standing there all grown up and pretty."

Meg pushed out a smile.

"Where's your grandmother?"

"Took some flowers to church. She should be back any time now."

For several long, awkward moments, Meg watched the members of Dad's family glance at one another and then at her.

Finally Donna stuck out her hip and planted a balled fist on it. "So what's your mama got to say 'bout you movin' here to Stanford?"

"My ma—?" Meg swallowed the rest of her question, remembering that Mom, Dad, and Donna had all grown up in this area and attended the same high school. It was a well-known fact that Mom had always longed for the bright lights of the big city, and she often referred to Donna as "The Princess of Prudery." Central Kentucky, of course, was her kingdom.

"I'm sure Tricia had a few choice words about your comin' here to teach," Donna added.

"You've got that right. She said I lost my—" Meg withheld the expletive. "—lost my mind."

Her stepmom appeared genuinely amused. "I figured. Some things never change. So where's she living now?"

"Arizona. She's with a guy named Greg. He's a plumbing contractor or something like that."

"Think this time it's for real?" Donna's sincere tone surprised Meg.

She rolled her shoulders in response. "Who knows?"

No one spoke. During the prolonged silence, Meg watched Ryan amble to the fridge and pull out a pitcher of lemonade.

"I want some, too," Kelly said.

"Yeah, son, make that three." Dad caught his son's gaze. "Aw, heck, just pour five glasses."

"None for me. Thanks." Meg lifted her mug. "I'm still working on my morning coffee."

Four heads turned toward her and regarded her as if she'd grown a pair of horns.

Molten-hot humiliation crept up Meg's neck and spread across her face. "Um, I'm not lazy or anything. It's rather involved. I'm sure the story would bore you to tears."

"Well, now, I'm sure that's not true." Dad recovered first and gave her one of his easy smiles. "In fact, we'd love to hear you ramble on for a while. We're all too tuckered out for talking. Kelly and Ryan each own a horse, and after the ridin' and groomin' and cleanin' the stables—"

"Which we all do as a family," Donna put in.

Meg picked up on the word "family," and her broken heart crumbled a little bit more.

Dad just smiled. "Well, we're pretty worn out this time o' day."

"I'm sure you are." Meg hoped her voice didn't sound as cynical as she suddenly felt.

"Ryan and I give riding lessons, and we actually get paid for it."

Kelly lifted her glass of lemonade to her lips. "Do you ride, Meg?"

"No. No, I don't."

"Well, maybe I can teach you how some time. I mean, seein' as you're going to live here and we're—you know, sisters and everything."

Sisters. Meg forced herself not to gape. She had expected the cold-shoulder treatment, but instead her sixteen-year-old half sister was attempting to reach out.

"Sure. I'd like that." Meg couldn't keep the surprise out of her voice.

"Okay." Kelly drank down a good portion of her lemonade. She wiped her mouth with the back of her hand. "And then maybe you can help me shop for a homecoming dress."

"Shopping?" Meg was floored all the more. "Okay. I like shopping."

Donna cleared her throat. "Who says you're going to the homecoming dance, missy? Dad and I are still thinkin' on it."

"But, Mama, I'm sixteen now—"

"We'll discuss this later." Dad sent Kelly a look of warning. "I'm sure Meg doesn't want to listen to us have this debate right now." He clapped his beefy hands. "How 'bout we go out on the screen porch and set awhile instead?" He glanced at Meg. "When your grammaw comes home, she'll kick us out of her kitchen anyhow." He looked at his wife. "Ain't that right, honeybunch?"

"That's right." Donna smiled up at him.

With ice clinking in their now-sweating glasses, they ambled outdoors. Meg followed her stepfamily, thinking this might not be such an interminable evening after all.

* * * * *

Cammy wheeled her chair closer to the open window. Daddy and Mrs. Foster stood on the lawn, talking, and Mrs. Foster had raised her voice. She sounded mad.

"Oh, whatever, Vance. I don't believe you. 'Not meant to be'? Please! You could at least be honest with me and tell me the real reason you don't want to see me anymore."

Honest? Cammy leaned forward, straining to see through the screen. Obviously Mrs. Foster didn't know Daddy very well, because he was always honest. Whatever he said, Mrs. Foster should believe him.

"This isn't about us, is it? It's about *her*." Mrs. Foster pointed at the house. "You let her run your life. If she doesn't like something or *someone*, you move heaven and earth to fix it."

"You're right. I do. Because that's my responsibility as a father."

Cammy realized they were talking about her now. She moved her chair in closer, careful not to be seen through the window.

"She's spoiled, Vance."

Cammy couldn't quite make out Daddy's reply.

"You dote on her. You're not helping her learn to be independent. You're enabling her physical disabilities by giving in to her every whim."

"She's eight years old, Nicole! She's been through a lot, and she deserves to be happy."

Go, Daddy! Cammy felt a smile stretch across her lips.

"And what are you going to do in about five or six years when she starts developing as a woman?"

"Guess I'll cross that bridge when I get to it."

"You're a fool, Vance. There's no man on earth who can take care of a disabled young woman, work a full-time job, and still have any sort of normal life. I think you should reconsider that Christian group home idea. Maybe not now, but—"

"I told you before, it's out of the question. I refuse to send Cammy to an institution."

Uh-oh, Daddy sounded like he was mad now. Cammy sat up

a little straighter.

"It's hardly an *institution*. It's a group home, and it's staffed with skilled personnel. Trained women. Christian women who can care for Cammy."

"For heaven's sake, she's not a vegetable!"

"Don't you dare use that tone with me, Vance Bayer."

Cammy cringed. She didn't like hearing people argue. It scared her. Tears stung her eyes, and she rubbed them away. Mrs. Foster sure didn't understand. But Cammy did; she knew what an "instooshin" was. There were some kids at day camp from an instooshin. But they had more stuff wrong with them than just their legs not working right.

"I'm sorry." Daddy sounded sorry, too. "I think we need to leave it right there. It's a shame things didn't work out between us, but I can see that they never will."

"Oh, Vance—"

"It's no use, Nicole. I think my capability to love another woman died with Angie three years ago."

Mrs. Foster was silent for a minute, and her voice was softer when she spoke again. "You haven't given me much of an opportunity to prove you wrong, Vance. Nine or ten short weeks?"

"Any longer isn't fair to you, Nicole."

More silence.

"Come on. I'll walk you to your car."

"No, wait—please." Mrs. Foster sounded like she might cry, and Cammy felt like she'd cry right along with her. She didn't like Mrs. Foster, that was true enough, but she didn't like seeing people sad more than anything.

"It's over, Nicole. Let's both move forward."

Nobody said a word for what seemed like forever, and Cammy stretched her neck to try and see what they were doing.

Suddenly they passed by the window, and Cammy saw that Mrs. Foster was crying now. Cammy wiped away a tear of her own. Too bad Mrs. Foster couldn't learn that Cammy was able to do lots of things; she didn't have to go to an instooshin. She could take care of herself and Daddy, too. And someday, when she walked again, everybody who didn't believe it would see it for themselves.

Cammy had dreams about walking, like Joseph in the Bible who had dreams from God that came true! When it happened for real, Mrs. Foster would be sorry she said Daddy should send her away. Cammy loved Daddy and she knew he loved her right back.

Mrs. Foster's car started up, and moments later Daddy passed by the window again. Cammy had to act fast; he better not find her by the window.

She gave a hard push on the wheels and moved her chair quickly backwards. Then she maneuvered it around, banging into the table as she did so. The lamp on top of it wobbled back and forth and Cammy prayed it wouldn't crash onto the floor.

She held her breath.

Seconds seemed like hours.

Whew! She let out her breath. It didn't fall.

But just then, Daddy walked in from outside. He glanced at her and then his eyes moved to the open window. Suddenly Cammy felt her face get hotter and hotter.

"I certainly hope you weren't eavesdropping, young lady."

Cammy gulped, then crossed the first two fingers on her right hand. Her friend Sasha Donahue said it was okay to fib if you crossed your fingers, but only if you use your right hand. Not the left one.

"Well?" Daddy folded his arms. "Were you listening to my conversation with Mrs. Foster?"

Cammy shook her head. "Oh, no, Daddy. Not me."

Chapter Six

....

Morning sunshine splayed through the kitchen window and caused the cheery yellow curtains that framed it to appear almost neon.

"Wasn't it fun last night, getting together with your dad, Donna, and the kids."

"Hardly kids," Meg said as Grams refilled her coffee cup. "Ryan will graduate from high school this year."

"Amazing, isn't it?" Grams set the carafe back into the automatic maker. Then she took her seat at the table across from Meg. "It's difficult for me to believe that you're finished with high school and that you've earned your college degree. I'm so proud of you—proud of all my grandkids."

"That's very obvious, Grams." Meg smiled into her coffee before taking a drink. "As for last night, I have to admit that I enjoyed myself. Even Dad seemed to warm up as the evening progressed."

"Things are different between the two of you now. You're a grown woman."

"And I'm no longer a ping-pong between my parents."

"No. No longer that." Clouds of compassion filled Grams' gaze.

Meg forced a grin. The last thing she wanted was pity. "Well, with your help, I'm making my own way now. A new way, different from my mom—maybe even my dad, too. I believe it was Albert Einstein who said that insanity is doing the same thing over and over and expecting different results. I'm breaking free of the insanity."

Grams set her palm over Meg's hand. "You've got a good attitude: Live and learn. You're wise for your young age. Sometimes it takes folks a lifetime to come to that conclusion."

"Thanks, Grams." The compliment bolstered Meg's self-confidence, and again she felt lucky to be there.

"Anybody home?" Tom's voice wafted in from the back door. Seconds later he walked into the house.

Meg took in his neat appearance, dark gray suit, and somewhat coordinating tie. "My, my, don't you look spiffy."

He gave her an amused grin before turning to Grams. "She's got your sass. I'll say that much for her."

Meg laughed. In addition to her dad, stepmother, and half siblings, she'd become better acquainted with Tom last night, too.

Grams stood. "Want a quick cup of coffee?"

"Naw, I had my fill." He tapped the face of his wristwatch. "And I think we best be headin' over to church about now."

"We're both ready to go."

"I figured." He looked at Meg again. "With all the clocks in here, who could lose track of time?"

"For sure."

Meg and Tom shared a laugh while Grams rolled her eyes at the both of them. "Everyone's a comedian this morning."

"Hopefully the same will apply to Preacher Wilkerson," Tom quipped.

Meg continued to grin.

"Some Sundays he drones on till noon."

"Tom Haynes, that's a very disrespectful thing to say about our pastor."

"Can't help it 'cause it's true." He winked at Meg.

She smiled.

Grams clucked her tongue at him as she strode into the dining room. "I'm going to fetch my purse and then we can be on our way."

Meg pushed her chair back and collected her own small but fashionable brown handbag from the kitchen table. She slipped its skinny leather strap over her shoulder, remembering the day she'd discovered it in one of her favorite secondhand shops.

Grams returned and together they walked outside to the car. During the drive to church, Meg soaked in the lush scenery through the tinted window, happy that she'd made positive inroads with her dad and his other family last night. It was evident from their behavior that they were making an effort to get to know her, too. They seemed interested in her and what she had to say. Ryan asked questions about applying for college scholarships. Kelly talked fashion and suggested she and Meg go shopping sometime. This morning Meg awoke with a lighter heart, and for the first time, she felt like she actually belonged to the Jorgenson side of her family.

Tom pulled his older model Lincoln Town Car into the lot and parked. Meg peered at the structure. A red-brick church set on a hill with the countryside all around. A picturesque scene, for sure. But Meg still couldn't figure out why Grams and Tom made the fifteen-minute drive to this church when they passed at least ten on the way—including the church Dad and his family attended right in Miracle. Of course, theirs was more modern-looking, and Meg had learned last night that Grams and Tom felt it was too "lively" for them.

They walked to the entrance and Tom politely opened one of the white double doors while Meg and Grams stepped inside. A waft of cool air met them, and Tom muttered about the air conditioning always being set too low. Grams ignored his grumbling and led them into the sanctuary. Meg immediately spotted the little girl she'd met on Friday night. It was hard to miss her since her wheelchair was parked at the end of a pew in the center aisle.

Meg smiled as she passed by, and the child's face lit with enthusiasm. Meg couldn't help laughing to herself as she scooted into the padded pew after Tom and Grams. Even from where she sat two pews up, Meg could hear the girl begging her dad to let her sit next to her "new teacher."

"You've made quite the impression on little Cammy Bayer," Grams remarked, patting the back of Meg's hand.

"I guess I have." Meg smiled, thankful that Grams reminded her of the girl's name. *Cammy.*

The choir began to sing with enthusiasm. Afterwards, the pastor made his way to the pulpit and began delivering his sermon.

Meg suddenly recalled a time when she was about Cammy's age. She was visiting Grams, and the two of them sat on the sofa. Grams had her large, brown-leather Bible in her lap. She had read several passages and talked about sin and hell and death. Everything ugly in the world. Then she told Meg about heaven and peace, love and joy. All things so beautiful that no one could even come close to imagining them. To Meg's little girl's ears, it sounded like a Cinderella wonderland where Jesus Christ was the King. She wanted to believe it was all true—and she did believe, at the time. Then Grams said a prayer that Meg repeated. It had something to do with asking Jesus into her heart. To this day she remembered that unique connectedness she felt to Grams—and to God afterwards. Amazing how a remnant of that special feeling still remained.

Of course, she knew now that there was no Cinderella wonderland, and peace, love, and joy were questionable.

The service ended and a wave of embarrassment hit Meg when she realized she'd daydreamed during most of it. Everyone stood, and after a final musical number, the pastor dismissed the congregation.

Cammy rolled her wheelchair and blocked the end of the pew before Meg could make her exit. "Hi, Miss Jorgenson."

"Hi." Meg was tickled by the glowing adoration on the child's face, and she hoped all her students would react this way. "How are you this morning?"

"Fine." The little girl continued staring.

"Well, Cammy, you have a pretty name."

"Thanks." A slow smile crept across her small face. "I know your first name is Meg. Is that your nickname?"

"Yes, and I'm surprised you remembered it."

Cammy seemed pleased with herself. "I remember lots of things."

"I can tell, and to answer your question, Meg is short for Meghan."

"That's a pretty name, too."

"Thank you."

Meg watched as Cammy inspected her outfit. It was one of the better ones Meg owned: A turquoise and cocoa zigzag-patterned sleeveless dress with a coordinating short-sleeved jacket.

"You wear nice things," Cammy said in a voice so soft Meg almost didn't hear her. The little girl's gaze traveled down Meg's legs and landed on her brown ankle-strap pumps. "Someday I'm gonna wear high heels, too." She lifted her blue eyes and stared into Meg's face. "Daddy said ladies can't walk so good in high heels, but I know I will. Just like you walk good in 'em."

For a few seconds, Meg felt dumbstruck, but soon she recalled from her studies in college that it wasn't uncommon for physically challenged children to pretend and imagine what life would be like for them without their disabilities.

Cammy opened her mouth to say more, but her father appeared beside her. Meg recalled meeting him on Friday night at the Depot Restaurant, but she'd been a bit overwhelmed and couldn't recall his name.

Victor? Vaughn?

He gave her a polite nod. "I hope Cammy hasn't been talking your ear off." He seemed a tad embarrassed.

"Oh, no, we had a lovely conversation." Meg smiled at Cammy again.

"Maybe I can sit next to you in church next week." Eagerness lit her blue eyes.

"If I'm here, sure. That'd be fine."

. "Goody!"

"There was an 'if' in Miss Jorgenson's reply." He pulled his daughter's chair back, out of the way so Meg could slip out of the pew. "Just keep that in mind."

"I will, Daddy."

He looked at Meg and, as if he sensed her struggle, stuck out his right hand. "Vance Bayer."

"Vance." She placed her hand in his. "Good to see you again."

An awkward moment lagged before Grams took hold of Meg's elbow.

"My, my, June Hatfield is out of the hospital." She glanced at Vance. "Please excuse us. I want my granddaughter to meet one of my dearest friends."

"Don't let me keep you." He inclined his head in a polite fashion.

"I might as well sit back down," Tom muttered. "Once you and June get to gabbin', it's hours till yer finished."

"Now, Tom, I promise I won't be too long. Just rest your bones a little longer."

With that, Meg found herself being propelled toward the front of the church.

* * * * *

With Cammy secured in the backseat, Vance pulled out of the church's parking lot. He'd taken a good tongue-lashing from Nicole Foster just minutes ago, and he was still stinging. She'd seen him talking with the new teacher in town after the service and had accused him of "dumping" her for Meg Jorgenson. Good grief! He and Meg had exchanged no more than ten words. But Nicole had plenty of choice words for him anyway—even after Pastor Wilkerson's message this morning. Of course, Vance never meant to hurt her, and he tried to explain that he had no designs on Meg Jorgenson. Why couldn't Nicole see that their relationship just wasn't going anywhere? The breakup was for the best.

"Daddy, do we have to go to Aunt Debbie's for lunch?"

"What?" Vance snapped from his musing.

"Aunt Debbie. Do we have to go to her house now?"

"Yep. I promised we'd be there."

"Why?"

"Because she asked us to come and we're family."

"But I heard old Mrs. Jorgenson tell young Miss Jorgenson that they were going to the Cracker Barrel in Danville. Why can't we go there, too?"

"Because it costs money for gas and more money to eat out, and that's not in our budget. Besides, I told your aunt Debbie that we'd go to her house for lunch."

"Oh, phooey, phooey, phooey."

Vance grinned at his daughter's exclamation.

A few moments of silence lapsed, and Vance could practically hear the gears turning in her eight-year-old mind.

"She's pretty, isn't she?"

"Who?"

"Miss Jorgenson. Do you think she's pretty, Daddy?"

"Yes. Yes, I do."

"I think she's pretty, too. And guess what? She has the nicest ankles I ever saw on a lady. And no stockings, just bare legs."

The image that flashed through Vance's mind caused him to loosen his necktie and unbutton the very top of his dress shirt. "Man alive, I hope Debbie made something go-od for lunch," he drawled, steering the subject away from Meg and her shapely, bare legs. "I'm starved."

"And, Daddy, Miss Jorgenson's bare feet were in the prettiest high heels with pointy toes." Cammy released a long sigh. "Boy, I sure do love high-heeled shoes."

"Pointy toes? High heels? They sound painful. So, what do you think Aunt Debbie made for lunch?"

"I don't know." A pause. "So you think she's pretty, too, huh?"

"Who's that, punkin?" Vance grinned. "I can't imagine who you're talking about."

"Daddy!"

Vance laughed, hearing Cammy's exasperated sigh.

"Miss Jorgenson."

"Oh, right. Yeah, like I said, she's very pretty."

"Prettier than Mrs. Foster?"

Vance peeked at Cammy in his rearview mirror. She might look innocent enough, but he knew a set-up when he heard one. He returned his gaze to the road ahead. "Everyone's pretty in their own special way. I've told you that a hundred times."

"I think Miss Jorgenson is the prettiest lady in all of Kentucky now that she moved here."

"Hmm. . .we'll see if you feel that same way after your first math test."

"I hate math."

"I know." Vance chuckled again.

"I bet Miss Jorgenson will help me with my math. I'll probably be her best student."

Vance prayed his little girl wasn't setting herself up for a terrible disappointment. Cammy had a lot of competition for the Teacher's Pet title. Lots of smart kids in Fairview Academy. He wondered if Meg Jorgenson was experienced enough to avoid favoritism in the classroom.

Reaching his sister's ranch-styled home, he drove his van into the driveway and parked. He noticed Debbie's boyfriend's pickup truck on the street, and Vance wondered if his sister was serious about the guy.

He hopped out of the van and slid open the side door. He released the security straps that held Cammy's wheelchair in place and then leaned on the switch near the door. Soon, both his little girl and her wheelchair were being lowered to the ground on a custom-made platform.

"All set?"

Cammy nodded and pushed herself toward the door. After closing up the van, Vance wheeled her chair the rest of the way into the house. Once inside, Cammy maneuvered herself toward the spare bedroom in which she kept a few toys for whenever she visited. Cammy was no stranger here, as Debbie babysat her a couple days a week.

Entering the living room, Vance greeted his sister's current boyfriend, Gerry, with a nod. "How're you doing?"

"All right." The stout man with a wide midsection got up off the couch and extended his right hand. "How's business?"

"Can't complain." Vance clasped Gerry's hand in a friendly shake.

"I saw there's a motorcycle in front of Hank's that's for sale."

"Yep. Engine's rebuilt." Vance lowered himself into the armchair.

"You repair it?"

"Part of it."

"Bet it's worth the price then."

Vance sat on the sofa and relaxed. "Definitely worth the price."

An announcer's voice suddenly drew Vance's attention to the wide-screen TV in the corner of the room. Gerry had tuned in to one of the sports channels, and Vance soon found himself distracted by the ballgame. The topic of the conversation shifted to sports, and Vance decided it felt good to not have to think or make decisions about who was prettier, Nicole Foster or Meg Jorgenson. All he wanted to do was relax and let the aroma of onions and frying beef that wafted from the kitchen whet his appetite.

At long last, his sister announced that supper was on the table.

Vance trailed Gerry into the kitchen. His gaze immediately found Cammy. "You doin' all right, punkin?"

She nodded and her blue eyes sparkled with mischief.

Her expression put Vance on the alert.

Debbie crossed the room and set a plate of thickly sliced meatloaf on the table beside a bowl of mashed potatoes and another serving bowl filled with tossed salad.

She straightened and blew several strands of white-blond hair off her perspiring brow. "I hear there's a new, single teacher in town who's quite the fashion statement."

Vance caught his sister's emphasis on the word "single."

"You heard right." He hoped he sounded noncommittal as his gaze returned to his daughter. Instinct told him something wasn't quite as it should be. He drew his brows together and frowned. What was different about Cammy?

Then he realized it: Gone were her white kneesocks that matched her frilly printed dress. Her long, thin legs were bare right down to her white patent leather shoes. Vance could only guess whom she was emulating, and he quickly deduced that his sister had been Cammy's accomplice.

He kneaded the back of his neck while his sister's laughter rang through the room. Next he watched as Cammy's cheeks turned pink.

Suddenly Vance had a hunch that he was up against a force far greater than he ever dreamed: Miss Meghan Jorgenson's influence.

Chapter Seven

....

"Well, Retta, you done a good job showin' Meggie around these last couple weeks," Tom said as he lit the tobacco in his pipe. "Ever'one knows her now."

"And?"

"And half the town is smitten with her and the other half's so envious they're as green as Martians."

Sitting across from him at the picnic table while her clean laundry flapped in the morning breeze, Loretta paid him no mind. "Don't be silly. There's no such thing as Martians."

Tom guffawed, releasing a cloud of smoke.

She smiled at her own retort. "Seriously, Meggie's going to do just fine. I think she's perking up some, too."

"I reckon she is at that."

"The poor thing. She had a rough time through the years, particularly with that awful man in Chicago. She had thought he'd end up a great poet like Carl Sandburg, but he turned out to be nothing but a two-timing bum."

"Now, Retta. . ."

"It still riles me, Tom, when I think of how that crude man hurt her. Hmph! Wants to be a college professor, one of those long-haired uppity types."

"Meggie admitted to making bad decisions where that boy's concerned. Important thing is she's learnin' from them and movin' on."

"I'm so proud of her."

"You are? A body'd never tell from the way you act." Tom sent her a wink.

Loretta waved her hand at him and his sorry attempt at humor. "Well, the best thing is Meggie's away from that scoundrel. Now he'll have to figure out how to support himself. About time, I'd say."

"Ever' man has his rough edges. Takes the love of a good woman to smooth 'em out. Meggie ain't that woman in this instance. God knows it's a right good thing she found it out at her young age. She still has a full life ahead of her."

"And that's just what I'm saying."

Tom puffed on his pipe, and Loretta suddenly thought about her dear departed husband, Jeb, gone for nearly two years now. She felt her smile grow as the memories of him and their life together took shape in her mind. He'd certainly had some "rough edges" when he was young, but he never cheated on her like Meggie's boyfriend. 'Course they never cohabitated, either. Folks just didn't do those sorts of things back then unless they wanted a scandal. Regardless, Jeb had always been faithful, even while they were courting.

The memory of him faded, and, looking at her dear, prune-faced neighbor now, Loretta recalled that once upon a time he'd had a few rough edges too.

At first, she could barely stand living on the farm next door to the rowdy newcomer from out West, until she became acquainted with him and his young daughter, Eugenia. Tom hadn't ever married, and when Eugenia's mother died, the poor dear came to live with the daddy she'd never even met. What a shock for both of them, but mostly for Tom, since he'd been a drifter most of his life. Settling down hadn't been easy, but he managed, thanks to Jeb. Jeb and his firm, albeit soft-spoken, ways.

Loretta breathed in deeply of the sweet country air, made sweeter still, somehow, by the rich, masculine smell of tobacco from Tom's pipe. "Those were the days," she murmured.

"Sure were," Tom replied, as if he'd been right there, riding beside her down Memory Lane. "Sure were."

* * * * *

Meg stapled the last brown cardboard letter onto the bulletin board in what would be her classroom this school year. She stepped back and admired her handiwork.

WHAT I DID ON MY SUMMER VACATION.

She tipped her head, inspecting the stapled words. Hardly original, but she hoped her third graders would find it fun to write a short essay about their experiences these last few months. In reading them, Meg imagined that she'd learn something special about each of her seventeen students.

She glanced at her wristwatch. Twenty minutes until the teachers' luncheon in the school cafeteria, followed by a meeting with the principal.

Meg walked to the bank of windows at the back of her recently constructed classroom. The school had been built only a few years ago, and everything still felt new—including the central air conditioning. The classrooms seemed bright and cheery, so unlike the dismal brick structure in which she'd taught in Chicago. How glad she was to have left the city behind.

She peered outside to the playground and spotted a couple of girls, perhaps high school aged, sitting on the swings, gabbing and giggling. At first look she thought they were smoking, but she soon realized that they had candy suckers in their mouths. She almost couldn't believe her eyes; the girls seemed so innocent compared to the youth she worked with last year. Had she helped any of her former students? She'd probably never know.

A wave of gratitude filled Meg as her gaze traveled beyond the teens and the play yard to the rich, green countryside and gently rolling foothills. This small town was out of a storybook, and she felt lucky to be here. She hoped Grams was right about everything having a purpose.

"Looks like things are coming together in here."

Meg startled and whirled around to find a skinny brunette standing in the doorway.

"I'm Leah Lawton," she drawled. "I'm the fourth grade teacher."

"I'm Meg Jorgenson."

Leah's thin eyebrows drew together. "You're not from around here, are you?"

"Formerly of Chicago, Illinois."

"I thought I detected one of those Midwestern accents. Kent Baldwin, the new gym teacher, has one, too. He's from Minneapolis."

"I haven't met him yet."

"Well, you can't miss him." Leah strode slowly forward. "He's a big strappin' fella with an all-over tan," she drawled, "and he's wearing a yellow polo shirt and navy blue shorts that go down to his knees." She paused and glanced over one slim shoulder before adding, "He's got the finest legs I ever saw on a man."

Meg bit her lower lip to conceal her mirth. She couldn't decide which was more humorous, Leah's remark about the new phys ed teacher or her chatty, Kentucky accent.

She swallowed a laugh. "I'll watch for him at lunch."

"You do that, but like I said, you can't miss him." Leah tucked several strands of her long, woodsy brown hair behind one ear. "Are you married?"

Meg shook her head. "Very single."

"Ah." Leah nodded. "Me, too. Kids?"

"None."

"Me, neither." She walked the rest of the way into the classroom and sat down on the edge of Meg's large wooden desk. "I've been corresponding with a guy in the military who's over in the Middle East. I email him every day, you know, try to keep up his spirits and all."

"That's nice of you." Meg crossed her arms. "What branch of service is he in?"

"Marines. His name is Dave and he drives one of those huge tanks. He's sent me all kinds of pictures of himself and his buddies. He seems like a great guy. A hero." She glanced down at her sandaled foot. "But, I don't think his computer works too well over there because I've sent him photos of me and he still e-mails back."

Meg didn't get it. "What do you mean?"

"My figure. I'm so thin. Hardly a curve on me. I fight to keep every last pound on my bony hips."

"Oh, please, spare me." Meg held up a hand. "Since I've moved in with my grandmother a couple of weeks ago, I've packed on almost ten pounds."

"I don't mean to embarrass you, but it looks like it's going to all the right places."

"Thanks, and I'm not embarrassed." She could tell the other woman was friendly, but not in a dubious way. "But the truth is, I can barely squeeze into my blue jeans."

"I can hardly keep my jeans from falling down."

They shared a laugh, and in that moment, Meg had a hunch she'd found a friend in Leah Lawton.

* * * * *

Labor Day arrived and Meg dressed for the picnic to which she'd been invited. According to Grams, every year the Owenses invited their "church family," neighbors, and friends to a large outdoor picnic on their sprawling farm near Cedar Creek Lake.

"They roast a hog and everyone else brings food to share. It's a fun time with games and whatnot," Grams had added.

Yesterday Meg had learned that Leah would be there, and Leah asked the new gym teacher, Kent Baldwin, to come along. Meg was glad she wouldn't be the only newcomer at the picnic.

She wiped her fingertips over her perspiring brow. Already the day was hot and muggy, and Grams didn't have air conditioning. There wasn't much of a breeze coming through the second story windows either. Unfortunately it wasn't much cooler downstairs.

Meg dressed, keeping the balmy weather in mind. She pulled a white tank top over her head and slipped into a lightweight, multi-colored, crinkled cotton skirt. Completing the outfit, she stepped into her favorite white leather flip-flops.

"Do I look okay, Grams? Like a respectable school teacher, albeit a comfortable one?" Making her way into the kitchen, Meg noticed her grandmother wore a sleeveless blue and white seersucker dress.

Grams pivoted around from where she stood at the sink, grabbed a towel, and dried her hands while giving Meg a once-over inspection. "You look real pretty. But some of the girls your age join in the softball game. Are you sure you wouldn't rather wear something else? And take your swimsuit in case you want to go out on the lake."

Meg shook her head. "I don't own a swimsuit. And it's too hot for sports today. I'm thinking I'll be doing the Southern belle thing—sit at a picnic table in the shade with a glass of iced tea or lemonade." She stepped farther into the room. "If I still lived in Chicago, I'd probably find an air-conditioned place with a view of the lakefront and enjoy a good book and a wine cooler on a day like today."

"We can offer you the lake view and a book." Grams grinned. "But the Owenses never serve alcoholic beverages at their picnics, and a person can't legally purchase beer or wine or any liquor at all in Lincoln County. That includes Miracle."

"Wow, I never knew that."

"Yep, we're a dry county."

"Feels awfully wet today."

Grams had the good grace to smile at Meg's well-intentioned pun.

"So now I'm curious." Meg leaned against the kitchen table and folded her arms. "Is Prohibition still alive and well down here? I've never heard of a 'dry county.'"

"Not Prohibition. It's not a government mandate. It's the people's choice. You see, there have been so many tragic drunk driving accidents in years past, including the one that injured little Cammy Bayer, and, well, everyone in the county just voted to be dry."

"Interesting."

"That won't be a problem for you, will it? I mean, it is an easy drive into Danville. That's in Boyle County, and they're not dry."

"I think I'll make do as long as chocolate's not banned." Meg had never been a habitual drinker.

Suddenly the clocks in Grams' home began to chime, ching, and gong, and Meg jerked from her ponderings.

"You all right, hon? You seem a bit jumpy."

"I'm fine." Meg laughed at herself for reacting to her grandmother's noisy collection. She thought she'd be accustomed to it by now.

"Maybe you're nervous about the picnic today. If so, don't be." Grams gave her a warm smile. "Everyone who'll be there adores you almost as much as I do."

Meg grinned at the compliment. "I appreciate your saying so and bolstering my confidence. But I think they like me because of you. Everyone I've met respects you, Grams."

"Oh, not everyone."

Meg raised her brows, her curiosity piqued, and she made a mental note to pry the details out of Grams sometime soon. It was becoming a regular hobby to learn more about her family and increase this newfound sense of belonging.

"Look at me just sitting here watching you work." Meg wagged her head at her thoughtlessness. What can I do to help you, Grams?"

"Want to make the fruit salad?"

"Sure." Meg plucked a knife from the butcher block holder on the counter and began cutting into the watermelon.

"Ellie Owens said there's another new teacher at Fairview Academy. Apparently he'll be at the picnic today."

"She must be referring to Kent Baldwin, the new phys ed teacher. He's the only other new teacher I'm aware of."

"Phys ed? Is that like physics?"

"No, physical education. As in gym class."

"Ah. Well, does he seem like a nice man?"

"Nice enough, I guess. I met him at the teachers' luncheon last week." Meg didn't add that something about the guy troubled her. Perhaps it was his *savoir-faire* around women that kicked up her defenses. She abhorred those Don Juan types. Still, she was determined to be polite and friendly. After all, he hadn't actually said or done anything offensive; it was just his attitude. "Kent's got an impressive resume—for a phys ed teacher."

"Really?"

"Uh-huh. He was in physical therapy before earning a master's and going into education. I mentioned Cammy's disabilities at our luncheon, and he promised to develop a program suited to her needs."

"How very thoughtful of him."

"Yeah, I thought so, too."

"Ellie said he's quite handsome."

Meg sported a grin and placed a portion of the watermelon she'd finished cutting into a stainless bowl. "I s'pose some would say he's a head-turner, all right."

"Hmm. . ."

"And he knows it, too."

"I gather he's not very humble."

"Not in the least, but—" Meg gave it a moment's thought "—he doesn't seem like an outright jerk."

"Well, there's something to be thankful for."

Meg continued to smile. Grams always found "something to be thankful for." Most likely due to her strong religious beliefs.

And, speaking of religion. . .

"Grams, tell me more about the Bayers."

For the third Sunday in a row, Cammy begged to sit beside Meg in church. Yesterday Vance finally allowed it, although he sat in the pew behind them. Odd, but throughout the service Meg could practically feel his gaze boring holes through the back of her brand-new linen blouse. "What do you want to know about them?"

"Well, I guess I'm curious about Vance."

"Oh?" Grams arched a brow.

"I'm just wondering, that's all."

"Okay." Grams still wore a bit of a smirk. "What particularly are you wondering about?"

"Well, for starters, is Vance a nice person?"

"Very nice. I knew his dad better, of course. He went to school with my boys." Grams finished peeling a sink full of potatoes and now began chopping them into small pieces for the potato salad. "But I do know that Vance was something of a hellion in high school. Always in trouble. The whole church prayed for him and prayed often. And then—" Grams chuckled. "Why, it was beyond our wildest dreams. God used all that time Vance spent with those Lincoln County sheriff's deputies, and one day he straightened up and decided to go into law enforcement. He graduated from high school and started college, and that's where he met his wife, Angie. She really was a lovely person. So you can imagine how sad we all were when—"

Grams paused. At Meg's questioning look, she continued.

"About three years back, Angie was killed in the terrible wreck that left Cammy paralyzed. She'd been on her way home from visiting friends when a drunk driver crossed the center line and plowed right into her car."

"How horrible."

"It truly was."

Meg cleaned up the mess from the watermelon. Next she began slicing the peaches.

"But back to Vance. He had still been taking a class here and there after Cammy was born, but after the wreck. . .well, needless to say, he never finished college. Instead of law enforcement, he works at Hank's, a small engine repair shop, and does a little fixin' on the side."

Meg, personally, wasn't so much impressed by someone's higher educational background—or lack thereof. Not anymore. Not after living with Dillon and experiencing firsthand what a knob a guy with a master's degree could be. "Who takes care of Cammy?"

"Vance's sister Debbie helps out, but from what I understand, Debbie has her own personal issues."

"Like what?"

"Like a brute of an ex-husband and a little boy with ADD."

Meg winced. Sounded like a handful, and watching a physically challenged niece on top of it had to be rough.

"And I guess this isn't gossip exactly—I suppose you should know, being Cammy's teacher and all, but Vance has been seeing a lot of Nicole Foster this summer. I heard from Myrna Westphal, who's Cammy's Sunday school teacher, that the little dear doesn't like Nicole. Unfortunately, from what I understand, the feeling is mutual on Nicole's side."

"Maybe she's just uncomfortable around a physically challenged child. Some people are, you know"

"Maybe."

Meg recalled meeting the woman that first Friday night she went out to eat with Grams and Tom. She remembered Cammy's expression of hurt and resentment and knew just how that little girl felt. "I've been on one end of those triangular relationships more than once. It's not fun."

"I'm sure it's not. But, come to think about it, I haven't seen Vance and Nicole together for some time now."

"Hmm." Meg realized she hadn't seen the couple together, either.

"Well, needless to say, losing his wife in such a tragic way changed Vance forever."

"How could it not?"

"Exactly. Everyone in town helps out when we can. The congregation at Calvary Hill even raised the money Vance needed for Cammy's wheelchair."

"That was nice," Meg said. "I'm sure Vance appreciated that."

"We do try to help out when we can. We team together and clean his house and prepare occasional meals—the poor man can barely cook. Lending a hand is what the church body is for. Though, as a rule, we stay clear of people's personal lives."

"Ri-ight." Meg attempted to stifle a laugh but failed. "Now try to convince me it never rains in Kentucky, either."

Grams sucked in a breath, stopped her chopping, and stared into Meg's face. "Why, Meggie Jorgenson, just what are you implying?"

She watched Grams wrestle with a grin, which only widened her own smile. "Oh, nothing. It's just that I've heard more than God's Word at your church." She batted her lashes for full effect. "At this rate, I'll get to know everything about everybody in Miracle in no time."

Grams looked away and resumed slicing the vegetable, held fast in her capable grip. "Tom's right," she muttered on a facetious note. "You are a sassy one."

Chapter Eight

....

"She's here! She's here!"

Cammy spotted Miss Jorgenson the minute Daddy's van rolled to a stop on the Owens' farm. Lots of people were here, and lots of kids, too, but Cammy saw Miss Jorgenson first. "Do you see her? She's wearing a flowery skirt."

Daddy turned off the van. "I see her." He twisted around and stared at Cammy through the two front seats. "Remember what we talked about this morning?"

"Yes." Cammy tried to hold in all her excitement. She felt like a shaken soda can ready to bubble over the top.

"It's not nice for a little girl to make a pest of herself around her new teacher. You need to give Miss Jorgenson a chance to make friends her own age."

"I know." Cammy thought Miss Jorgenson had lots of time to make friends her own age. "Miss Lawton is one of Miss Jorgenson's new friends. She sat with us in church yesterday."

Daddy sucked in some air in a way that let Cammy know he was growing short with her. She didn't want him to get mad. That would make her even more late to join the picnic and see Miss Jorgenson.

"I'll be good, Daddy. I promise."

The almost-mad look on his face disappeared like magic. "I know you will, punkin." He smiled.

Then he climbed out of the van and opened Cammy's door, lowering her wheelchair down to the gravelly ground. She could hardly wait. This would be so much fun. Cammy loved picnics and birthday parties and Thanksgiving and Christmas and school.

Her gaze zeroed in on her new third-grade teacher. She looked hard but couldn't tell if Miss Jorgenson was wearing high heels today. Cammy hoped she was.

Placing her palms around the wheels of her chair, she attempted to push it over the light brown dirt and all the small rocks, but it was hard, and she soon felt tired. She felt mad, too, that this dumb thing wouldn't take her where she wanted to go. Dumb. Dumb. Dumb.

"Dad-dy, help me!"

"I'll be right along, Cammy. Have some patience."

She puffed out her lower lip. Sometimes it was hard to have patience. Like now. She just hoped Miss Jorgenson wouldn't walk away and then Cammy would have to find her again. But wheelchairs didn't ride over bumpy ground too good. She wished she could just get up and run over to the picnic area.

"Hurry, Daddy!"

It felt like hours later that he pushed her chair across the yard. Cammy's teeth clacked together during the rough ride, but soon they reached the smooth walkway that led to the wide tent and the tables and chairs.

"Vance! Good to see you!"

Cammy watched Mr. Lattimer walk up to them. He was Bethany's dad and he had a fat nose that almost always had yucky hairs inside of it. Gross. Gross. Gross.

"I was going to give you a call this week," he told Daddy. "My tractor engine quit working. Didn't gimme a warning or nothing. Just quit."

"Does it make any kind of sound at all?"

"Kind of a grinding noise."

While Daddy and Mr. Lattimer talked motors, Cammy's gaze

roamed around, taking in the boys playing baseball, the red and yellow inflated bouncy house, the dancing sprinkler, and the waterslide. Next she saw Sasha, Rosie, Lindsay, and—"

"Hi, Cammy."

She turned real quick to see Miss Jorgenson right beside her. She had crouched down so her face was real close. A humungous balloon of happiness filled Cammy's insides. Miss Jorgenson actually came over to talk with *her*! Cammy didn't have to be a pest after all!

"I'm real glad you came to the picnic."

"Me, too."

Cammy looked hard into Miss Jorgenson's face. She had blue eyes— just like hers. And freckles on her cheeks, shoulders, and splattered all across the top of her chest.

Cammy's gaze slid down to Miss Jorgenson's skirt that was wrinkly on purpose, and it had every one of Cammy's favorite colors in it.

And then she saw them. Miss Jorgenson's toes peeking out from under her skirt. She didn't wear high heels today, but she had happy-red polish on her toenails.

Cammy suddenly wished her toenails were polished, too.

"Did you eat yet?" Miss Jorgenson asked.

Cammy shook her head. She was still thinking about nail polish and wondering if Daddy would let her have a bottle. Aunt Debbie would put it on for her, but Cammy'd probably have to say she'd wash the dishes first. Aunt Debbie always said one favor deserved another.

"Would you like me to fix a plate of food for you? Tell me what you like to eat."

"That's not necessary."

Cammy's gaze swung over to Daddy, who stood on the other side of her wheelchair.

"I don't want you to go to any trouble."

Miss Jorgenson stood. "It's no trouble, Vance. In fact, I can fix a plate for you also."

"Um. . ."

Cammy frowned, wondering why Daddy's face looked sunburned all of a sudden. Was he going to turn away Miss Jorgenson's offer?

"Daddy, let her go to the trouble. Please? I'm hungry."

"Well. . ."

"Listen, Vance. I'm happy to do it. I've been fixing up plates all afternoon and having a great time of it. Tom said I inherited a love of feeding people from my grandmother. It's the first time in my life that I didn't mind being compared to my grandmother."

Miss Jorgenson gave a little laugh, and Cammy thought it left a nice sound in her ears. It wasn't at all like Mrs. Foster's laugh. Hers sounded like she wanted Daddy to fix her lawnmower for free.

"Thanks. I appreciate it. Cammy and I both do." Daddy cleared a sudden frog from his throat and glanced around the picnic area. "Guess we'll find a place to sit."

"There's a table by the grills that has an empty bench."

"Sounds good."

While Miss Jorgenson left to get their food, Daddy walked behind her chair and began pushing her toward the smoking barbeques. Cammy wondered what was wrong with him. He was acting weird, weird, weird. Like he forgot how to talk. Daddy never acted like that before. He always knew the right things to say.

Oh, well. She couldn't think about that now. All she could think of was this way-fun day.

* * * * *

Meg set down two green plastic plates heaped with baked beans, grilled hot dogs, macaroni salad, and Grams' famous potato salad and fruit salad. One plate she deposited in front of Vance. It contained both a hot dog and hamburger. The other plate of food, a smaller-scaled version, she set in front of Cammy. Then she sat on the bench opposite them at the picnic table.

"So, what do you think?"

"I think I won't have to eat till Thursday," Vance quipped.

"I think, yum!" Cammy dug in with enthusiasm. But hearing her dad clear his throat in a tone of reminder, she paused to say a quick, "Thank You, Jesus, for this food." Then she tucked her napkin inside the neck of her orange T-shirt.

Meg bit her lower lip to keep from smiling, but the fact that Cammy knew to use her manners at all was a credit to Vance's parenting skills.

Reaching for the plastic bottles of ketchup and mustard, Meg placed them in front of Vance and Cammy. "I'm happy to fix a plate for your girlfriend, too. I overhead one of the men say that they'll be shutting down the grills soon."

"No—" Vance shook his head. "I, um, don't have a girlfriend."

"Not anymore," Cammy blurted. "Not since—"

"Cammy." There was an unmistakable warning note in Vance's tone.

The girl pressed her lips together, but Meg got the idea. He and the blonde had broken up after all. Had he severed the relationship for his daughter's sake? If so, Meg's opinion of Vance increased a notch or two. But was he hurt about it? Disappointed? Angry?

Meg shook herself. On to a new subject. "There's dessert, too—cookies, brownies, and all sorts of cakes. I just couldn't fit everything on a single plate."

"Cammy and I appreciate your kindness, but you're the one new in town. We ought to be serving you." Vance looked chagrined. "Cammy and I can go up and get dessert later. Don't want to trouble you."

"No trouble. In fact, I get a lot of pleasure out of watching other people eat." She glanced at Cammy and smiled. "Maybe it carries over from when I used to waitress in high school."

"You were a waitress?" Cammy wiped her mouth on the paper napkin and swallowed her bite of beans. "Where?"

"In St. Louis."

Cammy's eyes grew large. "Did you ever know a girl named Laura Downing? She was in day camp with me when I was in first grade. Her dad got a job in St. Louis and they had to move."

"I think my waitress days were a little before your time." She glanced at Vance and they shared a grin before Meg looked back at Cammy. "I'm talking about ten years ago."

"Oh." Cammy shook her head, and Meg noticed that her short black hair was even curlier in the humid weather. "Then you wouldn't know Laura Downing."

"No." Meg was amused by the eight-year-old's logic.

"I thought I heard you were from Chicago." Vance slid a forkful of baked beans into his mouth.

"I am. But I'm really from all over, I guess. I was born here, and after my parents divorced, my mom moved us to Louisville. From there we went to San Diego, then back east to St. Louis, and we finally ended up in Illinois. I completed my senior year of high school in Bloomington."

"Sounds like your mama had a good case of wanderlust."

"That's a nice way to put it." Meg sent him a smile.

He smiled back. "My life's been uneventful in comparison to yours. I've lived all my born days in Kentucky."

"Lucky you."

"Me?" He laughed. "You're the one who got to live in different states and meet all sorts of people."

"True, but it's hard to constantly move and make new friends, only to leave them behind and never see them again."

Vance momentarily ducked his head. "Guess you've got a point there."

"You could email them," Cammy said with a positive note ringing her voice.

"You're right." Meg looked her way. "And some of them I did email for a while. But life has a way of moving along, and friends you never get to see face-to-face end up going their own way while you go yours."

"Makes it hard for you to get close to folks now, I imagine."

Meg tipped her head. "Not really. It's just super-hard to say good-bye."

She saw Vance's bottom lip jut out as he contemplated her remark. She wondered what he was thinking about. Or who. His former girlfriend?

He caught her eye, but before he or Meg could say more, Kent Baldwin approached the picnic table.

"Mind if join you?"

"Not at all." Meg scooted over, nearer to Cammy, and Kent sat down. Meg had greeted him when he first arrived, and it didn't take her long to make an interesting discovery: Kent was the only guy at the picnic wearing a sleeveless shirt. It was bright yellow, and it emphasized his tan and his muscled biceps. Meg had a hunch that neither the color nor the style were selected by happenstance.

The bench dipped from the weight of his frame.

Meg made the introductions. "Kent's the new phys ed teacher at Fairview Academy."

"Good to meet you."

"Likewise," Kent said, reaching across the table. Self-assurance oozed from his every pore.

He and Vance clasped hands.

"Meg's been telling me about Cammy. She's a special girl, and

I'm working with Earl to apply for some state funding for new gym equipment suited to her physical needs."

Vance appeared impressed. "That'd be great. Wouldn't it, Cammy?"

The girl nodded, but Meg sensed she didn't quite understand.

"We exercise every night." Vance's tone didn't sound defensive, just explanatory. "But I guess more exercise can't hurt as long as her limitations are taken into consideration."

"And they will be." Kent shifted with enthusiasm. "My goal is to get Cammy involved in the sports aspect."

"Goody!" That much the child comprehended.

Meg smiled at Cammy's reaction. Since her luncheon with the principal, she felt one hundred percent more confident about teaching a child with physical disabilities this year. Meg had learned that the school district provided a HCA, or a "handicap assistant," who would help Cammy do things like use the restroom. The woman also accompanied the child on field trips, and as she also worked as a secretary in the school's office, she was on-site all day. Meg could just concentrate on being a good teacher.

Kent's focus remained on Cammy. "What do you usually do when the other kids have gym time?"

"I dunno." She shrugged. "We never had gym time before. Just recess."

"That's all going to change this year," Kent said, rubbing his tanned hands together in anticipation. "I guarantee you, Cammy, that you and all your friends will love gym class."

"But you'll love math and English more," Meg said. Somehow she couldn't resist teasing Kent. Knock him down a few notches.

"I know I will cuz you'll be my teacher for those subjects."

Meg smiled and flicked a triumphant glance in Kent's direction. He grinned, and as his brown eyes openly appraised her, it was obvious that he liked what he saw. Meg, however, hardly felt like melting beneath his gaze.

Kent slipped his arm around her shoulders. His palm felt warm against Meg's skin.

She tensed.

"Let's round up some people for a game of volleyball." His tangy cologne overpowered the smell of smoking burgers. "What do you say?"

The words "smooth operator" rang melodiously in Meg's ears.

She shook off his hold. "No volleyball for me. Much too hot and humid."

"What about you, *Cammy's dad*?" Kent asked. "You up for a game of volleyball?"

Vance lifted his gaze. "You know," he drawled with a slight smirk, "I can honestly say that I have never played a game of volleyball in my entire life."

"Then how 'bout giving it a go? Good ol' country boy like you? You shouldn't have a problem swatting at a ball. What do you say?"

Meg pulled her chin back, staring at Kent in surprise. The invitation sounded more like a challenge.

Vance didn't react one way or another. "I don't think so. Thanks anyway."

Meg wasn't sure if she imagined it, but she sensed an awkward tension beginning to build between the two men, and she didn't want to be part of it. She stood from the table. "Want some lemonade, Cammy?"

"Sure."

"Vance?"

"Can of anything cold will do me just fine."

"Nothing for me," Kent said. "I have volleyball players to recruit."

Meg set off to fetch the cold drinks, and when she returned, Kent was gone. Sitting in his place was Leah Lawton.

A wave of relief rushed over her. Meg had learned from experience that smooth operators came in all shapes and sizes, Dillon being the latest and greatest. But she wasn't about to befriend or fall for another self-absorbed guy who just wanted a good time and, in Dillon's case, a meal ticket.

She handed Cammy the blue plastic glass and set a can of cola in front of Vance. Meg thought he seemed genuine. Was he?

She gave him a polite grin.

"Thanks. At this rate, I'll have to leave you a tip," he joked.

"Services are on the house." She wagged her index finger at him. "But only for today."

He smiled at her in reply. He had a nice smile, too, Meg decided. It appeared sincere, non-threatening. . .

"Thank you for the lemonade, Miss Jorgenson," Cammy said politely.

"You're very welcome." Meg stooped beside her chair. "When you're done eating, I'll take you by the play area and maybe you can introduce me to some more kids who'll be in our class this year."

"Okay!" Cammy's eyes lit with excitement. "I know practically everyone here."

"You're not playing volleyball, Meg?" Leah batted her lashes before setting down her sweating can of diet cola on the table and wiping her hands on her denim, knee-length skort. "I'm thinking about it."

"No volleyball for me today." She pushed strands of her hair from her damp forehead.

"I second that! But it seems Kent's convinced every unattached female in Stanford to play in spite of the heat. Look at 'em all, following him to the volleyball net like a string of ducklings." Her gaze shifted and she peered across the table at Vance. "Sorry, fella, but you've got competition."

The humor wasn't lost on him, and he chuckled. "Guess I'll learn to deal with it."

A moment later, his hazel eyes found Meg's, and it was odd how she felt riveted to his stare.

"Miss Jorgenson—"

Meg tore her gaze away from Vance's and became aware of Cammy tugging on her shirt.

"I'm ready to go, Miss Jorgenson."

"Me, too." She stepped around Cammy's wheelchair and chanced another look at Vance. "It's all right, isn't it—if I take her near the play area?"

"Fine. But, um, stay clear of that volleyball area. I wouldn't want Cammy to get hit or knocked over."

"Not to worry." Meg watched as Cammy released the brake on her chair. "We'll stay clear of it."

Silently, she added, *And as far away as possible from Kent Baldwin.*

Chapter Nine

....

Vance had swung himself around on the picnic bench and now lazed back, his elbows resting on the table. Once he felt convinced that Nicole wasn't going to show up today, he began to relax. He knew she'd been hurt over their breakup, but he didn't relish witnessing another public scene such as the one in the church parking lot a few weeks ago.

Peals of laughter suddenly captured his attention, and he looked toward the play area. His gaze seemed adhered to Meg Jorgenson like melted gum on his shoe. He had to admit to feeling curious about her. She sat in the sand, interacting with a gathering of kids. She had a special way about her, that's for sure, and he had a hunch she'd be one of those teachers whom students remembered for the rest of their lives. She took an interest in each child, including Cammy, and what eight- or nine-year-old didn't enjoy an adult's rapt attention?

Thoughts of how she greeted him and Cammy when they first arrived at the picnic circulated through his head. He decided he certainly didn't mind Meg's doting at mealtime. Not one bit. What's more, he enjoyed the way she brushed off that new gym teacher's advances. Rather amusing to see, actually.

Vance tried to hide his slow grin by rubbing his fingertips across his mustache.

An instant later, his buddy Boz gave him a friendly rap upside the arm before sitting down beside him. His name was really Eddie Poedell, but as a kid he had curly orange hair that stuck out on the sides like Bozo the Clown's. Hence, the nickname "Boz."

"You get a load of the jock playing volleyball with the girls?"

"Mmm-hmmm."

"He had the nerve to take off his shirt. The old ladies are aghast."

This time Vance didn't even attempt to conceal his mirth. He glanced at his husky friend and they shared a chuckle.

"I don't know about you," Boz said, "but I work too many hours to get tan like Mr. Muscleman over there. I mean, I might get a little sunburned when I mow the lawn." He leaned forward. "Who has time to lay out in the sun all day?"

"I think it's more like fifteen minutes a day at the *tanning salon.*"

"Aw, man—" Boz looked embarrassed. "I shoulda known."

Vance laughed again.

Boz sat back. "Well, the guy's the talk of the town, and it's irritating, you know? I mean, all I'm going to hear about at home is how out of shape I am and how built Mr. Muscleman is. Tara'll want to join that new fitness center by the Goodwill. Next thing ya know, she'll be feeding me nothing but fancy grass trimmings and a piece of meat the size of my thumb."

"Might not hurt."

"Which one? The fitness club or the diet?"

"Both."

Boz removed his cap and whacked Vance.

A few other friends sat down and joined the bantering. Then Jeff Short extracted a fifty-dollar bill from his wallet and gave it a surreptitious wave.

"Here's betting that Mrs. Jorgenson's granddaughter and Musclehead over there are an item by the end of the year," he said, sitting forward in the green lawn chair.

Vance knew his buddies didn't mean any harm, but he shook his head at their antics all the same. "Listen, you guys, shouldn't we be reaching out to the new teachers, instead betting on them?"

"A friendly wager never hurt anyone."

Vance shrugged, and his gaze skipped to where Meg still sat in the sand with a circle of children around her. The view reminded him of a serene watercolor painting, even with his young daughter bound in her black wheelchair. Cammy always stuck out in a crowd because of her disabilities, but the smile on her face right now shone as brightly as the other kids'. The sight did Vance's heart good, but somehow it irked him to imagine Meg romantically involved with Kent. He wasn't really sure why.

"So are you in, Vance?"

"Nope." He pulled his gaze from Meg.

Boz nudged him. "You don't have to pay right now."

"I'm not betting, okay?"

His chums inched backwards, and Vance immediately regretted his sharp tone.

"What's eating you?" A frown creased Jeff's brow.

"Nothing. I'm just not betting."

"We're just havin' a little fun."

"Go on, then. Have your fun." Vance stood and made his way to the table filled with every kind of dessert imaginable. He didn't feel hungry, but he selected a few peanut butter cookies off a platter anyway.

Boz had followed him. "So what's going on with you? You seem tense."

"Aw, nothing."

"Is it Nicole? You heard the news then, huh?"

"What news?"

Boz winced. "I hate to be the one to tell you this."

"Just spit it out."

"She's back together with that professor in Stanford that she used to date. Tara said he didn't get married like he planned, and instead, he's hooked back up with Nicole."

"Well, then, maybe the two of them are meant to be." Vance raked his fingers through his hair. He wondered if Nicole had been seeing the professor while he was still dating her. But then he decided he didn't care one way or the other. He honestly wished Nicole the best and hoped she'd find happiness.

"The way I see it is," Boz began, "she just wants to get married again in the worst way. She talked about it a lot when we'd all get together."

"I know, but that wasn't what scared me off. It's like I told you— Nicole is no Angie."

"Of course not. No one will replace *her*. But in time you'll find the right woman and the two of you will have something special together." Boz gave him a friendly slap between the shoulder blades.

"Yeah, maybe."

In spite of himself, Vance's gaze wandered back to where his daughter and Meg sat near the play equipment. The idea of asking Meg out sometime sent a thrill right through him, but he knew they were opposites in many ways. She was big city, he was a country boy. She had her college degree, and Vance didn't even finish his second year at the University of Kentucky. He had quit school so he could marry Angie, and Cammy was born the next year.

Yeah, he could see where Meg and the new gym teacher might appear more compatible, and as he and Boz walked back to where their friends sat, Vance couldn't fault them for betting on the match. And yet, he wasn't so naïve about life that he didn't sense a spark of interest coming from Meg each time they made eye contact.

Unless, of course, the heat of the day just got to him.

"I'm going over to the cooler." He glanced around at his buddies. "Anyone else want a cold drink?"

* * * * *

All she wanted was a cool bubble bath when she got back to Grams' house. Meg imagined how marvelous it would feel to shed her clothes and relax in a tub filled with fragrant, silky soap. It'd sure beat the smell of hot grills and sweaty humanity that prevailed around the picnic area at this late hour.

"I've got three red, white, and blue tablecloths around here," Grams said as they packed up their belongings. "Don't let me forget them."

"Okay."

Meg watched as her grandmother strode away, collecting a plastic bowl here and a stainless pan there.

Despite the heat, it had been an enjoyable day. Meg liked the people she'd met today. She admired their old-fashioned values, their patriotism, their loyalty to God, family, and church—qualities so indicative of the area.

"You never answered my question."

Meg stopped clearing plastic plates, glasses, and Styrofoam cups from off one of the picnic tables and stared at Leah Lawton. "What? What question?"

"About Kent. Aren't you the least bit interested in him?"

"Nope. He's too full of himself. Besides, I didn't move to Kentucky because I'm looking for love. On the contrary. This teaching position means everything to me. I want to succeed at it, grow as a person, and stay put for once in my life."

"Well, I want that, too, except for the staying-put part. I wouldn't mind traveling some. But add a husband and a few kids to that equation and I'll be the happiest woman in the world."

Meg arched a brow. "A husband like Dave the marine, perhaps?" She couldn't help turning the tables on her new friend.

Leah expelled a dramatic sigh. "Pathetic, isn't it? I'm falling in love with a guy I've never met."

"You've met. On the Internet."

"I'm talking about *in person*." Leah's face pinked, and Meg knew it wasn't from the warm, thick evening air. "My parents are worried. Dad says it could be a case of bait and switch. You know, like Dave put up a picture of his hunky buddy, except in real life Dave is a hound—or worse, a man with ill intentions!"

Meg thought it over while she resumed clearing the table. "Guess it's possible. But it's nothing that can't happen 'in person.' Just exercise caution and common sense."

"I believe I'm doing just that." Leah paused and placed a hand on her bony hip. "But why would a good-looking fella like Dave want a skinny thing like me? Dad says I better get some meat on my bones. But when I feel pressured to eat I lose my appetite. I wind up losing weight."

"Wish that would happen to me." Meg found it somewhat difficult to pity her willowy friend. "Like I said before, maybe Dave is drawn to slim women. Besides, it's what's inside of you that matters most."

Leah stopped in mid-motion. "You're absolutely right. God sees the heart. Maybe Dave will see mine." She continued with the clean-up. "I just need to draw on my faith."

Meg mulled over the reply. *To draw on one's faith.* She was trying to tap into that Higher Power, too. Was it God? Was He real, as her grandmother claimed? Meg felt she had no other options than to discover the answer for herself. She had a lot to prove, being a new teacher in a close community, and it wasn't easy forging out a future without hope and purpose. Even so, this faith business was uncharted territory for her.

"Grams says everything that happens in life serves a divine purpose." The comment came as an afterthought.

"I believe that, too."

"Then why are you still worried about Dave?"

"I—I don't know." Leah looked bemused. "I reckon it's just a bad habit."

"I reckon so," Meg imitated.

Leah paused and placed her hands on her hips. "We need to work on that Southern drawl of yours."

"What Southern drawl?"

"Exactly."

They laughed.

* * * * *

With the lights off in her first floor bedroom, Loretta lay awake, listening to the wind rustling through the treetops. Her window was opened just an inch or so, and she heard an infrequent rumble of thunder in the distance.

She also heard Meggie traipsing around upstairs, and the creaking floorboards were a welcome sound after years of silence. Loretta never thought she'd be thankful for noise. Not after raising three sons. But she was.

Snuggling further down into her bedcovers, Loretta closed her eyes and smiled. How proud she was of her eldest granddaughter! Her friends were all impressed by Meggie's intellect and mannerly ways, said everyone said she wasn't a thing like her mother, who'd brought shame upon the Jorgenson name. True, Meggie had made mistakes—who hadn't? But she was quick to accept her wrongdoings and move forward, while her mother had always blamed others for her problems.

"Treading in the cesspool of life." That's what Jeb used to say, and while Loretta agreed with him, she also pitied Tricia. From what Meggie had said in recent weeks, it sounded like the poor misguided soul hadn't changed much in all these years.

Still treading.

But Meggie clearly wanted more out of life, wanted meaning and purpose. She said she'd even distanced herself from her mother back in high school. Meggie learned to be responsible and did well in school. She graduated with honors and went on to college. She had such potential. Jeb would be so proud.

Meggie. Meggie. Meggie. What a joy that she had moved in. Just wait till she got reacquainted with her cousins—especially the twins. She'd get a kick out of those boys. They'd been toddlers when Meg saw them last. Loretta smiled, thinking of her two precocious red-headed grandsons. They always had something to say.

She stayed her mind on pleasant thoughts while strains of music wafted down from the second floor. She closed her eyes and, at last, drifted off to sleep.

Chapter Ten

....

The eleven-forty-five bell sounded, and Meg jumped so that she almost dropped the dry-erase marker in her hand.

She looked up at the modern-looking device, which had just droned out an electronic *don-ong*. "That thing certainly gets a person's attention."

Giggles and snickers emanated from her students.

Meg herself had to laugh. The first day of school, and so far everything had gone as planned—except for the fact that she'd lost track of time. Where had the morning gone?

"All right, class, put away your math books."

Sounds of textbooks slapping shut and desks creaking open filled the room.

Meg looked at Cammy Bayer, who sat in the front row wearing a floral-printed dress, pink anklets, and white leather sandals. She'd dressed up for the first day of school.

She sent Cammy a smile before her gaze traveled on. The other girls, too, wore dresses today, while the boys looked clean and pressed in casual slacks and polo shirts. A few boys actually wore short-sleeved oxfords, although the shirts didn't stay tucked into their trousers once mid-morning recess time came along.

Absorbing the sight, Meg felt like she'd stepped into another world. At her old school in Chicago, most of the boys wore ragged jeans with holes in the knees, wrinkled tees, and hair that never saw a comb. A majority of the teenaged girls dressed in ways that even a young woman like Meg thought pushed the limits of decency.

Meg understood that there was a difference between grade school kids and high schoolers, but she'd determined weeks ago that life here in Miracle was nothing even remotely akin to life in the south side of Chicago. Everyone here was functioning at a slower pace, not racing ahead in life's fast lane. Here conservative views on issues prevailed, everyone owned a Bible, and if you didn't attend church, you were either physically ill or dead. It all ran contrary to what Meg was accustomed to, and for that very reason, she welcomed it.

She fixed her gaze on Cammy again. "You may leave for the lunchroom and get a head start. We'll catch up."

"Yes, ma'am."

And that was another thing: All the kids said "yes, ma'am" when spoken to. How refreshing.

Meg watched the little girl maneuver her wheelchair towards the door. "Okay, class, let's line up."

The students did as she bid them, with only nominal pushing and shoving from a few rambunctious boys.

Heading up the queue now, Meg narrowed her gaze at those wearing the mischievous grins. "We're going to walk quietly and quickly down to the lunchroom, and I don't want to see any nonsense. Got it?"

"Yes, Miss Jorgenson," came the unanimous reply.

Meg hid her smile as she pivoted, then led her class into the hallway.

Susie Fletcher slipped her small hand into Meg's. "Can I sit with you at lunch?"

"Sure." She glanced at the girl, whose beige plastic-framed glasses were sliding down her nose.

"Can I sit with you, too?" The request came from Erin Hollister.

"Yep. Lucky for you both I have two sides."

"What about me?"

Meg glanced over her shoulder and glimpsed the pout on Laura

Blakemore's freckled face. "You can sit next to me tomorrow."

"And me, too," said Ginger Widdenstamp.

Meg realized she'd need a date book at this rate, but it warmed her heart that her students asked to sit next to her at lunchtime. They liked her, wanted to eat with her!

Yet another difference from last year.

Chatter and childish laughter filled the cheery cafeteria. Over the din, however, she heard a male voice calling her name. Turning on her heel, she saw Kent approaching her.

"How's your first day been?" he asked.

"Great, so far."

"Mine's been insane." He cupped her elbow. "I'd like to speak with you."

"Well, um. . .I promised my kids I'd eat with them."

"Just for a moment."

Before she could protest, he'd propelled her into the hallway.

"Listen, I know you'll understand this, being from the other side of the Bible Belt like me." He smirked.

Meg didn't find the remark amusing. "What's going on?"

Dressed in black dress shorts and a red T-shirt, he widened his stance and rocked slightly from side to side. Meg was reminded of a comedian on stage about to tell a joke.

"I wanted to find a coffee shop this morning, right? A simple thing. So I stopped and asked directions. A couple of guys said it was down the block and to the left, across from the 'tar store.'" He paused. "Tar store." He shook his head. "I drove around for a full five minutes before I realized there was no tar store. It's a *tire* store." Kent put his hands on his narrow hips. "Can you believe it?"

Meg forced a polite smile. "Guess I've always been accustomed to that good ol' Kentucky drawl. I was born here and my dad and grandmother, along with a host of relatives, live here."

"Well, more power to you. But get a load of this: a guy can't even get a six pack of beer around here!"

"I know. It's a dry county."

"One of my neighbors told me that when the weather gets bad, the cops go out and collect the few homeless people around here and put them in jail, feed them. Like it's some kind of hotel."

Meg thought it was quite the humanitarian gesture. "What's wrong with that?"

Kent leaned forward. "I feel like I died and went to Mayberry R.F.D." She grinned.

Kent wagged his blond head. "I am suffering from culture shock."

"Think assimilation." This time Meg gave him a parting smile as she stepped around him.

He caught her by the elbow. "Have dinner with me tonight." All traces of humor had fled, and Meg recognized the look in his darkening green eyes. "We'll drive to Lexington and go to my place afterwards for a nightcap. You can help me. . .*assimilate*."

She pulled from his grasp. "Are you crazy? We're at school. You can't ask me out in the hallway like we're in some nightclub." She kept her voice low, but irritation threatened to get the best of her.

"Relax. No one's around."

"Still."

Kent raised his brows. "Is that a yes or a no?"

"Definitely a no. Now, if you don't mind, my students are waiting for me."

Meg re-entered the lunchroom. She picked up a plastic tray and got in line for a serving of baked chicken legs, white beans, biscuits, and, for dessert, a slice of apple pie. She tried to forget Kent's none-too-subtle proposition as she accepted a plate from the jolly-looking cook. But then worry began nibbling at her when she considered the possible consequences of Kent's foolishness just now. He must have lost his mind.

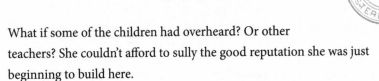

What if some of the children had overheard? Or other teachers? She couldn't afford to sully the good reputation she was just beginning to build here.

Fortunately, no one did hear—Meg felt confident about that much.

She pushed aside the unfortunate event and sat down in the chair which Susie and Erin had saved for her. She concentrated on their girlish prattle and soon forgot all about Kent Baldwin and his dinner invitation.

* * * * *

Meg glanced at her sterling-banded wristwatch. "Cammy, if you don't hurry you'll miss the bus."

"Oh, no, Miss Jorgenson, I don't take the bus home. My daddy picks me up after he gets off of work."

"Hmm." Thoughtfully, Meg crossed the carpeted classroom floor and stared out the bank of windows. She saw scores of students climbing into the long yellow vehicle. Only one school bus serviced the small school, and it was contracted through a private company. "What time does your dad get off work?"

"About four thirty."

Meg resigned herself to the fact. "Well, all right, then—"

"I could sit in the office, but I'd much rather stay here with you."

Flattered, Meg turned from the windows and smiled at Cammy. "That's fine. I planned to stay here until about five anyway. How about you finish your homework while you wait?"

Meg glimpsed the affirmative bob of Cammy's head and then strode to her own desk and sat down. Gathering the pages of arithmetic that her students had completed this morning, she began correcting each one. She made an encouraging comment on each child's paper, even if the grade was low. "You'll do better next time." "Good penmanship." "Great job." Meg wanted her students to know that she cared about them. In return, they might start caring about her opinion and work harder, learn more.

Meg came to Cammy's worksheet, graded it, and felt a frown pucker her brows. The child had earned an F.

"Cammy, did you have difficulty with your math sheet this morning?" With no one else in the classroom, Meg felt free to discuss the matter with the girl. "You're so smart. What's up with this grade?"

She shrugged. "I guess I'm dumb in math."

"You're *not* dumb. Let's do the worksheet over again. I'll help you this time." Meg found an extra copy of the math sheet. Pushing to her feet, she made her way over to Cammy, whose desk was wider and higher than the other children's so it could accommodate a wheelchair.

She pulled a chair alongside Cammy.

"I always get bad grades in math."

"How about if we change that this year?"

Cammy appeared skeptical but didn't refuse.

Number by number, equation by equation, Meg explained the principles of addition and subtraction. Cammy understood that much about arithmetic. She just grew impatient trying to arrive at the correct sums. So Meg made a game of it, making up little rhymes by which Cammy could remember the sums. Pretty soon Cammy played along.

In no time, the worksheet was completed, and Meg marked a large A+ at the top.

The sudden sound of a man clearing his voice drew their attention away from mathematics.

"Daddy, I got an A+ on my arithmetic!"

"Good for you, punkin." He strode into the classroom, bidding Meg a hello with a slight inclination of his head.

She smiled a greeting while taking note, again, of his uniform:

trousers and shirt of the same khaki color and fabric. His first name was embroidered in red thread atop the left breast pocket. She couldn't help remembering what Grams said yesterday about how Vance began his education in law enforcement but, because of circumstances beyond his control, settled for small engine repair. Was he satisfied with his life, even though it hadn't turn out the way he planned? He seemed like a relatively contented man, and Cammy was a spunky, happy little girl. Something was obviously going right for him.

Vance stood by wearing one of his almost bashful grins.

"Lovely weather since the storm rolled through last night," Meg ventured. She still sat beside Cammy and now helped her pack her notebook and school supplies. "Nothing like a good thunderstorm to clear the air."

"A lot of truth to that." Vance approached and took hold of the handles behind his daughter's wheelchair. Leaning forward, he placed a kiss on top of Cammy's head. "Tell your teacher good-bye for now."

"Bye, Miss Jorgenson."

"Bye, Cammy."

"I can't wait till math tomorrow."

Vance paused, chuckled, and shook his head. "Never thought I'd hear her say that." He looked at Meg, still smiling. "Math's her least favorite subject."

"My *worst* one, too." The pleased expression seemed pasted to Cammy's impish features. "But not anymore!"

"That's music to my ears." Meg stood as the Bayers moved toward the doorway.

"See you in the morning," Vance said with a parting dip of his head. "Have a good night."

Watching them go, Meg couldn't remember the last time she felt so encouraged in her chosen profession.

* * * * *

Cammy took a large bite of her taco. "I'm so glad you—"

"Chew your food before talking." Vance hid his grin.

She swallowed her mouthful. "Daddy, I'm glad you picked up tacos on your way home. I was starved all day cuz I didn't eat lunch."

"Why not?"

"Well. . ." Cammy took a deep breath.

Vance sat back on the kitchen chair. He had a feeling a long, involved explanation was on its way.

"Miss Jorgenson let me go to the lunchroom ahead of the class, but the elevator didn't come when I pushed the button. So then Mr. Gerler, the janitor, was walking down the hall and he used his key. The elevator came and when I finally got to the lunchroom, my class was already there and that's when I heard Miss Jorgenson and Mr. Baldwin talking. He asked her to go to dinner and show him how to 'similate.'"

"Similate? What does that mean?"

"I guess it means how to teach school," Cammy said with a shrug of her slender shoulders.

Vance hoped to God the pair weren't discussing anything immoral in the grade school hallway. No, Meg wouldn't do that.

But that gym teacher just might.

"Anyway, Miss Jorgenson told him no right on the spot."

"Told him no?"

"For the date."

"Ah." Vance felt oddly appeased, but he still felt the need to address the situation.

"Cammy Ann Bayer," he began, arching a brow. "Were you eavesdropping?"

She lowered her gaze.

"Well?"

"I. . .well. . ." At long last, she nodded.

"That's a naughty thing for a little girl to do."

"I only wondered if Miss Jorgenson and Mr. Baldwin are going to be boyfriend and girlfriend."

"That's none of your business." He kneaded the back of his neck, wondering why he felt so tense. "But when they were done talking, why didn't you go into the cafeteria, get some food, and find your friends?"

"Because then they'd know I listened on purpose and I didn't want Miss Jorgenson not to like me. You won't tell her, will you?"

"I can't make a promise like that, Cammy."

"Oh, Daddy—" Her face contorted with dismay.

"But rest assured that if I do speak to Miss Jorgenson, I'll be very nice about it. And I think she's the forgiving sort."

"Really?" Cammy looked hopeful again. "You're forgiving, too, aren't you, Daddy?"

"Forgiving, yes, but I'm still the disciplinarian around here, and you, missy, are going straight to your room after supper. I don't like this sneaky business. Some conversations are not meant for your ears—or anyone else's, for that matter."

Cammy pouted, but she didn't complain.

They ate in silence for a few strained minutes. Vance felt himself growing more irritated by the fact that the new gym teacher had the nerve to pursue a woman right in the school hallway. His irritation had nothing to do with the fact that it was *Meg* Kent Baldwin was after.

Or, maybe it did—a little.

The admission took him by surprise. Why should he care?

He didn't think he really did. He was just overtired, most likely.

In any event, he had to figure out the best way to handle this situation. Should he talk to Meg about it, or should he go directly to Baldwin and tell him to cool his jets on the job?

Vance took a bite of his burrito, mulling it over. Maybe it wasn't really that big a deal.

"Daddy, maybe you should ask Miss Jorgenson to dinner. She could come here and I'll make macaroni and cheese."

"Eat your supper." He nodded at the taco on her paper plate. "It's getting late, and we still have to get you out of that wheelchair, do your exercises, and get you washed up." Vance stood and discarded the rest of his supper in the trash. The evening wasn't even half done. "Is your homework finished?"

"Most of it. I just have to start on my essay about what I did this summer. It's due on Friday. Miss Jorgenson said that we'll have time during school to write it but that we oughta start it at home. I can't wait. I love to write stories. I just have to remember all the names of my camp counselors. Let's see, there's—"

"Cammy, eat."

She replied with one of her sweetest smiles. "Yes, Daddy."

Chapter Eleven

....

At Kelly's persistent request, Meg agreed to go shopping tonight. She ate a quick dinner and then drove over to Dad's place. His home sat on sprawling acreage with horses, pastures, and a large stable. As she pulled into the long, winding driveway, she recalled how Mom used to say they had to scrimp and scrounge for their next meal because Dad saved all his money for his "country ranch." Certainly her dad's horse ranch was modest, but Meg couldn't help wondering how much of her mother's remarks were true.

She parked and climbed out of the car, squinting into the evening sun as she walked toward the door. Donna's voice met her in the back hall.

"Come on in. Kelly's almost ready to go."

Meg made her way into the kitchen, where Donna was cleaning up supper dishes.

"How's the teaching coming along?"

"Just fine, thanks." Meg sat on one of the stools at the breakfast counter and watched her stepmother load plates into the dishwasher. "Can I help you with those?"

"Naw, I'm almost done. Thanks, though, hon."

Dad sauntered in. "Well, Meggie." He gave her a fatherly once-over. "I can't see any bald patches from you pullin' your hair out."

She smiled. "I can handle the kids here in Stanford."

"Not all of 'em are as nice as you might assume. Some are downright troublemakers."

"I know. I've got a few of those in my class."

Dad sat down on the stool beside her. "Sure you'll know how to handle 'em?" he teased. "You never got into any kind of trouble in school when you were little."

Meg felt herself tense. How would *he* know what she was like as a student? Why was he suddenly pretending that he had ever been more to her than a biological father she was forced to visit two weeks out of every year?

"Ryan and Kelly are good kids, too."

Meg didn't reply.

"But they're both still kids, Kelly especially. She's just sixteen, you know, and you're twenty-six. She looks up to you. You know that, right?"

"Are you insinuating that I'm a bad influence on her?"

"No, no." Dad set a hand on her forearm. "Don't get your dander up. I'm just informing you that, well, Kelly was raised different from you."

Meg glanced at Donna before looking back at her father. "Obviously."

Donna turned off the water and dried her hands on a dishtowel as she moved to the counter. "I believe what your dad's saying in his roundabout way is that Kel has school tomorrow, so we don't want her staying out too late."

Meg turned to her dad once more. "Is that what you're trying to tell me?"

"Well, yeah."

"Why didn't you just say so?"

"I don't know. Didn't want to offend you."

Meg sent a glance soaring upward and shook her head. She'd always preferred the direct approach, and this instance was no exception. "I have school tomorrow, too, so we definitely won't be out too late."

"I think the mall in Lexington closes at nine o'clock."

"Can we have until ten thirty so I don't have to speed all the way back to Miracle?" Meg had trouble keeping the sarcasm out of her voice.

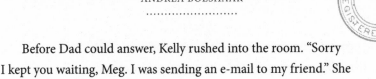

Before Dad could answer, Kelly rushed into the room. "Sorry I kept you waiting, Meg. I was sending an e-mail to my friend." She turned to Dad. "Emily Miles."

"Of course. Emily. Nice girl." Dad stood.

Meg did the same. She had that old feeling of being an "outsider" again. Along with it came the feeling that, in her father's eyes, she'd never measure up to Kelly, or even to Emily Miles, whoever Emily Miles was. Meg couldn't recall a time when Dad had ever dubbed her a "nice girl." She couldn't even remember if he had ever openly praised any of her accomplishments.

But maybe that was just because he hadn't known about them. Who would've told him? Mom didn't ever speak to him. And Meg herself had never been much of a bragger.

She tried to walk the proverbial mile in his shoes, to understand his position. Besides, it seemed that Dad was putting forth some sort of effort to get to know her—now.

Kelly raised herself up on tiptoes and kissed Dad's check. "Bye."

"Behave yourselves, you two."

"Oh, Daddy."

Meg grinned at her half sister's exasperation and followed her out of the house.

"And it's a ten thirty curfew," Dad called from the back door. "Remember that: ten thirty."

"Okay, Daddy. We'll remember." Then, after climbing into the car, Kelly muttered, "Whatever."

Meg couldn't help laughing as she started up her car's engine. But her smile soon faded. "I don't think he trusts me to take you shopping." She made a Y-turn and headed down the driveway.

"No, it's not you. Dad's just super overprotective. It really gets on my nerves." Kelly rifled through her purse, dug out a piece of chewing gum, and popped it into her mouth. "You're so lucky you didn't have to put up with all his rules and restrictions when you were my age."

"I'm not so sure about that." Meg turned onto the highway and pressed her foot on the gas pedal. "But if there's one thing I am certain of, it's that come rain, sleet, snow, or hail, I'll still have you back home well before ten thirty, or my name isn't Meghan Marie Jorgenson."

* * * * *

The following day, Vance dropped Cammy off at school earlier than he had the previous day. After mulling over the hallway incident, he decided he needed to discuss it with Meg. His daughter wasn't the only one in the community who liked to eavesdrop, and Meg ought to know about it.

A few raindrops began to fall from an overcast sky just as Vance wheeled Cammy into school. A minute or so later, they entered the classroom. Meg sat at her desk, writing something.

"Well, good morning," she said with a sunny smile.

"Hi, Miss Jorgenson. I got a lot of my essay written last night. Wanna see it?"

"If you don't mind, I'd like a word with your teacher first, Cammy."

She looked up at Vance with a pained expression.

He gave his daughter's shoulder an assuring squeeze and then looked over at Meg. "Have a minute?"

"Sure."

"Could we talk somewhere sort of—private?"

"How about the coatroom?" She stood, and Vance couldn't help noticing how her brown slacks accentuated her slender hips, while her ruffled beige blouse only made her other curves more pronounced. Vance could understand Kent Baldwin's eagerness to ask her out. He didn't condone it, but he could understand it.

"It won't be private for long. We'll have to hurry." Meg led the way into a narrow section of the classroom. Shiny stainless hooks lined the far wall, and wood benches had been placed below them. "What's up?"

She turned to face him, and Vance's insides suddenly felt like mush as he stared into her sky blue eyes.

"It's Cammy." He really disliked having to bring this up. "Well, she overheard something yesterday and, as a result, didn't eat her lunch. I thought you'd better know."

Meg grew paler with each word that came out of Vance's mouth. "I talked to Cammy and warned her not to eavesdrop in the future." He tilted his head. "Hey, are you okay? Maybe you should sit down."

Meg shook her head, and strands of her honey-blond hair slipped out of its clip. "I'm fine."

"Well, look, this probably isn't a big deal, but I felt you should know."

"I can't believe Cammy missed lunch, that poor thing."

"She survived."

"Look, I'm so sorry. It won't happen again. I promise."

"I believe you." Vance lowered his gaze, sensing he'd embarrassed her. He hadn't meant to. "I figured this whole thing wasn't your fault. Sounds like Mr. Baldwin oughta be the one apologizing. But I still thought I should give you a heads-up. People like to talk around here, you know?"

"I know."

He stared at his steel-toed brown boots for several long seconds before he looked back at her. "Would it help if I said something to Kent Baldwin?"

"That's your decision, but—" She pushed her shoulders back, standing a little straighter. "—I do intend to give him a few choice words of my own."

Vance rubbed the side of his jaw to conceal his grin. He almost pitied the guy just then.

"I appreciate your bringing this matter to my attention. As I said, it won't happen again."

"It's over and done with, as far as I'm concerned."

Her features softened. "Thanks, Vance. This job means everything to me, and I want the parents here at Fairview Academy to respect me. I think some have their doubts about me because of things that happened in the past, things I had no control over."

He sensed the indirect reference to her mother and the "things" she'd done. Everyone in town, thirty years old or older, had heard a tale or two about Tricia Lattice and the disgrace she had brought upon herself and her family. Her folks moved to Louisville after she left town, and most speculated it was because they couldn't bear the shame. Vance heard they'd both passed in the last ten years.

But any fool could see that Meg was different from her mother. Took after the Jorgenson side. Why, Loretta clucked about her like a proud hen.

"I think most everyone finds you a delight. I know I do." Vance realized what he had just said and wanted to swallow his tongue.

"Well, thanks, Vance. You just made my day."

The smile that lit her face changed his mind about being so forthright. A response like that, and he'd have to do it more often.

Meg walked alongside him back into the classroom. Vance approached Cammy and kissed the top of her head. "I'm leaving now. Behave yourself."

"I will, Daddy."

He sent a parting grin in Meg's direction, and as he walked outside, he barely noticed the steady drizzle.

* * * * *

While the kids were out at recess time, Meg penned a quick note to Kent, saying she needed to speak with him. She folded it, slipped it into his mailbox, and left the main office to rejoin the children and other teachers on the playground.

After school let out, Meg slipped away and checked her mail slot. Kent had replied: *We'll talk over dinner. Pick you up at seven. No need for directions. I know where you live.*

Meg stifled a groan as she made her way back to her classroom. Every muscle, joint, and fiber in her body tensed at the thought of having dinner with Kent. Well, she'd just have to turn him down at the doorway when he arrived at Grams' house. And how did he know where she lived, anyway?

"What's wrong, Miss Jorgenson?"

Meg looked up and spied the concerned expression on Cammy Bayer's face. She forced a smile and crumpled the note from Kent, tossing it into the waste basket. "Nothing's wrong. I'm just thinking about something."

Meg sat in her desk chair and tried not to dwell on her dilemma by correcting the spelling worksheets from this afternoon. She'd gotten through only two sheets when Cammy started asking questions.

"Did my Daddy tell you about—well, I did something I shouldn't have done."

"Yes, he told me."

Cammy's eyes grew misty and she looked as thought she might cry. Meg suddenly suspected that the child's guilt and remorse had been brewing all day.

"You won't eavesdrop again, will you?"

"No, ma'am." Cammy shook her head.

"Good, then we'll just forget all about it, okay?"

"Okay."

Meg turned her attention to the worksheets once more.

"Do you have a boyfriend, Miss Jorgenson?"

Looking up, Meg felt tempted to reproach Cammy for even asking, but she knew by now that this precocious girl didn't mean any harm with her inquisitions. "No, I don't have a boyfriend." Teasingly, she grinned and arched a brow. "Do you have someone in mind?"

"We-ell," Cammy drawled as she doodled with her pencil. "My daddy doesn't have a girlfriend."

"Oh, I see." Meg had certainly walked right into that one. She decided it might be best not to remark any further on the subject. "So do you watch any TV shows at night? What's your favorite?"

"Hannah Montana." Cammy tipped her head. "How come you don't have a boyfriend?"

After a moment's deliberation, Meg chose to be vague with her reply, sensing it'd likely get relayed to Vance. "I don't have time for a boyfriend right now. I'm concentrating on being a good teacher."

"Oh, you're a good teacher, Miss Jorgenson."

"Thank you, Cammy." Meg sent her a smile.

"I'm done with my essay. Wanna hear it?"

"Sure." Meg folded her hands above the stack of worksheets.

Cammy opened her desk, pulled out her folder, and poised herself over her piece of wide-lined paper. "'Last summer I spent lots of time over at my aunt Debbie's house. I don't like it so much over there because my cousin Tyler is the baddest boy in all of Lincoln County. My aunt has to yell at him and then he starts crying and Aunt Debbie turns up the TV so she can hear her soaps. That's why I like it better at day camp. My favorite counselor is Ruthanne. She tells me about all her boyfriends. Earl Ray is her best boyfriend. He plays lots of baseball and Ruthanne likes to go watch him play.'"

A fuller picture of Cammy's life formed in Meg's mind.

"'At camp I go canoeing or horseback riding in the morning. My favorite horse is Buckshot. I use a special saddle so I don't fall off of him. Then we have lunch. The cook's name is Gracie and she makes watery mashed potatoes, but they're still good. Sometimes I help feed the other kids cuz they're worser off than me. Some can't even swallow without a special machine to help them and they can't taste Gracie's mashed potatoes. One girl named Abby has a feeding tube in her. No one talks to her because she can't talk back. She makes noises, though, and I can understand her and I tell my counselor Ruthanne whenever Abby needs something.'"

Lowering her gaze, Meg suspected that Cammy's disability deepened her level of sensitivity toward others. Instead of feeling angry or bitter about her own disability, she was happy-go-lucky and willing to lend a hand to children like Abby. Meg felt impressed.

"'Some of the other kids like Abby live in an instooshin.'"

"A what?" Meg looked up and frowned in confusion.

"A instooshin."

"Hmm." Meg cupped her chin. "I'm not sure what you mean, but keep reading and perhaps I'll figure it out."

"Okay." Cammy found the place where she'd left off. "'I don't belong in one of those instooshins even though Mrs. Foster told Daddy to send me there.'"

Prickles of unease climbed Meg's spine.

"'She wanted to get rid of me so she could marry Daddy and so one of her kids could have my bedroom. Michael said he'd tear down my Hannah Montana posters and paint it a barfy blue. But that won't happen because Daddy doesn't go on dates with Mrs. Foster anymore—'"

"An *institution*? Is that what you're trying to say?"

Cammy bobbed her head. "I heard Mrs. Foster tell Daddy that and Michael said it lots of times."

"Who's Michael?"

"Michael Foster. He thinks he's so cool cuz he's twelve and older than me."

"Ah." He sounded like a bully, but Meg carefully guarded her reaction since she didn't know the full story. "Keep reading."

Cammy stared back at her page. "'—and that was the best part of my summer. Now Daddy and me can live happily ever after. The End.'"

"Well, Cammy. . ." Meg didn't know quite what to say.

The little girl watched her, awaiting approval.

"You wrote a very detailed and interesting essay. You're a good writer."

"I write stories all the time. I draw pictures for my stories, too."

"You're aware that your essay isn't supposed to be a story that's made up in your imagination. It's supposed to be the truth."

"My essay is the truth. Honest!"

"All right. I just wanted to be clear about the assignment."

"Yes, ma'am. Can I hand it in now?"

"Don't you want to show it to your dad first?" Meg wanted to be sensitive about the information her students shared with her, and she felt Vance should be aware of his child's candidness. "The part about Mrs. Foster and your dad might make him feel bad. You may want to rewrite that portion."

"My dad doesn't feel bad. He said he didn't love her."

"Well, maybe you should let your dad read your essay just to check your spelling and grammar before you hand it in. All right?"

Cammy gave a roll of her shoulders. "Okay." She slipped the loose page into her folder and leaned over to lift her backpack off the floor just as Vance entered the classroom.

"Hi, Daddy."

"Hi, punkin." He placed a kiss on the top of Cammy's head before nodding a greeting to Meg.

"I personally made sure Cammy ate lunch today."

"Miss Jorgenson sat at my lunch table."

"I'm sure you enjoyed her company." Vance mouthed the words "thank you" over Cammy's head. Slinging her backpack over one shoulder, he pulled her wheelchair away from her desk and turned her around.

"Bye, Miss Jorgenson." The little girl twisted the upper half of her body around and waved.

"Bye, Cammy."

* * * * *

While Tom sat at the kitchen table, sipping a cup of coffee, Loretta listened to Meg relay her dilemma about the new gym teacher's invitation to dinner. Clearly she didn't want to go out with the man, but he hadn't given her much of a chance to politely decline.

"It's only the second day of school, and already this guy has gotten me in trouble with one of my students' parents." She let out a groan. "I wish he'd go back to Minnesota."

"Can you speak with Earl about it?" Removing a cookie cutter from the utility drawer, Loretta began cutting out rounds of biscuit dough and laying them on a pan. Biscuits and beef stew were on the menu for dinner; it was a good day to turn on the oven. Rainy, chilly, and bone-achingly damp. "Earl's always been a fair-minded man."

"I need to talk to Kent first. If the situation doesn't improve, then I'll get our principal involved."

"Very wise decision," Loretta said, feeling proud of Meggie.

"I think Kent's a reasonable guy. I hope."

"I don't think the school district would have hired him if he wasn't. And every unattached female in Miracle has stars in her eyes over him."

"Not this unattached female."

Tom grunted out a laugh at Meggie's retort.

Loretta glanced at her granddaughter in time to see displeasure cloud her countenance like the gloomy skies outside. "Meggie, you could ask Mr. Baldwin to stay to dinner here at the house. There's plenty of food, and I could hold off on the biscuits until he arrives."

"Why would I do something nice like that? I have a mind to tell him off when he comes to the door."

"No, no." Loretta shook her head. "That's not polite."

Meggie laughed. "Oh, yeah, I forgot about Southern hospitality and all that."

"You'll get the hang of it." Loretta suppressed a smile. "But, seriously, if you ask Mr. Baldwin to stay for dinner, you'll have the chance to discuss the matter of his boldness without being placed in any sort of awkward position."

Loretta could see that Meggie was considering it.

"Grams, are you sure?" she said at last. "I really don't want to go out to dinner with Kent, and since it's not 'polite' to tell him off at the door," she said with a teasing light in her blue eyes, "then inviting him in would solve everything."

One glance at Tom and Loretta knew he was enjoying Meggie's pluck.

"Of course I'm sure. He's welcome to stay for dinner. Besides, I love to entertain. Don't do enough of it."

"Your grammaw's in her element, cookin' and feedin' folks."

"Had a lot of practice," Loretta added.

"All right, I'll ask him to stay." Meggie's tone did not sound enthusiastic. "But I feel it's only fair to warn you, Grams. He strikes me as a man who prefers wining and dining and the glitter of nightlife to a cozy supper around the family table."

"I'll consider myself fairly warned."

"Reckon if he doesn't want to stay, Meggie, then you're off the hook," Tom said.

"One can only hope."

Tom replied with a snort of amusement.

"You know," Meggie began on a more serious note, "I thought about this during my drive home from school. Kent's the sort of guy my mom tends to fall for."

Loretta looked over and saw Meggie tuck several strands of hair behind one ear.

"Once, Mom lived with a guy she met while she managed a fitness center. He was a weight lifter and totally into himself. I used to eat my breakfast while he'd point out various muscles on his arms and chest that he was pumping up." Meggie rolled her eyes.

"During breakfast?" Loretta grimaced. "How ill-mannered."

"Manners? That guy didn't know the meaning of the word." Meggie's voice was thick with disgust. "Another time, Mom moved us in with a construction worker who was really buff."

"Buff?"

"Built, Grams. Muscular."

"Oh."

Tom hooted while Loretta tucked the word "buff" into her memory bank. She tried to keep up with the trendy vernacular of her grandchildren, but he thought it always sounded rather funny when she tried to repeat it.

"So this guy liked to work out on his off days, and eventually he became abusive to Mom and me. He'd lose his temper with zero provocation. Months later, Mom discovered the guy was injecting steroids. We moved out as soon as we found another apartment, but we had to leave when he wasn't around. We couldn't let him know where we were going because we didn't trust his temper. I was actually really frightened by that entire situation."

Loretta's heart felt tight in her chest. She had had no idea. "Oh, Meggie, I'm so sorry you had to live like that. I wish I would have known. I would have sent for you myself."

"It's not your fault. I actually thought I was pretty happy back then, if only because I didn't know better. In fact, I thought Mom's lifestyle— the boyfriends, the continual moving—was normal until I got to college and started meeting friends who had two stable parents living under the same roof."

Loretta shook her head while a sea of regret flooded her heart. "Maybe that's why you find Mr. Baldwin unappealing—he reminds you of that life."

"I'm sure you're right." Meggie strode to the refrigerator and took out a bottle of Diet Coke. Loretta had bought a twelve-pack of bottles after discovering the beverage was Meggie's favorite. "But it goes even beyond that. The way I see it, Kent dates women like it's a sport. I, on the other hand, am looking for something *real.*" She shook her honey-blond head and laughed. "Actually, I'm not even looking."

"Well, you might give the feller a chance," Tom drawled.

"I don't know. What's the point?"

"Perhaps Mr. Baldwin isn't looking to date at all," Loretta pointed out. "Maybe he's in need of a few good friends, seeing that he's new here in Miracle."

Meg looked skeptical. "I think Kent's looking for a good time. He doesn't strike me as friend material."

An instant later, Loretta chided herself for being naïve. Back in her day, nice men didn't look for a "good time," and the ones who did wouldn't pay any mind to a fine girl like Meggie.

"You really think Kent's all that?" Loretta found the idea ever so disappointing.

"And then some." Meggie grinned before setting down her bottle of cola. "But I'll be polite and ask him to stay for dinner. You and Tom can make up your own minds about him." She blew out a breath of resignation. "Guess I'd better freshen up a little bit before he arrives."

Chapter Twelve

. . . .

"Daddy, guess what?"

"What, punkin?" Vance scooped a small portion of the scrambled eggs he'd made for supper out of the frying pan and onto a plate.

"Miss Jorgenson doesn't have a boyfriend."

"How do you know that?" He scooped out a larger portion onto a second plate.

"She told me."

"Just came out and made the announcement, huh?"

"Well—"

"Sounds fishy to me." Vance opened the oven and removed the frozen Tater Tots he'd baked to go with the eggs. After sliding some onto Cammy's plate, he took a good number for himself. "Miss Jorgenson doesn't seem like a teacher who'd blabber on about her dating life."

"Well, I did sorta ask her." Cammy's cheeks pinked with the admission.

"Mmm-hmm. I thought maybe you did." Vance set the meal on the table.

"She wasn't mad, Daddy." Cammy looked at him with her huge blue eyes, rimmed with dark lashes. "She just came out and answered my question."

Vance took a seat at the dinner table. "It's not nice to ask people personal questions like that."

"But how else are you gonna know?"

"I don't have to know—and neither do you."

"But, Daddy—"

"Let's say grace so we can eat. I'm starved."

Cammy pressed her lips together, and Vance bowed his head and asked God to bless their food. He also placed a silent request for patience and wisdom where his well-intentioned daughter was concerned.

"Please pass the ketchup."

Vance set the bottle within her reach and watched her glop some onto her plate. "Daddy, don't you like Miss Jorgenson?"

"Sure, I do." He salted and peppered his eggs and Tots. "But this isn't about me. This is about you, a little girl who should not be asking her teacher personal questions."

"I just wondered if she had a boyfriend cuz I can tell she likes you." Cammy narrowed her eyes. "I saw her look at you real funny."

"Oh, yeah? What do you mean by 'funny'?" He hated the way his inquisitiveness got the better of him.

"We-ell, when you were packing me up today, Miss Jorgenson looked at you sorta like Evie Mathews looks at Henry Preston—and they're getting married!"

"You're makin' that up."

"Am not. Miss Jorgenson did look at you like that."

Vance covered his smile by forking in a mouthful of food. In spite of his teasing, he knew what Cammy meant about those interested glances that passed between Meg and himself. He wasn't exactly stupid when it came to women; he sensed her attraction and was well aware of his own, especially since the Labor Day picnic. And this morning. But he just couldn't envision a relationship between the two of them ever going anywhere. A big-city schoolteacher and a widowed, country hick repairman with a high-needs daughter. Right. And what if she decided she didn't like living here? Why waste time, money, and a whole lot of energy to court a woman who's likely to move on anyway?

He ignored the tweak of disappointment.

"Daddy, maybe you should ask Miss Jorgenson on a date before someone else does."

Vance forced a chuckle "Too late. I'm sure she's already got a string of suitors."

"Maybe so. Max Bixby's in my class and he sure is sweet on her." Cammy giggled. "He picked some flowers out of his mama's garden, and they were still gobbed with mud when he gave 'em to Miss Jorgenson this morning. Everyone knows Mrs. Bixby's sure to warm his backside when she sees her flowers missing. But Max didn't even care."

"Love'll do that to a man—makes him take all leave of his senses." Vance laughed, realizing he'd seen the rather peculiar bouquet on Meg's desk. Its roots floated along the bottom of the clear glass vase.

"Daddy, how 'bout we ask Miss Jorgenson over for dinner sometime?"

"We'll see."

Vance finished his supper and wiped his mouth with a paper napkin. The topic of Cammy's new teacher caused him to eat faster than usual.

Standing, he excused himself from the table and walked his plate over to the sink. As he rinsed it off, he grew uneasy at the thought of Meg coming here to his humble abode. Not that he felt ashamed of his home. Not at all. Except for the old, worn-out chair that had belonged to his father, the place was in decent shape. Angie had fixed everything up so nice and pretty with stencils, borders, and papered walls. Of course, the carpet had been removed and flooring installed once Cammy learned to maneuver her wheelchair. Still, the Bayer home was presentable enough for company, and Vance missed the days when Angie would invite their friends over for dinner or a holiday party. He'd light the fireplace, and they'd laugh and sing while Angie strummed her guitar.

But what would Meg think about it? Nothing better than a shack in her eyes, no doubt. He'd heard she used to live in a fancy penthouse overlooking Lake Michigan. Why she left all that to come to Miracle was beyond Vance's comprehension.

"Cammy, is your homework done?"

"Yep. . .except, Miss Jorgenson wants you to read my essay and make sure I spelled all my words right."

"Okay, where is it?" Vance turned from the sink and regarded his sweet-faced daughter. Her eager blue eyes and heart-shaped face resembled Angie's so much that sometimes he didn't know whether to smile or shed tears of renewed sorrow for his wife.

A moment later he wondered what Angie would think of Meg Jorgenson.

"My essay's in my backpack."

"What?" Vance reined in his wayward thoughts in time to see Cammy pop a Tater Tot into her mouth.

"I said, my essay is in my backpack."

"Oh, right." He glimpsed her plate of food. "Girl, you are one slow eater."

"Well, my stomach is kinda tired of eggs and Tots, Daddy. You still make good dinners. It's just this one."

"You're sick of my specialty?" Vance teased her, well aware that cooking wasn't his strong point. The kitchen had always been Angie's domain.

"Sorry, Daddy, but it's true."

He wondered if Meg could cook. Then he wondered why in the world the woman kept pervading his thoughts.

Once again, he forced his mind to shift gears. *Cammy's essay.* He located her Hannah Montana backpack in the dining room, unzipped it, and pulled out the pages in question. He'd seen Cammy working on the assignment last night.

He began reading about his little girl's summer vacation, enjoying Cammy's spunky style. However, he took an immediate dislike to the description of Debbie's babysitting methods, the yelling and the daytime soaps. He found a few misspelled words and felt proud of Cammy's benevolence at day camp. But when he came to the part about his relationship with Nicole and figured out what Cammy meant by the word "instooshin," he could hardly believe his eyes. He had to read the last part of the essay again.

"Cammy Ann Bayer!" Horrified, Vance stormed into the kitchen. He took a deep breath, taming his rising temper. "How could you write something like this? And show it to your teacher!"

His daughter looked back at him with an expression of baffled innocence. "It's not made up. It's the truth."

"But you made Nicole, your aunt Debbie, and me look like monsters."

"Oh, no, Daddy, you're not a monster. You're the best daddy in the world. But sometimes it's hard at Aunt Debbie's all day with nothing to do, and you already know why I don't like Mrs. Foster."

"Look, you have to be careful what you tell people." Vance pulled out a chair and sat down. "I think you're correct when you write in your essay that you watch too much TV at your aunt's house. From now on, there'll be no TV on school nights."

"But, Daddy—"

"It's only homework and—" He thought quickly. "—and some of those missionary biographies from the church library. That imagination of yours is on a major diet."

"But—"

"Life isn't some fictional drama filled with villains and heroes."

"But there's good people and bad people in the world."

"True, but Nicole Foster and your aunt aren't the bad ones." He shook his head and softened his tone. "Punkin, Mrs. Foster never wanted me to place you in an institution."

"Yes, she did. I heard her say so."

"When?"

"Well, I don't remember exactly all the other times, but I did hear her say so that last day she came here."

It took a few seconds, but Vance suddenly recalled the exact day to which his daughter referred. "So you were eavesdropping after all."

Cammy swallowed hard.

"You lied to me. You said you weren't listening to our conversation."

"It was just a fib, Daddy, and I crossed my fingers really tight."

Vance didn't get it. "Come again?"

"Sasha told me that if you cross your fingers when you fib it's not a lie."

"That's not true. A lie is a lie is a lie." Vance shook his head at her. "I'm disappointed in you."

"But I didn't mean it."

He sat back in the chair and the last of his anger melted away. "Cammy, if you lie to me—and a fib is a lie—then I can't trust you anymore. That means that if you tell me something, even if it's the truth, I'll always have a hard time believing you."

She sucked in her bottom lip and a worried frown creased her brows.

"Look at me."

She did.

"Don't ever lie to me again, okay?"

"Yes, Daddy."

Vance could tell by her misty eyes that his words had reached her heart. "Now, as for Nicole. . .Cammy, you're wrong in believing that she wanted me to send you away. Sure, she was emotional the day we broke up, but I believe she was only thinking about you, about what's going to happen when you become a young lady. She's worried that I won't be able to take care of you when you get older because, well, I'll be older, too. She merely suggested the idea of a Christian group home—for when you become a woman and you have to learn how to get a job."

"But I'll be walking by then, Daddy, and I'll do all the taking care of *you*."

Sadness sprang up inside him. It'd never happen. Not with the injuries Cammy had sustained in the car accident. Vance had seen the X-rays himself. Sure, he'd been in shock after losing Angie and seeing his daughter battered and bruised, but he still recalled hearing "SCI" or "spinal cord injury" over and over in reference to Cammy's injuries.

Then the doctors broke more bad news to him: His little girl would never have the use of her legs again.

Since the accident, Vance had been faithful about taking Cammy to her medical appointments and physical therapy, much of which he learned to do at home. Her legs continued to grow normally, but her prognosis hadn't changed. She'd never walk again.

Reaching out, he captured his little girl's hand. It appeared so small and fragile as it lay in his much larger palm. "It's good to hope and dream, sweetheart, but—"

"It's not a dream. Not pretend. Jesus said that if we pray, believing that what we ask will come true, He'll do it. My Sunday school teacher said so."

Vance released her hand and slowly began rubbing his whiskered jaw. He couldn't very well argue with Jesus. "Listen, I'm going to clean off the table and then I want you to rewrite your paper."

"But I wrote the truth."

"Not quite. You didn't know all sides of the story—just your side. And that's not fair to everyone involved."

Cammy jutted out her bottom lip and folded her arms. *Stubborn little thing.*

Vance set out to reason with her. "You brought up Jesus—would He want you to drag someone's name through the mud just because you didn't see eye-to-eye with her? And what about forgiving and loving your enemies? Jesus taught those things, too."

Cammy thought for a moment, and he watched her resolve weaken. When she looked up at him, Vance recognized his sensitive and obedient little girl again.

"O-kaay. I'll write it over again."

"That's my girl."

Adoration shone in her eyes. "I'll always be your girl. Right, Daddy?"

"That's right." He sent her a smile.

"But—"

Vance had started to stand and paused halfway up. "But what?"

"But maybe Miss Jorgenson could be your other girl."

"Cammy—" Vance narrowed his gaze.

She rolled her shoulder in a prissy sort of shrug. "Well, I did say *maybe*."

Chapter Thirteen

....

At five minutes past seven, the doorbell rang. Meg couldn't seem to help dragging her feet to answer it. When she did, she found Kent standing on the stoop beneath the white aluminum awning. His light jacket was unzipped, revealing a pea green polo shirt that matched his eyes.

"Come on in." She stepped aside while he crossed threshold, and she noted his tan trousers. She found it a tad humorous to see him attired in something other than shorts.

"Hungry?" He pressed an innocuous kiss on her cheek. "I've got a taste for Mexican. How's that sound to you?"

"Actually—" Meg closed the door, noticing how his upscale cologne suddenly overpowered the aroma of Grams' stew. "—my grandmother made dinner already, and I thought you might like to join us."

"Here?" He leaned forward. "You're kidding, right?"

"Serious as a heart attack."

Kent winced.

Meg held her breath, hoping he wouldn't stay. But before he could reply, Grams entered the room. She had changed clothes and now wore a pair of black slacks, a maroon turtleneck, and a multicolored, quilted vest.

"Mr. Baldwin. So nice to see you again." At his puzzled expression, Grams expounded. "I'm Loretta Jorgenson. You and I met at the Labor Day picnic."

"Oh, right."

Meg had a hunch he didn't recall meeting Grams. "I live with my grandmother for the time being," she explained after he sent her another curious glance.

"Really? And here I thought you were renting this place."

"If I were renting, I'd live closer to school." She tipped her head. "How did you know where I lived, anyway?"

"Oh, I had some time to waste last weekend so I looked up various teachers' addresses and did a few drive-bys. Acquainted myself with the area, you might say."

Yeah, right. Meg kept her sarcasm to herself. Miracle wasn't exactly on the main drag. Kent must have purposely tracked her down.

She watched his gaze dance around the dining and living rooms. "Quaint."

"I'll take that as a compliment," Grams said, her tone tinged with pride. "I want my home to feel cozy." She smiled. "Did Meggie tell you that you're welcome to stay for supper? It'd be an honor to have you as our guest. Wouldn't it, Meggie?"

"Sure." She put more feeling into the reply than she actually felt. "What do you say, Kent?"

"Well, um. . ." His gaze ping-ponged between the two ladies.

Again Meg hoped he'd opt to dine elsewhere—and alone, since she had no intentions of eating Mexican food tonight. The savory smell of Grams' beef stew had been making her mouth water for more than an hour.

"Well, okay, then. I'll stay." He chuckled in a way that conveyed the awkwardness of the moment. "What the heck."

Meg veiled her disappointment while Grams introduced Tom, who had just made his way in from the back porch where he'd been puffing on his pipe. The scent of tobacco followed him, tickling Meg's nostrils.

"Good to meet you formal-like. I seen you at the picnic."

"Nice to meet you as well." Kent shot an uncertain look in Meg's direction. No doubt he assumed Grams and Tom were regular country hicks.

"Please have a seat, Mr. Baldwin," Grams said. "Can I get you something to drink?"

"Gin and tonic would be great, but if you don't have that, I'll take a beer."

A crimson hue crept into Grams' cheeks. "I'm afraid I don't serve alcohol. Don't even keep it in the house unless, of course, you count my vanilla extract."

Tom chortled as he moseyed over to the thick wood-framed, six-cushioned couch. Meg always remembered it being there, up against the longest wall in the room. The deep brown and beige plaid piece of furniture had a boxy look to it, and its heavily shellacked arms were nicked and scared. A matching two-cushioned chair occupied a corner of the neutral-colored living room. Grams said she loved the set because, like her, it had survived three rambunctious little boys. Survived the grandkids, too.

"How about some coffee or sweet tea? Oh, and there's pop." Grams flashed a smile at Meg. "I've stocked up on the Diet Coke ever since I learned Meggie likes it."

Kent held up a hand, palm side out. "Don't touch the stuff." He winked at Meg and sat down in the chair. In the next moment he furrowed his brows and looked back at Grams. "Is sweet tea hot or cold?"

"Cold. But I could probably heat it up if you wanted."

"No, no. Cold is good."

Grams gave him a gracious nod of her head before regarding her relic of a neighbor. Tom seemed to blend right in with the décor. "More coffee?"

"Nope. I'm set, Retta."

Grams took off for the kitchen, and Meg took a seat in the wooden rocker. To her left, the book titled *Daily Strength for Daily Needs* lay on the table, right where Grams had set it after her "God time" this morning. Out of sheer discomfort, Meg slid it into her lap and flipped it open to today's date.

"So. . ." Tom stretched one thin arm across the top of the couch cushion. "Meggie says you're from Minneapolis."

"That's right," Kent replied. "Land of ten thousand lakes."

"Pretty country up there, I hear."

"It is."

"Harsh winters."

"Plenty of snow for skiing and snowmobiling."

"Too cold for me. Blood's too thin."

"You get acclimated after a while." Kent cleared his throat. "Isn't that right, Meg? You're all about acclimation—or rather assimilation."

Meg gritted her teeth and turned her attention to the day's Bible verse, Isaiah 38:14: "*O Lord, I am oppressed; undertake for me!*"

She found herself savoring the irony of the situation and added a plea of her own: *Please deliver me!*

"What are you reading over there?"

It took a moment for Meg to realize that Kent was speaking to her. She looked up at him. "I'm sorry. I'm being impolite. Some, um, poetry caught my eye."

"Let's hear it." Kent sat back and crossed his legs.

"Okay." Meg lowered her gaze to the page and read aloud.

"Being perplexed, I say,
Lord, make it right!
Night is as day to Thee;
Darkness is light.
I'm afraid to touch
Things that involve so much; —
My trembling hand may shake,
My skill-less hand may break:
Thine can make no mistake."

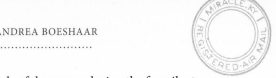

She mulled over the words of the stanza during the few silent moments that passed until Tom spoke up.

"Ain't no doubt about it; God minds our business better'n us."

"Indeed." Grams had re-entered the room and now handed Kent a glass of sweet tea.

Meg gently closed the book and replaced it on the table.

"You're a poetry lover, huh?" Kent's voice held a note of interest.

"Very much. There's no better catalyst for soul searching."

Kent took a few swallows of his tea. "This might surprise you, but I used to write lyrics for my buddy to set to music. I think our songs would have been big hits. They were that good." He shook his head, grinning at the recollection. "But the competition out there in the music industry is steep. So I went to college instead."

"Did you give up the music idea completely?" Grams seated herself beside Tom.

"Yep. I'm a guy who likes a sure thing."

"You don't strike me as someone who's afraid of a little competition," Meg said. "Sports and all that."

"I'll play the game only when I know I can win."

Figures.

The monologue continued with Kent recounting his life's achievements: hunting, fishing, boating, swimming. He'd apparently done it all and won awards to prove it.

Meg sighed with relief when Grams announced that dinner was ready.

In the dining room, the round table had been set with four pumpkin-colored placemats and matching napkins. The backdrop of the rain streaming down the windows made it feel decidedly like fall even though autumn hadn't yet begun.

They took their places and Grams served the steaming stew in heavy white porcelain bowls. Tom said grace and they began eating.

Meg wasn't shy about enjoying her first bite. The rich, slow-cooked beef practically melted in her mouth. "Mmm, Grams, this is the bomb!"

"The bomb? Is that good?"

"Uh-huh." Meg grinned and cut into a piece of potato, done to perfection.

"Used to be when folks mentioned bombs we'd think fallout shelters." Tom chuckled and passed the platter of flaky biscuits to Meg. Accepting one, she handed the plate to Kent.

"Honestly, that phraseology is so yesterday, Meg." Kent sent her an amused stare. "I thought you were from Chicago."

"I'm from all over, really."

"Then you should know better." His brown eyes twinkled.

"And what would you have said, Mr. Withit?" Meg couldn't help throwing out the challenge.

"Oh, I don't know. Maybe something like, 'Mrs. Jorgenson, your stew is delicious.'"

"Why, thank you—both of you." Grams smiled and dunked her biscuit in the thick gravy.

Kent threw a good-natured grin in her direction, and Meg had to admit to being amused.

"Tell us more about yourself, Mr. Baldwin." Grams wiped her mouth with the linen napkin. "How did you end up in the Blue Grass part of Kentucky?"

"That's a long and rather sordid tale. I'll spare you the details, of course. I'll only say that I made some mistakes and my marriage of seven years fell apart. It was a difficult decision for me, but I left my ex-wife and two kids in Minneapolis and moved here to, um. . .well, to let the dust settle, so to speak."

Meg quickly read between the lines. He cheated on his wife and ran away from his responsibility. Great guy.

"My kids are seven and three. They're young but resilient. In no time they'll forget all the ugliness that transpired between their mother and me."

Meg suddenly lost her appetite. She hadn't been much older than three when her own folks divorced. Didn't anyone believe in forever anymore?

"I have an older sister in Lexington," Kent went on. "A brilliant woman who's making money hand over fist—takes after my father, who founded Baldwin Manufacturing. But that's another saga for another time. Anyway, my sister runs an employment agency and with the South growing like it is, her business is skyrocketing. She's the one who told me about the teaching position here. I applied, and the rest is history."

"Don't you miss your kids?" Meg couldn't help asking.

"I miss them a lot. More than words can say."

Searching his expression, Meg thought he might actually be sincere.

When everyone finished eating, she helped Grams clear the table and set a pot of decaf coffee to brewing. Then at precisely eight o'clock, every clock in the house proceeded to whistle, chime, and gong.

"What in the world?" Kent sat back. His blond brows furrowed and he gaped at the commotion around him.

From the kitchen, Meg caught his shocked and bewildered expression, and the sight tickled her so she nearly doubled over with laughter. When the racket ceased, she tried to explain but couldn't manage to speak.

"Oh, for pity's sake." Grams rolled her eyes in dramatic fashion. Then she turned to Kent. "I have a clock collection that my granddaughter obviously finds hilarious."

"I'm sorry, Grams. It's just that Kent's reaction—"

"Don't blame it on me." He lifted a hand, curbing the rest of her reply.

Grams herself had a hard time containing a grin now. "You see, it all started when my boys were little."

"Oh, dear." Kent wiped his mouth with his napkin. "I'd better get comfortable. This could take awhile."

Grams looked embarrassed, and her forthcoming words seemed pasted to her lips.

"Don't mind Kent." Meg sent him an annoyed glance. He'd only been droning on about himself for the last hour. "I want to hear the story."

"Oh, Meggie, you've heard this story a hundred times."

"No, I haven't." Meg suddenly realized that, for whatever reason, she'd never thought to ask. Instead, she had politely accepted the racket as just *one of those things* about her grandmother's house.

"Go ahead, Grams. Tell us the story."

"Well, all right." She sat up straighter, more poised and dignified than ever. "Every year my boys would give me some sort of clock at Christmastime. I suppose it was all they could afford back then. But as the years went by, the clocks kept coming. One holiday I worked up the nerve to ask my sons why they felt compelled to purchase clocks for me. I was never a forgetful person. Always punctual."

Her eyes lit with fondness. "Turns out the idea sprung up from something I used to tell my boys when they'd laze around the house instead of doing their homework or their chores. I'd say, 'Lost time is never found again.'" She gave a little laugh. "So my sons set out to prove me wrong."

"Now she can't never lose time," Tom added. "She's got more of it than she knows what to do with."

Meg smiled at the amusing account.

Grams stood. "There's applesauce cake for dessert."

"I'll partake in a slice," Tom drawled.

"I knew you would," Grams retorted. "I made it just for you." She winked at Meg.

"Well, ain't that sweet, Retta. You just happened to remember applesauce cake is my favorite."

"You've only been pestering me for days to make it for you."

Meg reclaimed her seat at the table, laughing under her breath at the banter. She happened to look in Kent's direction, and he caught her glance.

"You, uh, planning to live here much longer?" he asked her, and something about his teasing tone irked her.

"I enjoy living with Grams."

"Hmm. Well, I'm purchasing a condo in Lexington."

"Oh, how nice for you." She made sure her tone was both polite and uninterested.

"I can't find anything I like locally."

"No?"

Kent shook his head. "Right now I'm renting one of those red brick townhouses on the edge of town. I feel like I'm in the slums. What's more, in order to get approved for visitation with my kids, I have to prove that I have a permanent residence. Renting doesn't qualify, according to my lawyer."

Meg pursed her lips. "I see." His divorce sounded messy.

"If I had my druthers I'd live in New York instead of Kentucky. But here I am, so I'll settle for the nearest big city. And this condo is great. Gated community on Highway 27 across from a huge mall. Tons of restaurants and things to do."

"I hope you'll be happy there."

"I will be." He leaned toward her. "You know what I'm talking about, don't you? I'm going crazy here in Stanford with nothing to do. You must be mad out here in the country."

Meg shook her head. "I love it here. It's peaceful. I'm not hearing the continual blare of police and fire sirens all night long. Instead I listen to the crickets."

Kent's full lips curved with a charming grin. "Meg, what I love about you is that you're sophisticated, worldly." He placed his hand on top of hers.

She pulled away. How could he "love" anything about her? He barely knew her.

"I know you'll never direct me to the—" He paused for effect. "—the 'tar store.'"

"Very funny." Meg glanced at Tom. He didn't appear to be paying much attention to Kent's flirting at the family dinner table.

"And I know you won't direct me *toad* Louisville, but *toad* Lexington," Kent continued, clearly enjoying himself.

Meg hid a grin. A good ol' Kentucky twang—like the way folks pronounced Miracle as "Merkle"—wasn't anything new to her. Mom had been born and raised in Stanford, so she talked the same way.

Grams walked in and set down the wooden serving tray. She proceeded to hand out plates of applesauce cake, each with a dollop of vanilla ice cream. Cups and saucers of coffee came next, along with cream and sugar.

"Looks good 'nough to eat, Retta."

Meg agreed as she forked in a mouthful. Tart, sweet, cold, and creamy converged on her taste buds. "Delicious, Grams."

"Not *the bomb*?"

Kent and Tom had a good chuckle, and Meg was actually quite impressed by her grandmother's comeback.

Suddenly a hard knock sounded at the back door. Puzzlement swept across Grams' face. "I wonder who that could be." She took off to see about the caller.

"So, you're moving to Lexington, huh?" Tom didn't even look up as he asked the question.

"As soon as I can." Kent eyed Meg. "The condo is great. Brand, spanking new. Spacious, and a balcony with an amazing view."

"Sounds real nice." Tom took another bite of his dessert.

Several moments later, Grams reappeared at the archway. Her blue eyes came to rest on Meg. "Vance Bayer is here. He'd like to speak with you about Cammy. Says it's important."

Chapter Fourteen

....

Meg excused herself from the table and strode into the kitchen, where Vance was waiting. She thought he looked uneasy. His russet brown hair was damp and his jacket was splattered with raindrops.

"You wanted to speak with me?"

He nodded. "Sorry to intrude like this."

"No problem."

"I would've called, but this isn't something that's easily said over the phone."

"All right." Feeling curious and a tad bit guilty to have been caught at the dinner table with Kent Baldwin, she pointed toward the screened-in porch. "Let's go outside so we're not overheard." She hoped she could explain. After all, it was Kent's dinner invitation yesterday that stirred up trouble and caused Cammy to miss her lunch.

Meg slid open the glass door and stepped outside. Vance followed. The gentle but steady hum of the rain filled the nighttime beyond the porch. Only the light from the kitchen illuminated the immediate area.

"Is this about what we discussed this morning?" Meg slid the door closed. "If so, I can explain—"

"No, it's about the essay Cammy wrote."

"Ah." Meg switched gears. *The essay. Of course.* "So you read it."

"I did." Vance jammed his hands into his jacket pockets. "We talked, and I explained things. I want you to know that Cammy agreed to rewrite her paper."

"Okay. It's not due until Friday. She's got plenty of time. We'll have class time in which the kids can write, too."

LOVE FINDS YOU IN MIRACLE, KENTUCKY

"Forgive me, Meg, but that's not what's eating me." He paused. "You see, I'm ashamed that Cammy shared such personal information with you. Personal and not quite accurate information, I might add."

Meg nodded. "I had a feeling Cammy's perception was a bit short-sighted."

Vance rubbed the back of his neck as if alleviating the tension there. "I appreciate that you gave me the benefit of the doubt. Some teachers wouldn't. You're new in Miracle, and you don't know me well. I wouldn't blame you if you read that essay and thought I was the worst dad in all of Kentucky."

"The thought never entered my mind, Vance. I might not know you well, but I know you well enough, okay? Besides, you gave me the benefit of the doubt when Cammy missed her lunch."

"Guess we're even then."

Meg smiled.

"But just for the record, my sister's babysitting skills aren't as bad as Cammy described. Sure, she has her faults, but—"

"But nobody's perfect."

"Exactly. What's more, and I swear it's the truth, I'd never institutionalize my daughter. Never." Vance's tone sounded thick with vehemence. "And Nicole never wanted me to send Cammy away. She just brought up the idea of a Christian group home as a possibility—for when Cammy's a young woman." He wagged his head. "But what Nicole never could seem to understand is that I have to take one day at a time. Sure, I plan ahead, but—" He raked his fingers through his hair. "—I can't decide something like whether Cammy needs to learn a vocation at a Christian group home a decade from now. I have to figure out what I'm going to feed her for supper tomorrow night."

Meg sent Vance a reassuring smile. "I can imagine how overwhelming life must be for you at times. But, as Cammy's teacher, I'd like to point out that college is a viable option for her. I can tell already.

154

She's extremely independent, and, even at her young age, she knows how to take care of herself." Meg folded her arms, still smiling. "She's one of the smartest little girls I've ever met, and she's a happy, well-adjusted child. That's a credit to you, Vance. So relax. You're obviously doing a fine job."

"Thanks. I think I needed to hear that." His gaze fixed on hers. "Especially after reading that essay."

Reaching out, Meg touched him on the sleeve. What a sensitive guy he was—and one who obviously cherished his daughter. Meg wished her own father had loved her even half as much.

"I'm glad you came over tonight, Vance."

"Well. . ." He ducked his head for just an instant. "I didn't mean to bust in on you, seein' as you've got company. Maybe I should have called first."

"It was a very impromptu dinner. Nothing I planned—or even wanted. You didn't 'bust in' on anything."

As if on cue, a car's engine fired up and the sound split the quietness of the night. Meg looked towards the driveway and saw white headlights, bright against Grams' garage door. They grew dimmer as the car backed away.

Kent had just left.

"Actually, I don't have company anymore." She looked back at Vance, whose expression was weighted with regret.

"I hope your guest didn't leave on my account."

"I hope he did." Meg laughed. "I'm teasing, Vance. Seriously, it's no big deal."

"Okay. If you say so—"

Still smiling, Meg realized just how relieved she felt now that Kent was gone. When she was near him, her senses operated on high alert. In Vance's presence, however, she felt comfortable and more like herself.

"On second thought, I've decided that you're going to have to make this up to me."

He put his hands on his hips and regarded her for a long moment. "What would you like me to do? I'm willing to apologize to Mr. Baldwin if necessary."

Meg had a hard time concealing her smile. "And how do you know that my guest tonight was Kent?" She saw him swallow a knot of discomfort and almost laughed out loud.

"Well, for one, no one around here drives a vintage red Corvette. And I've seen that same car parked in the school lot."

"Excellent deduction. But you don't have to apologize to him. How about staying for a cup of decaf coffee and some dessert instead?"

"Well, I—"

She tipped her head. "Or do you have to rush back home? Is Cammy alone?"

"No, no, I never leave her without adult supervision. Mrs. Donley from church came over to clean the house tonight, and she offered to babysit. Not that she'll really need to—I made sure Cammy was fast asleep before I left." He glanced at his wristwatch and deliberated over Meg's offer for a few seconds. "She was just getting started when I left. I guess I can stay for a little while."

"Good."

Feeling pleased with his decision, she looped her arm around his elbow and escorted him into the kitchen. Grams was rinsing dishes and loading the dishwasher while Tom stood idly by.

Meg rubbed her arms, staving off the chill she received from the damp night air. "Any applesauce cake and coffee left for Vance and me?"

"Plenty." Grams smiled at them both. "Go on and make yourselves comfortable and I'll bring it in."

"Thanks."

"Oh, and—I'm afraid Mr. Baldwin left."

"Yes, I saw him pull away."

"Said he had something he needed to do."

"I know you're real heartbroken 'bout that, Meggie," Tom said with a playful snicker.

She replied with a pointed stare, the same look reserved for mischievous boys in her third-grade class. Then she led Vance into the living room. Tom's chortles followed in their wake.

"Want to take off your jacket?"

In reply, he shrugged out of the blue-gray slicker and hung it in the closet. Then she crossed the room and, tucking one leg beneath her, took a seat beside him on the couch.

Tom trailed them in and lowered his lanky frame into the armchair. "Been meaning to talk to you, Vance," he said. "My gas weeder don't want to start."

"I told you last spring that you needed a new one." Vance brought his ankle to his knee. "That weeder's shot."

"Fool thang!"

Meg had been studying Vance's profile, his aquiline nose, the curve of his cheek, strong set to his jaw. Now she saw the corner of his mouth twitch, an amused response to Tom's exclamation.

"Ain't you able to fix it once more?"

"Maybe."

"I should just ask Eugenia to gemme a new weeder for Christmas."

Meg had heard that name mentioned a few times. "Eugenia is your daughter, right?"

"That's right." Tom smiled with pride. "She's a veterinarian. Lives in Louisville."

Meg was impressed.

Grams entered the room, carrying a serving tray. She set it on the rectangular coffee table in front of the couch. Meg repositioned herself so she could reach her dessert.

"Looks great, Mrs. Jorgenson. Thanks."

"You're ever so welcome, Vance." Grams sat down in her wooden rocker. "How's Cammy liking school?" She eyed Meg with a grin.

"Loves it. Loves her new teacher."

"I know she does."

Meg didn't think she'd ever felt more encouraged.

"Now about my weeder. . ."

"Oh, Tom, for heaven's sake." Grams' impatience couldn't be mistaken. "That piece of junk isn't worth a minute's time."

"You let Vance be the judge of that." He frowned at Grams before looking back at the other guest. "Whadda you think?"

Vance exhaled a breath of concession. "I'll look at it. How 'bout I pick up the weeder on my way home tonight? I can take it to work tomorrow, and maybe I'll get to it before the weekend."

Meg suddenly recalled what Grams had said about Vance being a reformed hellion. Remarkable, but Meg couldn't see a single trace of hellion left in him. Instead, she viewed him as mild-mannered, reserved, thoughtful, and kind.

"I'm much obliged to you, Vance."

"Sure thing." He took a gulp of coffee, and Meg thought the delicate cup and saucer looked out of place in his large, rough hands.

"Charlie Drake had his septic system all dug up," Tom said. "Never woulda guessed what he found inside that tank."

"I heard."

"Oh, please, gentlemen." A look of disgust fell over Grams' face. "Not in mixed company."

Too late. Meg's curiosity was piqued. "What was it? A dead body?"

"No." Tom ground out a low chuckle.

"Honestly, Meggie. What a question."

"Sorry, Grams," she said, smirking at her own morbid inference.

"Too many TV crime dramas." She looked back at Tom and then at Vance. "So, what did they find in the tank, then?"

"Seriously, you don't want to know." Vance sent her a glance from out of the corner of his eye. "Trust me."

"Meggie ain't the squeamish sort."

"Well, I am," Grams declared. "What's more, I have dishes to wash. Besides, I heard this story when I got my hair done. So if y'all will excuse me. . ."

"Yes, ma'am." Vance stood as Grams exited the room. He sat back down once she'd left.

Meg noted the polite gesture with a smile, then turned and bore her gaze into Tom. "Yeah? So what was it?"

"A hog-nose snake, that's what. Fat ol' thing. At least two foot long."

"That's disgusting." Meg shuddered and, in spite of herself, cautiously brought her other leg up off the floor until she was sitting cross-legged on the couch. "I hate snakes!"

"Ain't worse'n a dead body." Tom's reply came out in a series of chuckles.

Meg had to think that one over. "It's a toss-up, I'd say. The thought of either one gives me the willies."

Vance looked at her, amusement waltzing in his hazel eyes. "I just had a feeling you didn't want to hear the details of Charlie's find."

"Guess you're right." Meg pressed her back into the couch cushion, but then a morbid curiosity made her ask, "Was it poisonous?"

Vance laughed, his shoulders shaking, but Tom was the one who replied.

"Nope. And Charlie'd already seen one or two come through his plumbing."

"Snakes? Though his plumbing? That's *so gross!*" Meg covered her face with her hands as her mind whirred with possible scenarios.

She peeked at Vance over her fingertips. "That doesn't really happen here in Kentucky, does it? Snakes slithering through the pipes, coming up through the commodes?"

"No, no." Vance laughed hard, but then, as if reassuring her, he set his hand on her knee for several long moments. The warmth of his palm penetrated her slacks. "You've got nothing to worry about."

Meg didn't miss the meaningful stare he sent Tom.

"Eugenia used to enjoy a good snake discussion."

"Reckon that's why she's a vet," Vance pointed out, "and Meg's a third-grade teacher."

"Yeah, and a teacher from the city," Meg interjected, "where the plumbing is safe."

"Not so fast, there, missy." Tom wagged a gnarled finger at her. "You know what I heard about city plumbing? I heard—"

Tom's words were cut off by an orchestra of cuckoos and chimes, marking the hour. The cliché "saved by the bell" never seemed more appropriate.

"Nine o'clock already," Vance said. "I guess I should be going."

"So soon?" Meg had hoped he'd stay awhile longer.

"Morning comes real fast at our house."

She could well imagine.

Vance slowly rose to his feet. "I'll give you a lift home, Tom, since you're determined to waste my time on that old weeder of yours."

He chuckled. "Appreciate it, son." He got up and ambled toward the kitchen.

Meg stood as well. "I'm glad you stopped by, Vance."

"I guess I'm glad I did, too."

She smiled and he cupped her elbow, giving it a gentle squeeze.

For the following five seconds, he seemed to wrestle with what he wanted to say next. Finally he gave up. "Cammy and I will see you tomorrow."

"You sure will." She felt tempted to speculate on his unvoiced intentions but decided there was no point.

As they made their way toward the back door, Grams handed Vance two plastic containers. "One's beef stew and the other's some biscuits. Now you've got dinner for tomorrow night."

Vance accepted the leftovers with obvious gratitude. "This'll sure beat the meals I throw together. Cammy and I will enjoy it."

Good-byes said, the men took their leave, and Meg helped Grams with the rest of the cleanup in the kitchen.

"This has certainly been an eventful evening."

Meg agreed with a few bobs of her head. "So what do you think of Kent now that you've had a chance to get to know him a little better?"

"I think he's a lonely man."

"I don't think he's lonely." In fact, Meg doubted that he slept by himself more than a few times a week. It was like Dillon once said: *A guy can find a willing woman just about anywhere.* And who'd know better than Dillon, that two-timer.

Maybe Kent.

"We'll have to pray for him."

"Pray?" Meg found the idea a little weird. "Kent doesn't need anything from God. He thinks he is a god."

"But that's why he's lonely. Don't you see? When people fill up themselves with themselves, they're the most miserable wretches in all the world." Grams paused. "What hope does he have? That fine-looking body of his might well look like Tom's in another forty years."

The sudden mental image of Kent all wrinkly made Meg laugh. "I get the picture."

But she wasn't done yet. "Or he might find himself a victim of unfortunate circumstance and wind up like little Cammy Bayer in a wheelchair."

"Kind of gloom and doom there, Grams."

"No, just pointing out the need for hope, because I know the One who can provide it. That's why I mentioned praying for Mr. Baldwin."

"I get it. I'm not sure if you're right about Kent, but I understand your reasoning."

* * * * *

Later that night as she lay in bed, listening to the rain splattering against the rooftop, Meg recalled the words of the poem she'd read earlier in the evening. If she wasn't mistaken, the first couple of lines went something like: "Being perplexed, I say, Lord, make it right!"

So—could He?

She couldn't help examining her own life, with its less than perfect past, and Grams' analogy of Kent's somehow got folded into the mix. What fine messes people could make of their existences. Determination alone didn't seem like enough to make a change—make it right.

Was prayer the key to it all? Did it work? Did God really hear mortal man's requests and deign to do something about them?

She mulled it over awhile longer and then suddenly found herself at the defining moment of faith. It was either true or it wasn't, and either way, she'd have to believe.

Okay, God. I don't think I've done this before on my own, but. . .I'm going to pray.

Chapter Fifteen

....

Cammy's eyes stuck like glue to Miss Jorgenson as she erased the whiteboard, just the way she did every day after school. Right now she wiped away all the words from social studies. It was the last subject today, and Miss Lawton's class got to join in. When everyone was quiet, Miss Lawton read a letter from a soldier who was real far away from home. Then they made cards from colored paper for him and all his friends. Miss Jorgenson wrote on the white board: "Thank you for your service to our country." She said anyone could copy the words down if they didn't know what else to write. When they were finished with their cards, Miss Lawton said that she'd mail them and that the soldiers would be really glad to get the greetings, even from a bunch of second and third graders. She said that the soldiers might even write back!

Miss Jorgenson moved back and forth as she finished erasing, and Cammy liked the way her brown flowered skirt swirled around her legs. She liked her boots, too. They were wrinkly and soft-looking, like the skin on Mrs. Owens' bulldog named Buster. Cammy decided that someday she'd wear a pretty outfit like Miss Jorgenson's. Maybe she'd even be a teacher.

Miss Jorgenson swung around and smiled. "What are you doing this weekend, Cammy?"

She opened her mouth to answer, but the words got stuck in her throat when Mr. Baldwin walked into the room.

"T.G.I.F.," he said, clapping his hands together. His smile faded a little when he saw Cammy, but it came right back again.

"So how has your first week of school been, young lady?" He had a happy note in his voice.

"Fine." She couldn't help smiling back at him.

Mr. Baldwin sat on the corner of Miss Jorgenson's desk. "Ever been on a rowing machine, Cammy?"

She shook her head.

"Well, then, you're in for a treat. The school just purchased two rowing machines. We're going to have rowing contests. Boys against girls."

"Girls'll win!"

"We'll see."

"I can be a cheerleader for 'em while I watch."

Mr. Baldwin's smile grew, but his eyes got smaller as he looked at her hard. "You know, Cammy, you can do more than just cheer. Rowing is something you can do. It'd be good exercise. Would you like to give it a try?"

"Okay!" An excited feeling filled her chest. She hardly ever got to play games with the other kids unless they were spelling or math races. "I'd like that a lot."

"Great. I'll talk to your dad."

"Promise?"

"Of course."

"Daddy'll be here in a few minutes." Cammy hoped he'd hurry up.

"In that case, I'll wait."

Cammy's heart beat faster. A rowing machine. She wasn't sure what one was, exactly, but if she could help the girls beat the boys, it would be so much fun.

She saw Mr. Baldwin glance over his shoulder at Miss Jorgenson, but she didn't seem to notice. She sat down in Dustin Baker's seat since Mr. Baldwin's backside was taking up most of her desk.

"So," Miss Jorgenson looked at Cammy, "you were going to tell me what you're doing this weekend."

Mr. Baldwin answered. "I'm driving to my sister's place in Lexington. Would you like to come along, Meg?"

"No, I've got plans. Thanks."

"Hanging out with your grandparents?"

Cammy watched Miss Jorgenson's cheeks turn as red as candy apples.

"If you must know, I'm going horseback riding with my sister tomorrow, and then I'm attending a baby shower with Leah on Sunday afternoon."

Cammy perked up. "Is it for Jenny Washborne?"

"Yes, it is."

"She goes to our church."

"That's right. She does." Miss Jorgenson's red spots started fading and she smiled.

"Way too much excitement for me," Mr. Baldwin said. He sounded like he was kidding, but Cammy wasn't sure. "I'm just going to a cocktail party tomorrow and hobnobbing with Lexington's most affluent people."

"What's a cocktail party?" Cammy had never heard of them before. But Aunt Debbie went to a candle party once and another time she had a makeup party at her house.

"It's a fancy get-together," Miss Jorgenson explained. "People get all dressed up and eat itty-bitty meatballs on toothpicks."

Mr. Baldwin laughed, and his big voice filled up the whole classroom. "So I gather you'd rather be horseback riding than hobnobbing, huh, Meg?"

She shrugged. "I'm not a good hobnobber."

"I think you underestimate yourself."

Miss Jorgenson lifted her shoulders up and down like she didn't care one way or another.

"Well. . ." He slapped the tops of his legs. "I'd better be on my way." He stood. "I'll see you Monday. Have a good weekend, ladies."

He pointed a long, tanned finger at Miss Jorgenson and winked. Then he looked at Cammy. "Bye."

"B—Bye." Sadness covered her like a blanket. She couldn't believe he was walking away.

She looked at Miss Jorgenson and blinked.

"What's wrong, Cammy?"

She gulped, determined not to be a baby and cry.

"Cammy?"

"M—Mr. Baldwin said he'd talk to Daddy about me rowing on the new machines. But now he's gone."

For a moment Miss Jorgenson seemed out of words. She glanced at the empty doorway and then back at Cammy. "I'm sorry, honey, he must have forgotten."

"But he *promised*."

"I know he did." Miss Jorgenson pressed her lips together, and Cammy wondered if she was mad at Mr. Baldwin now.

"Don't worry. I forgive him." Cammy couldn't keep her bottom lip from jutting out, but she knew it was the right thing to do.

"Listen, Cammy, don't feel bad. There's plenty of time for Mr. Baldwin to discuss the rowing idea with your dad. The school just placed the order. The machines won't arrive for a while."

The sadness inside her rushed away once Cammy realized that what Miss Jorgenson said was true. She felt like smiling again. Then Daddy arrived and it occurred to her that she didn't have to wait for Mr. Baldwin to talk to him; she'd tell Daddy about the rowing machines herself!

* * * * *

Meg listened as Cammy relayed Kent's offer to Vance. She didn't see any reason why the little girl couldn't row. She could be lifted carefully out of her wheelchair in order to use the bathroom, and she had some control of her hips—thus her squirming with excitement now as she told her dad she was going to play with the other kids.

"We'll see," he said. "I think I need a little more information before making a decision."

"Okay, Daddy."

Meg smiled as she watched father and daughter interact. She had a feeling that, to a point, Cammy had her daddy wound around her pinkie.

"Guess what? Miss Jorgenson's going horseback riding and to Mrs. Washborne's baby shower."

"Sounds like she'll be busy." Vance grinned.

"Well, not so busy," she said, feeling awkward all of a sudden. "It's horseback riding tomorrow and the baby shower Sunday afternoon." She didn't know why she felt the need to explain.

Vance narrowed his gaze and appeared contemplative. "That's right; your dad owns horses."

"Yep. They live about four miles away from my grandmother, in Miracle, and my sister and brother give riding lessons on Saturdays." It felt strange to call Kelly and Ryan her "sister and brother." However, they were her family, and Meg had decided it was high time she publicly acknowledged the fact. "Kelly offered to give me a freebie tomorrow. Little does she know that I've only been on a horse once or twice in my entire life."

Vance sported a wry grin. "Then I expect you'll be moving kind of slow come Sunday morning."

"I expect you're right." She laughed in spite of herself.

"Daddy, can we go watch Miss Jorgenson get lessons tomorrow?"

"I don't know if she wants an audience, punkin."

"I wouldn't mind. Come and watch if you'd like. Need directions?"

"Naw, I have a general idea of where your dad's place is located."

Meg interpreted the reply to mean Vance really might show up. She looked at Cammy and realized the little girl's pleased expression mirrored her own.

"Well, we'd best be going, Cammy," Vance said, stooping to help her collect her things. "Got a lot to do tonight if we want to go watch Miss Jorgenson tomorrow." He paused and tossed Meg a playful smile. "Like charge up the video camera."

"Ha, ha. Very funny."

He chuckled and Meg tipped her head, thinking she glimpsed a speck of hellion in him after all.

* * * * *

"Is that Vance Bayer over there?"

Meg looked at her dad and then over at the lawn chairs set up on the other side of the corral, where he and Cammy sat in the shade of a large willow tree. "That's Vance, all right."

"Thought it was." Dad grinned. "I'll be dogg'd. I haven't seen him in a long, long while. What's he doin' here?"

"He's been here for a couple of hours." Meg had spent all but the last forty five minutes with him and Cammy, Grams and Tom. They'd all watched the other students ride.

"I been busy in the back with paperwork. Didn't see him arrive. What's he doing here anyway?"

"Well, Cammy—that's Vance's daughter—is in my class this year. She wanted to see my first riding lesson. When Grams heard, she insisted on coming, too, and then, of course, Tom came along. Donna was nice enough to set up some chairs."

Smiling, Dad looked from his unexpected guests back to Meg. "And you didn't seem a bit nervous, even with those folks watching. You did just fine." He squeezed her shoulder.

Meg felt surprised by his praise and show of affection. "I guess I did okay, except for my none-too-graceful dismount." She wondered if she'd imagined it.

Dad chuckled. "Looked all right to me. I've seen far worse."

"Thanks." Meg knew she had a lot to learn, but she'd had fun.

The horse beside her stomped and snorted as if impatient to return to the hilly pasture behind the stable. But first Ryan had to unsaddle her. With the mare's reins in her fist, Meg had been heading into the pole barn, in which the stables were located, when she'd encountered her father.

"Easy, girl." Dad rubbed the horse's nose, then patted her neck. "Nothing to get excited about."

Meg realized how tense she felt and thought he might as well have been talking to her. "I don't mind saying I'm a little timid around horses. They're so big and seem so powerful."

"They are that, but they're also like any of the good Lord's creatures. Just got to get to know 'em, that's all."

"Makes sense."

"Sure. So now you just take that horse in to Ryan and then help yourself to a bottle of soda. There's an ice chest around by where we built the office." Dad threw a thumb over his shoulder as if pointing out the way.

Meg smiled. "Good idea. Thanks."

She tugged on the reins, and the horse began following her into the barn. Walking by neatly stacked hay bales, Meg marveled at the difference in her father's attitude toward her today. Maybe he trusted her a little more since she'd gotten Kelly home on time the night they'd gone shopping. Maybe he was just in a good mood.

And everyone thought women were moody!

Several feet away, she spotted Ryan and waved to get his attention. When he saw her, he stopped what he was doing and came over.

"So, how was your first lesson?"

"Went well, I think."

"Yeah?" He arched his reddish gold brows. "Think you'll get on a horse again sometime?"

"Sure." Meg smiled at the challenge.

Ryan seemed pleased by her response. "Well, when you're ready, I'll take you riding on the trail instead of just round 'n round in the corral." He began leading the mare to her stall. "The trail out back is way more fun to ride."

Meg followed. "I'd like that, Ryan."

Stepping on the lowest plank of one of the stall walls, Meg peered over the top and watched Ryan unbridle the animal. When her brother glanced at her, she saw a resemblance between him and herself. Odd, but she'd never noticed it before. She suddenly wished she'd been closer to both him and Kelly while they were growing up.

As if guessing her thoughts, Ryan said, "You're different, you know?"

"I am? How do you mean?"

He shrugged and then sent her a sheepish grin. "You're nice."

Meg laughed. "I don't remember ever being *not* nice."

"Not outwardly maybe, but I always thought you were—well, kinda snooty. You never wanted to do anything with Kel and me. Every time you came to visit, you'd stick your nose in a book and ignore us."

"Sorry. I always felt—" Meg paused to collect the right words. "—well, I felt out of place when I'd visit."

"Understandable."

Meg left it there, deciding not to elaborate on how the whole divorce situation affected her. Mom always said that Dad resented her because she demanded alimony and child support from him, and, consequently, that he resented Meg, too. Mom also said Dad just went along with the visitation thing because the courts forced him to see his kid once in a while.

The hurt, the bitterness, and the anger had worked their way so deep into Meg's heart, that during those annual visits with Dad and his other family, she erected an emotional wall around herself. Grams was the only one she ever allowed inside.

Grams. Thank God for Grams!

"So what changed? How'd you come to decide you wouldn't feel out of place when you moved back?"

"Honestly? I didn't give it a whole lot of thought. I left a bad situation in Chicago, and I knew Grams' place would be safe, so to speak. I wanted this teaching position, and Grams assured me that everything would work out. I simply hung onto the hope that it would."

"Are you sorry you moved here?" Ryan glanced at her before lifting the heavy leather saddle off the horse's back.

"I'm not sorry one bit. I love it here so far."

He paused. "I'm glad." He heaved the saddle over the top of the next stall's wall. "It's kinda nice having an older sister. Maybe she'll even let me borrow her car sometime—" His blue eyes twinkled with mischief. "—when my truck's not running."

"Yeah, maybe she will." Meg sent him a good-humored grin. "*Maybe.*"

He chuckled but appeared momentarily distracted as he gazed around the stall. "Hey, listen, I gotta fetch something. I'll be back in a minute."

"No worries. I gotta fetch something, too, namely a cold soft drink."

"Go for it." Ryan pointed out the way, and Meg hopped off the plank.

She walked down the dusty, hay-strewn aisle between the flanks of stalls. Each step was laden with purpose—she was thirsty and hoping to find a Diet Coke in what her dad called the "ice chest." But, rounding the corner fast, she didn't find her father's office like she expected. Instead, she slammed right into Vance Bayer.

"Whoa," he said, catching her by the upper arms and saving her from falling backwards.

"Oh. Wow. . .sorry about that." She stared up into his face.

"You okay?" His hazel eyes melded into hers.

"Fine."

A long moment passed. Neither seemed able to move. With her

hands splayed across his chest, Meg felt his heart beating beneath her palm. Her own heart began hammering with anticipation when she guessed what would happen next. It seemed so inevitable. . . .

Slowly, he lowered his head. She lifted her chin, and when their lips met, Meg's limbs felt as wobbly as Grams' strawberry Jell-O. His arms slipped securely around her, and she sagged against him. She couldn't recall ever enjoying a kiss more.

Then all too soon, it seemed, Vance pulled his head back. The headiness of the moment waned and Meg blinked, taking in his baffled expression.

"I don't know what came over me. . ."

"Or me either. But, whatever you do, don't apologize, Vance."

"All right." His expression showed a mix of relief, shock, and amusement. "I won't."

She noted his reluctance to release her, and she allowed herself to enjoy being held close. She fingered the tiny white buttons on his denim shirt and decided that weak-kneed romances weren't just for characters in novels. They really happened.

The sudden sound of a man clearing his throat caused them to step apart. Meg pivoted and saw her father standing with his hands on his hips and an indiscernible expression on his face.

"You two find what you're looking for?"

At the sound of his harsh tone, Meg tensed. She had a hunch he was assuming the worst. But she and Vance hadn't done anything wrong. In fact, being held in Vance's arms felt anything *but* wrong.

"Vance, if you're looking for a soda, it's in the ice chest over there." Dad inclined his head.

Without a word, Vance strode to the ages-old chest, opened the lid, and slid out a couple of bottles of soda. "Meg, are you thirsty?"

She slacked up on her jaw enough to reply. "Yes, and anything diet will do. Thanks." She looked back at her father, who continued to regard them both without a trace of cordiality. What in the world was his problem?

Meg knew she couldn't let this go. It was time she and her father talked.

Vance handed her the cold bottled beverage and Meg gratefully accepted it. "Will you excuse my dad and me for a few minutes?"

"Sure." He looked from one to the other with confusion on his face.

"I'll meet you back outside."

Vance nodded, once to Meg and again toward Dad. Then he left.

Meg returned her gaze to her father. "I'm not a child anymore." She kept her voice calm and even. "I'm an adult. It just so happens I care for Vance and—well, he obviously likes me, too. What's so terrible about that?"

"I never said anything was terrible." But the scowl on his face showed no signs of fading.

"You don't have to say a word. You look like an ogre standing there. You probably scared off poor Vance. He's a nice guy."

"Never said he wasn't."

This conversation was going nowhere fast. "So what's the problem?"

"Well, if there is a problem it'd be with Vance. He came in here looking for something and I reckon he found it."

"It? I'm hardly an 'it.'" In a flash, Meg knew exactly what her father insinuated. "You think I'm my mother's daughter, don't you? Well, I'm not what you think. Yeah, I've made some mistakes. But God knows I just want what everybody wants: love, peace, happiness, success." Her feelings of injustice mounted. "You know, you can stand there and judge me, but if you would have bothered to get to know me in the last twenty-six years, you'd know that I'm not my mother. I'm *me*!"

Turning, she marched toward the worn wooden door. She had just yanked it open to leave the barn when Dad caught her around her belt loop. He swung her around to face him.

"Listen here, little girl—and, yeah, you'll always be my little girl. I don't care how old you get. I do know you, better than you think, and as your daddy, I reserve the right to be a—an ogre to anyone who gets the idea he's gonna manhandle you."

"Vance didn't 'manhandle' me."

"Good, because that boy's known his share of trouble and I'd hate to think he's backsliding."

"So sharing a kiss makes us bad people?"

"Maybe. Maybe not. Now, this is what I've told Kelly. I told her—"

"Oh, spare me, will you? Kelly is sixteen."

"I told you, age don't matter."

"And I'm telling you that I don't need this daddy lecture at this point in my life." Meg stared hard at her father, her throat constricting with a sudden onset of emotion. Tears of hurt and frustration began burning the backs of her eyes. "Where were you ten years ago when I needed—and wanted—your protection? You weren't a part of my life then."

Her father's features softened. "I tried, Meggie."

"No, you didn't."

"You're wrong." He glanced at his boots before lifting his gaze.

"You always paid your child support, is that what you mean to say? That's how you were there for me, making sure guys didn't 'manhandle' me? And my once-a-year weekly visits to your neatly kept horse farm in the country? That gives you daddy rights over me?"

He ran a hand through his rust-colored hair. "I tried." His voice sounded hoarse, weary. "I really tried. . ."

She wasn't sure what that meant, *he tried*, but she decided not to pursue the matter. Not now. Not here. Besides, she already felt a stab of guilt for flinging the past at him, especially as the rest of his family had been so warm and welcoming since her arrival in Miracle.

"Okay, Dad, well, look—" She searched for the right words. "I'm sorry if I offended or embarrassed you by kissing Vance. I'll be more careful in the future. But despite what you might think, I do care about how you and this whole community view me. I want to be a respected and effective schoolteacher."

Dad rubbed his jaw, looking thoughtful.

"As for the rest—" Words seemed to fail her. There seemed to be no way to verbalize the intense feelings that had surfaced. She gave up. "Let's just forget it, all right? The past is dead and gone and maybe I was wrong to resurrect it."

With that, Meg exited the stable. She couldn't help letting the door slam shut behind her as she left.

Chapter Sixteen

....

Vance tinkered with the engine from Arnie Stiller's ATV, but his heart wasn't in his work. True, it was a gloomy Monday morning, and his own motor wasn't fully functioning yet. But the reality was that his thoughts were stalled on Meg and on what had transpired between them a couple of days ago. That kiss had taken them both by surprise.

All day Saturday he'd had a hard time taking his eyes off of her. Her golden hair and expressive blue eyes, combined with her quick wit and genuine warmth, had all worked together to capture his senses. He hadn't felt so enamored since the days he and Angie dated, and he had a hard time coming to grips with the fact.

Was falling in love again a real possibility? Kissing Meg made him believe it was. His thinking had turned.

He only hoped Meg didn't have regrets. They hadn't exchanged more than a few sentences since Saturday afternoon. Sure, she had assured him that everything was "fine," but he sensed that it really wasn't. And he felt responsible. In addition, he had to admit that Paul Jorgenson still made an imposing figure. When he started up with those authoritative glares, Vance didn't know whether to laugh or turn tail and run like a delinquent thirteen-year-old boy.

Well, at thirty-three, he wasn't a boy. But twenty years ago it was a whole different story. Back then, he *was* a delinquent, and fathers had good cause to be concerned for their daughters with Vance anywhere in the vicinity. All that had changed when he turned his life over to God. Studying the Word changed his thinking. Even so, he knew that plenty of times folks around here got their minds stuck in the past and couldn't distinguish between then and now. Seemed Meg's dad was one of those folks.

He picked up a nearby rag and wiped the grease off his hands. Another cup of coffee was in order.

In the shop's staff lounge, he filled a plastic mug with dark, steaming brew from the automatic maker that ran practically all day long. Taking a sip, he thought about this morning when he'd dropped Cammy off at school. Meg had seemed as pleasant as always. Her smile could make him forget the dreary weather. Her eyes were the color of a cloudless sky.

"Hey, Bayer!"

Vance jerked to attention as Andy Smith walked into the lounge. As one of the salesman who worked out front, he wore dress pants, shirt, and tie, whereas the repairmen in the shop, like Vance, sported uniforms and overalls that were usually stained with motor oil.

"Some dude's in the store, asking for you," Andy said, eyeing the coffee.

"Repair question, or what?"

"No clue. Go talk to 'im, will you?" Andy walked to the coffee maker and began filling a cup. "He's being kind of insistent and won't tell me anything."

"All right." Vance dragged himself from the lounge and, coffee in hand, walked into the brightly lit storefront. Shiny new items hung neatly on hooks and, on the adjacent wall, various automotive parts lined the shelves. As he entered the area, he almost missed a step when he saw Paul Jorgenson waiting for him.

Vance greeted him with a polite nod. "What can I do for you?"

"Wanted a word with you." His casual but professional attire resembled Andy's, and Vance had the feeling that Meg's dad had come here straight from his job at the Panasonic plant in Danville. "Got a minute?"

"Sure."

"How about we step outside?"

Vance set down his coffee mug behind the counter, then held out his arm toward the glass-paned door. "After you."

As he stood on the pavement beneath the shop's canvas awning, Vance watched the older man shift his weight from one foot to another. He seemed to grope for words.

Finally, he said, "Meg told me I needed to apologize to you. I thought it over and decided she's right. You two aren't children."

"Apology accepted."

"Now, hold on." He raised his hand to forestall further remarks. "I ain't finished yet."

Vance grinned and folded his arms.

"Me and Meg had a talk—well, first she told me off, and I might have deserved it. But last evening she come over to the house, and we had one of those ol' heart-to-hearts, you know? Shoulda talked like that years ago. But, well—it's hard with kids. And then they grow up—"

"I think I know what you're trying to say." Vance had to respect the guy for dialoguing with Meg. Said a lot about his character.

"Meg said you're a fine man and I believe you are."

"Appreciate it." Vance was encouraged to hear he was still in good standing with her.

"And to show you I mean it, I want to ask you and your little girl to my house for supper tonight. Meg'll be there, too."

Confusion engulfed him. "But I saw Meg this morning and she didn't mention—"

"That's because she wanted me to do the apologizing and the inviting."

"I see." Vance sent him an empathetic grin. He knew firsthand that it wasn't easy to choke down one's pride, but Paul was doing a good job. "I'm grateful for your invitation, and Cammy and me'd love to come to supper tonight. Thanks. "

He bobbed his head, looking genuinely pleased. "Come about six thirty."

"Will do." The thought of seeing Meg again on a social level sent a thrill right through him. One thing was for sure, he'd be watching his p's and q's this time.

Paul stuck out his right hand.

Vance accepted it in a friendly shake. Then he set his hands on his hips and gazed at the sky. As the store was on a hill, he could see a band of blue stretched across the horizon. "You know, I think the weather's clearing."

"Son," Paul drawled, "I think you're right."

* * * * *

Meg stood to help her stepmom clear the dining room table.

"Relax. You're company tonight." Donna glanced across the table. "Kelly will help me."

The sixteen-year-old pressed her lips together in displeasure, but she didn't argue.

Meg settled back in her chair and looked over at Vance. They exchanged polite smiles. An air of awkwardness filled the formal, oak-furnished dining room. She guessed the reason for the discomfort was the general unfamiliarity between these people. Small talk dominated the conversation. Still, she was glad that Dad suggested this dinner of recompense.

Lifting her water goblet, Meg took a sip and regarded Vance from beneath her lashes. He'd been kind enough to pick her up at Grams' house after he'd stopped home and changed out of his work clothes. Now, as he sat across the table from her, he didn't appear uncomfortable, although he'd been relatively quiet during dinner. His attire was just as subdued as his demeanor: faded blue jeans and a plum long-sleeved, button-down shirt. After Saturday's kiss at the stable, Meg felt sure she was falling for the guy. But was that wise? She'd recently ended a bad relationship, and Vance had just broken up with someone, too. Meg hated to think their attraction to one another could be some sort of rebound, and yet she wondered. She couldn't help feeling curious, too, about his deceased wife. Meg had never dated a widower before. Had Vance been a good husband? Was he faithful?

"What's your grammaw doin' tonight, Meg?" Donna asked, carrying in a plate of brownies.

"Not sure. Didn't have time to ask."

"Must be boring over there," Ryan said. He removed two brownies from the plate and shoved one into his mouth. They were hardly bite-sized.

Meg couldn't help grinning at her brother and the bulge in his cheek. "I haven't had time to be bored."

"My friend Sasha Donahue said you're going to her house for supper tomorrow night," Cammy said.

"That's right. I've gotten so many dinner invitations from my students that I'm going to have to create a special social calendar."

"How do you stand the excitement?" The sarcasm in Ryan's voice was unmistakable, but Meg caught the twinkle in his eye.

Kelly excused herself and rushed away from the table. Meg looked at her dad and then at Donna. Both shrugged.

"Her cell phone's probably ringing," Dad muttered.

"Daddy, can I ever get a cell phone?" Cammy asked from where she sat beside Meg. Although her wheelchair wasn't quite high enough for her to reach the table comfortably, the little girl never complained and had minded her manners all evening. "Maybe when I'm in high school?"

"I think we've got some time before deciding on that." Vance sent his daughter an affectionate wink.

"Cell phones are amazing as long as you keep them charged up and don't forget to turn them on," Meg said with a grin. "I miss more calls. I hardly use the thing."

"You are such an old lady, Meg," Ryan teased. "No wonder you're not bored at Grams' house."

Meg was tempted to retaliate by throwing a chunk of her brownie at him, but then she remembered that she was a dignified school teacher.

Ryan's blue eyes danced with amusement.

"So this is what it's like to have a pesky little brother, huh?"

"I wish I had a little brother," Cammy said.

Meg nearly choked on her mouthful of chewy chocolate. Vance turned a shade of crimson, and Ryan, Donna, and Dad laughed.

"Maybe you can get a puppy, instead," Meg offered diplomatically.

Cammy gasped, and an expression of sheer joy washed over her face. "Oh, I'd rather have a puppy than a little brother any day."

Chortles echoed around the table.

"Ta-dum!"

Everyone turned to see Kelly, standing at the doorway in a semi-formal dress, a slinky emerald creation that left very little to the imagination.

"What do you think? For the homecoming dance next month? Actually, it's only three weeks away."

"Looks like one of them things that goes *under* the dress," Dad said.

"A slip," Donna clarified.

"Right. So now you need to put on your dress, Kel. And I'd like to remind you that we have company."

"This *is* the dress, Daddy."

"Well, you ain't leaving this house looking like that."

Kelly huffed, placing her hands on her hips. "Meg, what do you think?"

"I think maybe I agree with Dad on this one."

"Ol' lady," Ryan muttered.

Meg feigned a glower. She'd get even.

Meanwhile, Kelly pouted out her disappointment. "Oh, all right, then. Let me model the other two dresses. Y'all can tell me which one you like best."

"Dad, please don't let her." Ryan scrunched up his face like he'd taken a bite of bad sushi.

Vance sat by, looking embarrassed.

Dad noticed. "How 'bout a little Monday Night Football for us fellas?"

"Sounds all right to me." Vance looked at his daughter and then at Meg.

"Cammy can stay here with us girls," she said, seeing the questions in his eyes. "We'll watch the fashion show."

"Yay, yay, yay!" Cammy cheered.

The men rose from their chairs and departed, Dad talking up his new, wide-screen HDTV.

Minutes later, Kelly returned. This time she wore a pearl dress with a high neckline, lacy bodice, and blue satin sash.

"Oh, my!" Cammy seemed awestruck. "That's the most beautiful dress I ever saw."

Meg disagreed. "You look like Mary Poppins, Kel." She started singing. "'Everyday's a holiday with you, Bert. . .'"

Kelly heaved a tired-sounding sigh. "Great. Just great."

Donna laughed, and Meg thought she'd never seen her stepmother so amused before. The woman actually looked pretty when she relaxed and smiled. Meg wondered why she'd never noticed before.

"Okay, I'll try on the last dress. I hope y'all like it," Kelly drawled, "or I'm back at square one."

"How 'bout some coffee, Meg?"

She nodded at her stepmom's offer. "Thanks."

"Cammy, would you like something more to eat or drink?"

"No, ma'am."

Donna strode to the kitchen, leaving Meg alone with Cammy.

"Someday, when I walk, I'm going to wear a pretty Mary Poppins dress like that one Kelly just had on!"

"You liked it, huh?"

Cammy replied with a vigorous nod. "And I'm gonna wear pointed toe high heels like the kind you have on sometimes and no socks."

Meg smiled, laughing to herself. She realized, and not for the first time, just how much influence she had on her students. They watched her, emulated her. It was a gigantic responsibility and one she took seriously.

Donna brought in the coffee, and Meg stirred cream and sugar into her cup.

Kelly sashayed back into the dining room, wearing her third semi-formal gown.

Meg immediately liked it. "Now we're talking!" The sleeveless dress had a tasteful V-neck, princess seams, and silky fabric in a gorgeous teal color. A black sash that tied at the waist and tulle that rimmed the hemline gave the piece just the right amount of contrast. "That one gets my vote."

Donna nodded. "I think your daddy might even let you out of the house wearing that dress."

Kelly beamed. "Good. Then I'll return the other two dresses to the store."

"Black shoes, black purse, and you'll be good to go," Meg added.

"I can't wait." Kelly pirouetted, a dreamy smile on her face. "I'll be dancing with Bobby Addison." She paused and glanced at Meg. "He's on the football team."

"He's a nice young man," Donna injected.

"I'm sure he is or Kelly wouldn't be going to a dance with him. Dad'd see to that."

"You can say that again." Kelly sent her mom a glance of annoyance. "I've got to have the strictest parents in all of Kentucky."

"Your daddy's the strict one." Donna sipped her coffee.

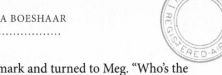

Kelly seemed to ignore the remark and turned to Meg. "Who's the best guy you ever went to homecoming with?"

"Um, well, to be honest, I never went to a homecoming dance."

"You didn't?" Cammy peered up at her. "Why not?"

Kelly regarded her with a puckered little frown. "Yeah, why not? You're pretty. Bet you had lots of boyfriends."

"Not really." It felt a little odd being totally candid when she'd spent the last twenty-six years erecting a wall so her stepmom and half sister couldn't get into her life. But she quickly reminded herself that those days were gone—and so was the wall. "I moved around so much that I never had the chance to get to know any boys well enough to attend dances with them. And, to be completely honest, I was also what you might call a 'nerd.' One of those brainy kids who hung out with other brainy kids and read books in her spare time."

"Nerd?" Kelly wrinkled her nose, causing Meg to laugh.

"I like to read books." Cammy's voice held an enthusiastic note.

"I know you do, and reading's terrific, isn't it?"

"Uh-huh."

Meg leaned sideways and slipped Cammy a quick hug around the shoulders. Gazing back at Kelly, she said, "But I'll have you know that I did to go to the prom my senior year of high school. I went with some friends. We didn't have dates, so we all went together as a group."

"I'm going with a group, too, but Bobby's my date." Kelly expelled a wistful sigh and swung her hips from side to side. "I might like him more than my horse, Rosebud."

"Whoa-oa," Meg quipped. "This guy must really be somebody!"

"He is."

Meg looked at Donna. "Is Ryan going to the homecoming dance also?"

"Sure is." Kelly was the one to reply. "He's going with Brenna Leopold. He's been sweet on her since they were twelve. But Daddy didn't allow dating until we turned sixteen. But even now, Daddy doesn't let us go anywhere un-chaperoned and if we're not home by curfew, he comes looking for us." Kelly's expression said she felt thoroughly disgusted. "Why can't he trust us?"

Because he trusted my mother and she betrayed him.

Meg stared into the stoneware mug she cradled in her hands. In talking with her father last night, she'd gleaned a lifetime of knowledge. They weren't so unlike, she and Dad. Once bitten, twice shy, as the adage goes.

"I can't stand it sometimes," Kelly rambled on. "Daddy smothers me."

"Did you ever think that's his way of showing he loves you?" Meg asked, having arrived at the same conclusion herself. "He wants to protect you so you don't make wrong decisions and ruin your life."

"I'm not going to ruin my life." Kelly tossed a glance upward.

"It's happened to the best of folks," Donna said without looking at her daughter. Instead, she slowly stirred the dark brew in her cup.

Kelly obviously didn't feel like discussing the issue. "Well, what's important is that I'm going to homecoming with Bobby. I'll know I'll remember it for the rest of my life."

Meg grinned. "I'll check back with you in about five years, okay?"

Donna smiled and sipped her coffee.

"You know, Meg," Kelly stood and crossed her arms. "I feel bad that you never went to a homecoming dance." She seemed genuine, her tone sincere. "You missed out."

"No, I didn't. I had fun. Just in a different way."

Vance entered the room just then. He rubbed his palms together, and his gaze made its way around the table until it landed on Meg. "I think it's time to head home."

"Let me guess; it's halftime."

Vance narrowed his gaze at the retort before returning one of his own. "Can't fault a man for using his time wisely." He paused. "Especially

since *he's* driving."

Meg feigned a wince. "Touché."

"What's 'touché' mean?" Cammy asked.

"It means," he replied, "that it's time to thank the Jorgensons for the nice evening and get along home. It's a school night."

"Very true." Meg stood and collected her purse and raincoat. As she said her farewells to her family members, each gave her a small hug.

Once again, the show of affection was unexpected, even overwhelming. But Meg welcomed it. She felt encouraged. Blessed.

Blessed? That word had never had a place in her vocabulary before. Meg couldn't help thinking that Grams was rubbing off on her more than she realized.

The night air was warm and muggy as they walked outside to the Bayers' van. Then, with Cammy and her wheelchair safely secured, they began the trek home.

"Thanks for meeting me at my dad's for dinner tonight. I hope you and Cammy had a nice time."

"Very nice. I'm glad it worked out."

"It did. More than you know."

"You'll have to fill me in on the details sometime."

"I'd be happy to." Meg said no more. After all, there wasn't much that Cammy missed.

"Did you have a good time at the Jorgensons' tonight, punkin?"

"Yep. I liked the fashion show the best. I can't stop thinking about that beautiful white dress with the blue sash. I'm gonna wear a dress just like it one day when I go to a homecoming dance."

"Do you think your dad will allow you to attend homecoming when you're Kelly's age?" Meg turned and regarded Vance's shadowed profile as he sat behind the steering wheel. She couldn't resist teasing him. "He seems like the kind of father who won't let his little girl date until she's at least thirty."

"You got that right."

"But, Daddy, I'll be grown by then."

"I recently learned it doesn't matter how old you get," he said.

When he looked her way, she glimpsed the smirk on his face.

"Touché again." She shook her head. "Man, you're on a roll tonight."

He chuckled.

When they arrived at Grams' house, Vance pulled into the driveway. He parked and killed the engine.

"Cammy, I'm going to walk Miss Jorgenson to the door. Will you be okay here for a couple of minutes? I won't be but a few feet away."

"That's okay, Daddy."

"Good." He climbed out of his seat and walked around the van to politely assist Meg. Together, they took slower strides than usual to reach the backdoor.

"So, do you think you might find some time for me in that social schedule you're putting together?"

They halted when they reached the entryway.

"Oh, I think maybe I can do that." Meg grinned and tipped her head. "What do you have in mind? Not horseback riding, I hope. I still feel like my legs are permanently bowed."

Vance ground out a little laugh. "No, I was thinking more along the lines of dinner for two."

Meg warmed to the idea. "I'd like that."

"So would I."

A few seconds lapsed in awkward silence.

"I'm relieved to know things between you and your dad are okay."

"Never been better." Meg smiled at the surprising outcome. "I guess Grams is right; things really do happen for a reason. Because of our, um, misunderstanding, my dad and I are closer than we've ever been. He told me he tried to get custody of me. He even dug out all the documents to prove it." She was touched to the core that Dad would spend so much time and effort, not to mention money, on the attempt. Mom, however, won that battle. "Then he tried to get more visitation rights, but those attempts failed, too." She pause to collect her thoughts before gazing up at Vance. "I find it admirable, and, well, I believe he really does love me."

"It's a shame you ever wondered."

"Well, divorce'll do that to a kid, I suppose."

"I guess that's right."

"I'm sorry you got dragged into the fray."

"I don't mind."

Meg regarded him askance. "And you didn't mind sitting around the family dinner table tonight?" She thought of Kent and how he barely tolerated dinner at Grams' the other night.

"Dinner was great. I miss home-cooked meals and family sitting around enjoying 'em together."

His reply tweaked Meg's heart, and she suddenly felt extremely fortunate to have people in her life who loved her enough to butt in.

"But I'm looking forward to dinner alone with you one night, so we can get better acquainted. I just have to line up a sitter for Cammy before I can ask you out for a specific night. There's only a handful of folks I trust to stay with her."

"I understand."

Vance cast a glance at his feet and then one at his van. "And, um, in light of the fact that my daughter probably has her eyes pasted on our every move, I'll refrain from kissing you goodnight right now." He paused, looking back at her. "This time."

"I think that's a good idea. *This* time."

Beneath the golden glow of the light by the door, Meg could see his amused expression.

Then he reached out and gave her elbow a squeeze. "G'night, Meg."

"See you tomorrow."

Meg entered the house, closed the door, and leaned against it. She heard Vance back his vehicle down the driveway and realized she'd been holding her breath. She exhaled and smiled inwardly. Everything seemed so right, so perfect, that she wanted to savor the feeling of this moment.

Holding it close, she took it upstairs with her and cast it into her dreams.

Chapter Seventeen

....

Meg arrived at school the next day almost thirty minutes early. She opened her notebook computer and signed on to her e-mail. Grams didn't have WIFI—didn't even have cable television—so Meg was forced to check her messages at school on her own time. The truth was, she didn't mind. Sometimes she forgot to check her e-mail for days.

She scanned her messages and deleted the ones that appeared to be spam. After leaving Dillon, she had ditched her old screen name and created a new one. She'd made sure those people with whom she stayed in contact were alerted, and the rest could just guess as to where she'd moved.

She spied a note from her mother. It had been sent from Mom's e-mail address at work.

Haven't heard from you in a while. Are you OK? The condo that Greg and I are renting has a spare bedroom. You can come and stay with us as long as you'd like if you're going crazy, living with all those country bumpkins. If you're not going nuts now, I promise you will be soon. When I was your age, nobody could've paid me enough to live with my grandmother!

Meg felt grateful that she could reply to the contrary. *Hi, Mom. I'm just fine. I'm happy here in Kentucky and I love teaching grade school. Grams and I are getting along great, and I'm even getting to know Dad and his other family. I actually enjoy their company, and they've been very supportive of me.*

She paused, wondering whether to tell Mom she'd met a man who could make her heart skip. A moment later, she decided against it. Things were only budding between herself and Vance, and Meg didn't want

Mom to assume that this newfound happiness was contingent upon an *affaire de coeur*.

She ended the note with a simple *Love, M* and fired off the e-mail. She checked her other messages, and before long, students were trickling into the classroom.

* * * * *

Loretta sat at the kitchen table, trying to figure out how many family members were likely to come to the house for the Thanksgiving Day holiday—that is, if she invited them. Most years, her daughters-in-law either cooked or went to their folks' homes while Loretta's sons went hunting. But this year, Loretta wanted to do something different.

Besides, Meggie's birthday was the Wednesday before Thanksgiving, and a huge party was in order.

"Whadda you want to do all that work for, Retta?" Tom groused. His coffee cup sat half-drunk in front of him. "You'll have to wash dishes for days."

"Family, Tom. Family! It's a person's reason for being."

"No, it ain't. God's a person's reason for being."

"Well, of course, but God instituted family."

"And ours are grown and gone. So I say let's go out to eat on Thanksgiving Day."

"What about Meggie?"

"She can come, too, if she wants."

Loretta expelled a sigh of annoyance. Men just couldn't understand the importance of a family sitting down together and eating a well-planned holiday meal. Why, their ideal Thanksgiving Day would involve hunting deer for hours and then returning to the house to watch a football game on TV.

"I want Meggie to experience family like she never has before," Loretta tried to explain. "She and Paul finally made their peace." Just thinking about the miracle that recently transpired caused her to choke with emotion. "She's curious about her aunts and uncles and cousins. And it's her birthday."

"You know I'm just as happy 'bout that as you are, Retta, but Meggie's a growed up woman now. You can't plan things for her like she's gonna be sweet sixteen. Why don't you ask her what she might like to do over the Thanksgiving Day holiday and her birthday? She's a spirited little thing. Might just want to go huntin' with the fellas." Tom let loose a series of chuckles.

Loretta bristled at such nonsense, but she had to concede that her lovable, crinkly faced friend had a point. It might be best to consult Meggie before the actual planning process began. Tom had a keen sense of understanding when it came to people. He didn't say much, but when he did, folks listened.

Like on Sunday, during the ride home from church, Loretta had tried to convince Meggie to talk to Paul about the argument they'd had the day before at the stables. That girl was as stubborn as her daddy and refused. But later on, after lunch, Tom had offhandedly mentioned the biblical principle about not letting the sun go down on your anger, and before Loretta knew it, Meggie was driving her car over to Paul and Donna's place.

"Besides, you've got two months till Thanksgiving," Tom said, interrupting Loretta's thoughts. "What's the rush?"

She pushed aside the pen and scratchpad on which she'd been doodling ideas. "I don't know. I guess there is no rush." She stood from the chair on which she'd been sitting. "Maybe I'll just have a cup of coffee and a peanut butter cookie and think about Thanksgiving Day another time."

"You're a wise woman, Retta."

She grinned. "And birds of a feather—"

"—flock together."

* * * * *

Meg willed her tense body to relax as she stared out the bank of windows at the back of the classroom. Thank God this day was finally over! The school year was in full swing now, and her students' personalities were emerging. Two boys got into a scrape at recess today, so Meg had to send them to Mr. Sutterman's office. Then, during the spelling quiz, three girls in her class wouldn't stop whispering. Warning notes were on their way home for the girls' parents.

Meg rolled her shoulders, working out the stress in her muscles. It occurred to her that perhaps she'd been too strict today, and yet she knew that boundaries needed to be set early if she wanted the remainder of the school year to go smoothly. No doubt she'd be hearing from a few concerned, perhaps even irritated, parents.

"Meg?"

She turned from the windows just as Leah entered the room.

"Oh," her friend sighed, looking relieved. "I'm glad you're still here."

"What's up?"

"Can you give me a ride home? My car won't start."

"I'd like to, but I'm supposed to be at the Donahues' at six."

"I live right on the way."

Meg smiled at her friend. "Then I'm glad to give you a lift."

"Thanks."

Leah strode across the room, wearing khaki linen slacks, a matching short-sleeved top, and an olive-green vest. Meg noticed that she always looked professional, fashionable, and comfortable.

"Hi, Cammy."

The girl twisted in her seat and peered at Leah. "Hi, Miss Lawton." She went right back to work, copying her spelling words.

Leah leaned forward, her elbows resting on top of the bookshelf that was situated beneath the windows. "Nice that the weather cleared."

"Uh-huh."

A silver and blue customized van with an extended roof suddenly pulled into the parking lot. Meg recognized it at once. Leah obviously did, too.

They glanced at each other and grinned.

"Wouldn't it be fun to double-date sometime?" Leah whispered the question.

"Yes, it would."

"There's a dinner theater in Lexington—though I'm sure it's amateurish compared to anything in Chicago."

Meg lifted her shoulders. "Maybe we'll have to go sometime and find out."

Just as Meg was about to turn around and inform Cammy that her father had arrived, Nicole Foster showed up from out of nowhere. Meg watched as the woman took purposeful strides toward Vance, cornering him between his van and its open driver's side door. From Meg's vantage point, the conversation that ensued looked heavy, serious.

Meg exchanged curious glances with Leah.

"Maybe it's something about her oldest son, Michael. He's gotten into trouble here at school. He's got anger issues. Maybe. . .maybe Nicole needs a male opinion about what to do with him or something."

"That's quite a stretch, even for you, Pollyanna."

Leah elbowed her as repayment for the facetious remark.

Meg glanced back outside just in time to see Nicole slip her arms around Vance's neck and lean forward.

Her lips met his. And what was worse, Meg didn't see Vance putting up much of a fight.

Leah gasped and slapped her hand over her mouth.

"So that's how it is. Okay, I get it." Meg tore her gaze away. Touching Leah's elbow, she urged her friend away from the windows, too.

Cammy watched them with a worried frown. She'd obviously overheard bits and pieces. "What's wrong?"

"Oh, nothing, sweet pea." There was a melodious note in Leah's drawl.

"Your dad's here." Meg forced her legs to make their way to her desk.

"He is?"

"Yep, so it might be a good idea for you to pack up your things."

"Yes, Miss Jorgenson."

Cammy sent her a puzzled look, and Meg realized she'd sounded short. She wanted to amend her tone, but she couldn't seem to find something—anything—to say.

Long moments of impregnated silence hovered in the room.

Leah peered over her shoulder and out the window in an attempt to glimpse further activity. Meg wished she wouldn't even try. She felt embarrassed, confused, and incredibly disappointed. At this point, additional glances would only make her feel like she was spying. Though of course, if Vance chose to make out with that Foster woman in the school parking lot, then he could hardly accuse anyone of invading his privacy!

"I just can't help wondering how some people's minds work." Leah sat down in Jordan Smith's desk. "What are they thinking?"

"No telling." But Meg's own mind had already figured things out. Kissing her in the stables on Saturday, kissing Nicole right now in the parking lot—Vance Bayer seemed to be just as much a player as Kent, only coy and a hundred times more subtle. Meg could come to grips with the fact that Vance had lied to her, but how could he lie to Cammy, too?

Disappointment assailed her. She liked Vance. A lot. She'd looked forward to getting to know him better. But not anymore.

Vance walked into the room and Meg manufactured a polite smile. "Hello."

He inclined his head. "Hi, Meg."

She spun on her heel and began erasing the already cleared whiteboard. She supposed it wouldn't hurt to give it another once-over.

"How was your day?"

She wasn't sure to whom he spoke, but she allowed Cammy to answer the question.

"It was good, Daddy. And guess what? Jimmy Butterfield and Troy Thompson started fighting on the playground and had to go to the principal's office."

"I'm sure Mr. Sutterman took care of the matter."

"Boys'll be boys, eh, Vance?" The discomfort was evident in Leah's voice. "Not that it's okay to fight on the playground or anything, but you know what I mean."

"Yeah, I think I do."

Hearing the warmth and amusement in his voice, Meg stopped her cleaning and studied the eraser. She concluded there was no use mourning something that never was.

She forced herself to face Vance and watched him gather his little girl's belongings.

"Don't worry, Miss Jorgenson, Jimmy and Troy will be better tomorrow. They're not bad boys."

Meg realized she'd been frowning hard, but not because of her students. "I'm sure you're right, Cammy. Everything will be all right tomorrow."

Vance looked at her, and she saw the diffidence in his eyes. A result of guilt? Embarrassment? He'd done plenty of public kissing in the last four days. Maybe there was more hellion left in Vance than Meg had thought.

"Ready, Cammy?"

"Ready."

Vance peered over her head at Meg. "See you in the morning."

"I'll be here."

Vance backed up the wheelchair and steered Cammy toward the door. As he passed by the window, Meg saw him casually glance in the direction of the parking lot. Was it her imagination, or did he miss a step?

She looked at Leah, whose eyes missed nothing. Her friend pressed her lips together but didn't say a word.

Until they were alone in Meg's car some minutes later.

"Can you believe it? Nicole's out of her mind! Flinging herself at Vance like some hussy."

"It wasn't a fling. The move was very deliberate."

"You're miffed at Vance, aren't you? I can tell. But that was all Nicole in the parking lot. Talk about a sneak attack! Poor Vance."

"Sure, and Vance was as defenseless as a newborn baby, right?" A frown weighed on Meg's brow.

"He pushed her away."

"He did not. Looked to me like he kissed her right back."

Leah inhaled sharply. "Heavens, no! He pushed her away."

Meg didn't want to debate the issue, but it certainly seemed more like a romantic *tête-à-tête* than a "sneak attack."

"Listen, it doesn't matter." Meg squared her shoulders. "There's nothing between Vance and me anyway. We mentioned going out together sometime. Big deal. If it never happens, I'm okay with it. In fact, I just e-mailed my mother this morning, and I felt like it was really important to let her know that my happiness here in Miracle isn't dependent on whether I have a man in my life."

"What is your happiness dependent on?"

"On—" The question momentarily threw her. She had to think about it. "My happiness is dependent on my new job, my family," Meg aimed a grin at Leah, "and my friends."

"That's awesome, but—" Leah paused, appearing thoughtful. "Well, not to be a pessimist or anything, but jobs can be lost and family members and friends can desert you when you need them most."

"I know that." Meg couldn't help thinking that Dillon was a prime example of betrayal.

"Make a left up ahead."

Meg did as her friend bid her.

Still belted in, Leah scooted sideways in her seat. "So what do you hinge your happiness on?"

"Okay, let me rephrase my previous reply. My happiness is based on my success, teaching kids, and making a difference in their lives."

"Admirable, but, again, temporal."

"Huh?" Meg briefly took her eyes off the road and cast a quick glance at Leah. "What answer are you fishing for?"

"I'm not fishing, exactly. I'm just trying to make the point that true love, joy, and peace aren't derived from people or accomplishments. They come from having a relationship with God."

Meg thought it over. She'd heard a lot about having a "relationship with God" lately. But the philosophy seemed out of context here. "So what's God got to do with Vance kissing Nicole Foster in the school parking lot?"

"Well, love and happiness and all that."

"I don't love Vance." Meg shifted in her seat, suddenly uncomfortable. She felt like she'd just fibbed. But how could she have, when he barely knew Vance?

"Slow down. We're almost to my house. Make a right turn."

Following Leah's directions, Meg sped her car up the long driveway.

She was met by a neatly groomed yard and a long ranch home with white siding. "Pretty place."

"I wish you could come in. Maybe next time. You can stay for dinner."

"Sounds fun."

"Thanks for the ride." Unlatching her seatbelt, Leah opened the door and climbed out. "The Donahues live four houses down the road, but considering the surrounding acreage, that amounts to about a half mile."

"Got it."

"And the Bayers' house isn't far from the Donahues' place."

"You're telling me this, *why*?" Meg couldn't hold back the gibe.

"I don't know." Leah slung the strap of her leather satchel over her narrow shoulder. "Just thought that when you're done visiting with the Donahues, you could stop and say hi to Vance."

"He might have company."

"Only one way to find out." Leah flashed a grin. "See you tomorrow."

Before Meg could reply, her friend closed the door and headed for the side door.

Chapter Eighteen

....

Vance paced the kitchen while Cammy ate her dinner. He knew he made poor company this evening; he felt so flustered he could barely form a cohesive thought. So he'd taken Cammy out of the wheelchair and propped her up on the sofa in the living room. With a tray across her lap and a movie, *The Hiding Place*, playing on the TV, she was contented. She would, of course, have preferred an episode of *Hannah Montana* to the story depicting Corrie ten Boom's experiences with the Nazis during World War II, but as part of her punishment for lying, he had banned television on school nights. The DVD was a stretch, but in his preoccupation with what happened this afternoon, Vance made the exception.

This afternoon—unbelievable! What was Nicole thinking?

He ran his hand through his hair and walked into the dining room, where he paused, folded his arms tightly across his chest, and stared out the front windows.

She'd kissed him right there in the school parking lot! Vance had been so stunned, it had taken him several seconds before he could peel her off of him.

Next she said she loved him and didn't want to marry Professor Amir Gaspar. She begged Vance to give her a reason not to marry him.

He gave her not a single one. How could he?

She clung to him with tears in her eyes. While he pitied her, he mostly felt irritated and embarrassed. Nothing even resembling love filled his senses.

It definitely couldn't match what he felt when he kissed Meg. At that moment in the stables, the air around them seemed electrically

and magically charged. Vance hadn't experienced anything like it
since Angie died.

Never with Nicole. She'd been good company over the summer
months, and they'd shared some fun times with mutual friends. But how
in the world could she translate a few dates into *love*?

Vance rubbed his stubbly jaw before massaging the knot of tension
forming in the back of his neck. Engrossed in his thoughts, he barely saw
the bicycle riders outside, pedaling by his house.

He figured Meg probably saw the incident this afternoon. He sensed
her distance when he picked up Cammy. After a few subtle questions,
Cammy confirmed that both Miss Jorgenson and Miss Lawton had been
standing by the windows, talking, just before he arrived.

Great. Just great.

Maybe it was insensitive, but Vance cared more about Meg's opinion
of him than he did about Nicole's dilemma.

"Daddy, I'm done eating."

"Coming, punkin."

Vance steered his mind back to the here and now. He walked into
the living room and removed the tray. Carrying it to the kitchen, he set it
down on the table and decided to clean up later. For now, he'd sit through
the rest of the movie with Cammy. Afterwards, they'd do her physical
therapy, just as they did every night. Then he'd allow her to read for a
while. Once she fell asleep, maybe Vance would work up the nerve to
give Meg a call.

* * * * *

When Meg arrived home from the Donahues', she received the message
that Vance had called. But it was late, and she felt so stuffed with pork
roast, spoon bread, and rhubarb pie that she didn't call him back.

Instead, she waddled upstairs to her room and spent a few
hours reviewing tomorrow's lesson plan before crawling into bed.

The next morning, there was neither time nor privacy for her and
Vance to have a conversation. When school let out, Kent was hanging
around and finally spoke to Vance about Cammy and the rowing
machines. He added that the school's HCA, or handicap assistant, agreed
to stay by Cammy's side the entire time. Vance was hesitant at first, but
he finally gave his permission.

That evening, Leah convinced Meg to attend a home Bible study.
She said that it was attended by a small group of women around their
age, and that it was a great way for Meg to make a few more friends.

"Besides, with my car in the shop, I could use a lift. I'll pay for
the gas."

For whatever crazy reason, Meg agreed; however, her expectations
weren't high.

But when Sarah Berger, the hostess of the Bible study, began reading
a poem about how each individual was "fearfully and wonderfully"
made, Meg couldn't help but give her full attention. She'd always assumed
she was an inconvenience that had to be dealt with until she became
a self-sufficient adult. But hearing how God *created* her, just as Grams
created her intricate patchwork quilts with careful planning, dedication,
and great effort, struck Meg as quite profound.

"God put all the days of our lives together, knowing where each
piece goes." Conviction shown in Sarah's brown eyes, but her voice had
a sweet ring to it. "No one is a mistake, a fluke. In fact, each of us has a
specific work or purpose to fulfill." She read from her Bible then, citing
Psalm 139.

After the study, Meg mingled with the seven other ladies in
attendance. She'd already met several of them at church and decided they
were friendly and sincere.

"Think you'll come back next week?" Leah asked as Meg drove her home.

"I might. I feel—" Meg searched for the right word. "Uplifted."

"Cool. That's what it's all about." Leah paused. "Wanna bring the dessert next week?"

"No, because that would mean I'd have to bake, and who's got time for that?"

"Not me," Leah confessed. "And my mom works full-time, too, so I can't ask her." A pause. "If you haven't noticed, it's my turn to bring the goodies, and I'm trying to get out of it."

"I noticed." Meg bit back a laugh, but then an idea struck. "I'll bet Grams would whip up something. I'll ask her."

"You think? I mean, I don't want to impose."

"Grams loves to make food for people, but if she's too busy, she'll let me know. Besides, there's always the grocery store."

"Oh, no, no, no," Leah said with dramatic flare. "The Titus Two woman does not bring a store-bought dessert to Bible study."

"Titus Two?" Meg hadn't ever heard the phrase before. "Sounds like some buff thing Kent might be into."

"No, that's Midas," Leah said on a giggle, "not Titus."

"Not him, either. King Midas turned everything to gold."

"Hercules, then?"

"Yeah, in Kent's dreams."

Meg turned and drove her car up the Lawtons' driveway. By the time it rolled to a stop, whoops of hilarity filled the vehicle. Meg couldn't help envisioning Kent morphed into He-Man, and she laughed until her stomach muscles cramped.

Leah admitted to thinking of the same cartoon character. "Oh, my goodness, that's so funny!"

Meg wiped her teary eyes and audibly expelled the last of her mirth. "I must be overtired."

"I know I am."

"So what's Titus Two all about, for real?"

"It's a chapter—half a chapter, really—in the Bible. The Book of Titus. It instructs older women to teach good things to younger woman, and it encourages married women to keep their hearts in their homes, even if they have to work someplace and earn money."

"Keep their hearts in their homes." Meg pondered the idea.

"As opposed to being consumed by a career and looking outside their marriages and families for happiness."

"A lot of women would stay out of trouble if they took that advice." Meg thought of her mother. What would have happened if she'd kept her heart in her home? She and Dad might still be married.

Leah opened the car door. "So, about the Bible study—you'll come next week?"

"Sure."

"Great. It's a date."

"The only date I've got."

"Ditto."

Smiling, Meg watched her friend get out of the car and walk into the house. Then she drove back to Grams' place.

The back door was unlocked when she arrived, and she let herself in. A nightlight shone in the spotless kitchen, and on the stovetop Meg found a note saying that Vance had tried to get a hold of her again. But now it was after ten o'clock, so she decided it was too late to return his phone call.

The next two days played out much the same way, and the evenings were consumed by dinners with her students' families. On Saturday Meg accompanied Donna and Kelly to a mall in Lexington, where Kelly returned the two extra homecoming dresses. She came home with them, stayed for dinner, and—at Donna's insistence—agreed to spend the night. The two women stayed up late chattering, and it was good for Meg to finally have an in-depth conversation with her stepmother. She found herself liking Donna more and more.

The next morning, Meg attended Sunday service with her dad's family—her family, too, she reminded herself. In light of all that had happened between them, it seemed fitting to her that the church was located on Redemption Road. Meg had driven by the round, red brick structure scores of times since moving here, but she hadn't found the time to investigate it.

After church, they went to Grams' and enjoyed a chicken dinner together. Then they sat out on the wraparound front porch and talked over pie, iced tea, and coffee. Meg reveled in discovering such simple pleasures and felt lucky to find such peace here in Miracle.

All too soon, it was Monday again.

"Mornin', Meg." Vance wore an affable expression as he pushed Cammy's wheelchair into the classroom.

"G'morning, Vance." Meg smiled, hoping it didn't appear as tentative as she felt. Despite what he might think, she hadn't been intentionally avoiding him. But she had to admit that she wasn't overeager to converse about what she'd seen in the school parking lot last week.

She looked at Cammy. "Good morning to you, too."

Enthusiasm lit the child's blue eyes. "Hi, Miss Jorgenson."

Vance kissed his daughter good-bye. "Be good." He patted Cammy's shoulder, and Meg thought she looked both pretty and prim in her navy slacks and printed smock-top with its lacy collar. "Listen to your teacher."

"I will, Daddy."

He sent Meg a parting grin. "Have a good day."

"Thanks. You, too."

He walked out of the classroom without so much as a long look or one of his reticent grins, and he certainly didn't dally as though hoping to find a few private moments in which the two of them could talk. Meg felt a mild sense of relief—mixed with sadness. It was rather disappointing that Vance backed off so quickly. But it just proved that Leah was wrong and that Meg's assumption was correct: he still harbored feelings for Nicole Foster.

More children arrived for school, and Meg pushed aside her tumultuous thoughts. Acquiescence set in. After all, if things really happened for a reason, then maybe it was for the best.

* * * * *

Over the course of the next few weeks, Vance set out to prove two women wrong. Daunting, perhaps, but he was up to the task.

After discussing the matter with his trusted friend and confidant, Boz Poedell, as well as with Pastor Wilkerson, it wasn't difficult to put the pieces together. Nicole blamed their breakup on Vance's attraction to Meg. Meanwhile, Meg viewed him as some sort of dirty rotten scoundrel. Of course, both perceptions were way off target, so Vance aimed to set the record straight. He planned to do so by staying clear of both women, particularly Nicole. In the few months they'd dated, he'd never realized how desperate she was to, as Boz termed it, "tie the knot—as in, the noose around your neck."

No wonder Cammy had felt so threatened. Vance marveled that he'd been so blind.

As for Meg, it was impossible to avoid her, since he saw her twice a day and on Sundays at church. Still, he did his best to be formal but cordial, friendly yet distant, and his actions, or lack thereof, seemed to lessen the pressure between them. In fact, it lessened everything between them, including dialogue.

Even so, Vance couldn't help watching her from the sidelines.

She hung out with Leah Lawton, who'd always been known around town as "a good girl," and Boz reported that the two women were at his house when his wife, Tara, hosted one of the weekly Bible studies. Tara had nice things to say about Meg, and Vance listened to every word. What's more, he soon took note of the fact that Meg wasn't dating— and it wasn't due to lack of offers. Vance personally knew of at least two guys whom Meg had turned down. They'd come into the repair shop at different intervals and bemoaned their bad luck. Each time, Vance did his best to sympathize while secretly rejoicing.

And then there was Cammy. Her adoration for Meg hadn't waned, and every day she came home with some tidbit—and it never involved that new gym teacher, either.

Finally, one Thursday night, Vance's passive persuasion paid off. Things took a turn for the better.

It happened at Wal-Mart of all places. Meg was reading the tag on an article of clothing, and when she rounded the corner of one aisle, she nearly plowed him over with her shopping cart.

"Oh, Vance, I'm so sorry!"

"No harm done, but, um, I think there is a speed limit in here."

Amusement sparked in her blue eyes, and she slowed to a halt. She seemed reluctant to speak to him.

So he began. "How've you been? I haven't really talked to you in a while. I mean, other than discussing Cammy's performance in school."

"I'm fine. How're you doing?"

"Good." Vance shifted, feeling a tad nervous that he might say or do something to send her running again.

She glanced around. "Is Cammy with you?"

"No. I got her ready for bed, and a neighbor came over to babysit. I needed to pick up some things."

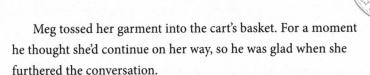

Meg tossed her garment into the cart's basket. For a moment he thought she'd continue on her way, so he was glad when she furthered the conversation.

"Are you going to the homecoming game and bonfire next week? I hear it's a big event for the high school alumni as well as for the students."

"Wouldn't miss it. I usually meet some buddies at the game." Vance's former in-laws were driving down from where they lived on the Kentucky-Ohio border for one of their short but frequent visits with Cammy. They'd already agreed to stay with her on Friday night.

"It sounds like fun. Kelly and Ryan have been telling me all about it."

"It's a good time." Vance regarded her askance. "The bonfire is always after the game on Friday night, and it's held at the Owens' farm."

"Same place as the Labor Day picnic."

"Right."

Vance saw the wistfulness waft across her features.

"Why don't you come?"

She shrugged. "Maybe I will."

"Is Kelly still excited about the dance next Saturday night?"

"Oh, yeah." Meg's eyes widened with emphasis, and a smile crept across her face. "Except she—" A faint blush pinked her cheeks. "I almost strangled her. Kelly called tonight—*tonight*—and announced that she had volunteered me to be a chaperone. Apparently they're short staffed."

Vance leaned on the end of Meg's cart and grinned. "You're saying you didn't jump at the chance to babysit a gymnasium full of teens?"

She gave her head an affirmative bob. "That's what I'm saying. But my relationship with Kelly is still sort of fragile. For the first time ever, she's looking up to me as a real older sister. Her friends think I'm 'cool,' and, well, I just couldn't let her down. I agreed to chaperone." She released a heavy sigh. "So here I am, drowning my sorrows in Wal-Mart."

The quip caused Vance to chuckle, but secretly, he was wondering who she'd go with.

Then again, maybe she didn't need an escort. Plenty of kids went to the dance without dates, and the single chaperones probably did, too.

Seconds later, he recalled Cammy mentioning something about how Meg hadn't attended homecoming in high school.

"If you need a date, let me know." The words tumbled out of his mouth before he could fully consider the idea, and he felt like a giant fool.

But Meg didn't seem to think so. "Are you serious?"

Was he? He cleared his throat. "Well, yeah, I mean—"

"It's such short notice."

"That's okay." He rolled his shoulders. "I'm available."

She paused and tipped her head. "Yes, so I've noticed." Her eyes went from sky blue to cobalt, and Vance picked up her meaning at once.

"I wasn't sure." Her tone was soft, her voice steady. "And I—well, I didn't want to play games. Been there, done that."

"I understand." He felt almost weak with relief. "How did you—"

"Leah. She saw—everything." Meg smirked. "And she finally convinced me that you were quite the innocent victim in that whole exchange."

Vance chuckled softly and shook his head. "You have no idea."

They were silent for a few moments until Meg finally spoke.

"I think I would like to take you up on your offer for next Saturday night. I think I'd feel less anxious about the whole homecoming thing."

"Good." He felt his smile grow wider. "Glad I can oblige."

She wheeled her shopping cart around. "So, where are you headed next?"

Vance retrieved his list from the back pocket of his jeans. "I need laundry soap."

"What a coincidence." Sarcasm dripped from each word. "It just so happens I'm heading in that direction myself."

Vance was tickled by her antics. "Imagine that."

* * * * *

Meg pressed Leah's number into the keypad of her cell phone while navigating her way out to the main road. Only a few cars were left in the wide parking lot. After checking out, she and Vance had talked outside until the lights went out and the store closed.

Meg listened while Leah's phone rang. At last, her friend answered.

"What's going on, Meg?" She sounded drowsy.

"Hope I didn't wake you."

"You did, but that's okay."

"I apologize for calling so late, but you're not going to believe what just happened."

"What?" Leah's voice perked up.

"Remember how we were discussing destiny and Divine Intervention last night?"

"Yeah?"

"Well, it just happened. Divine Intervention—at Wal-Mart!"

Chapter Nineteen

....

"Daddy, I want to go, too." Cammy jutted out her lower lip. Not fair. Not fair. Not fair!

"Punkin, the football game'll run until at least nine o'clock and then the bonfire lasts till midnight. Too late a night for you. You've been up since the crack of dawn and gone to school all day." He dipped his head and leaned forward. His spicy cologne tickled her nose. "Don't forget you got to go out to eat at the Depot tonight with me and your grandparents. That was special."

"Yeah, I guess." Cammy rolled her wheelchair back and peeked at Grampa Charlie and Gramma Liz. Right now they were watching *High School Musical* on the Disney Channel because Cammy had said she liked that show.

But she liked being with Daddy and Miss Jorgenson more than watching even her most favorite TV shows.

She turned back to Daddy. "Take me with you."

He hunkered down beside her so that his face was close to hers. "Punkin, it was your idea that I ask Miss Jorgenson out. But how are we supposed to talk and get to know each other better if I've got my little girl along with me all the time?" He smiled. "And, just like we planned, you can call me on my cell phone just before you go to bed. I'll put Meg on and you can say good night to her, too. Okay?"

"Okay, but—" Cammy glanced over her shoulder at her grandparents. They had said they were happy to see Daddy going out and having some fun. Cammy was, too. She just didn't like to be left out. "Daddy, I don't want to stay home."

"Listen, it was very nice of your gramma and grampa to agree to stay with you so I can go out with Miss Jorgenson tonight *and* tomorrow night. They drove a long way to see you, you know. They love you."

"I know. I love them, too."

"Good. Then you'll enjoy your time with them tonight."

"But, Daddy—"

"Now, don't whine. You be sweet, Cammy Ann. Make me proud."

Cammy felt her lower lip slipping out again. She didn't want to be mad, because she did love Gramma and Grampa. They bought her an American Girl doll. She was the most beautiful doll ever, with dark wavy hair and blue eyes like her own. Cammy could hardly wait to show her friends.

But she still wanted to go to the football game and bonfire. "What if—"

"Discussion's over, punkin." He stood and placed his hands on his hips. His voice told her it was useless to keep begging.

Cammy sighed dramatically. "O-*kay*."

Daddy tickled her and she giggled.

"That's my girl."

Peering up into his face, Cammy could see happiness in his eyes.

"You like Miss Jorgenson, don't you?"

"Of course I do. Otherwise I wouldn't be going out with her two times in a row."

Daddy turned and walked toward his bedroom.

Cammy rolled her wheelchair down the hall behind him. She passed Mommy's portrait on the wall and imagined her looking down from heaven and smiling. Mommy would like Miss Jorgenson. "Are you gonna kiss her?"

"Maybe."

A giggle bubbled up inside of Cammy. She hoped Daddy did kiss Miss Jorgenson, not just maybe.

Cammy closed her eyes. *Well, Jesus, our plan is going just fine.* She paused. *I just wish I could be there tonight to make sure Daddy and Miss Jorgenson fall in love. I just don't know how they'll manage it without me along.*

* * * * *

Meg walked along a winding dirt trail beside Vance. The Lincoln County High School Patriots had won their homecoming game, so everyone supporting the home team left the football field in good spirits.

Meg had enjoyed watching the game, especially when Ryan would take to the field. She felt proud of her "little bro," which she called him chiefly because the endearment irked him.

Vance's friends had made the game all the more fun, particularly Boz and his wife, Tara. They shared "back in the day" stories, and Meg got a sense of just how much of a hellion Vance had been. He had instigated the county's legendary "firecracker war," in which about twenty guys split up into two teams and shot bottle rockets and homemade explosive devices at each other. It was a wonder no one was maimed or killed.

"Nice night." Vance's arm brushed against Meg's shoulder as they ambled along the moonlit pathway.

Glancing up at the starry sky, she had to agree. "Perfect weather for a bonfire. Is it held here every year?"

"Uh-huh. For the last two decades the Owenses have hosted a bonfire after the homecoming game. I think it was their way of keeping an eye on their oldest son, Troy."

"Another reformed hellion-friend of yours." Meg nodded. She'd met Troy and his wife and kids.

"Right." Vance chuckled. "As you saw, he's driving the team of horses for the hayride."

"I saw. Looks fun. The hayride, that is."

Vance halted. "You want to take one?"

"No, this is nice. With a little privacy, we might actually have a real conversation."

The walked a few paces in silence.

"This week went by so fast." His tone held an apologetic note. "I'd hoped to stop by and see you, but I never got the chance. There was a lot to do before Liz and Charlie arrived."

"And Liz and Charlie are. . .?"

"I'm sorry. I should have been more clear—they're Cammy's grandparents. Angie's folks."

"Ah. . ." Meg wondered again about his deceased wife. What had she been like? Had Vance fully healed from the sorrow of losing her?

Somewhere off in the distance, a horse whinnied.

"What did Cammy's grandparents say about you going out with me twice this weekend?"

"They asked a few questions about you, and of course Cammy gave them an earful. They're satisfied that you're a nice person. You've certainly made an impression on their granddaughter, at any rate."

Meg smiled, pleased.

"Honestly, they're happy for me—happy to hear I'm getting out more. And, of course, they jumped at the chance to babysit and have Cammy to themselves."

Vance was silent for a moment before he nudged Meg with his elbow. "Follow me."

Leaving the trail, he took her hand.

"Where are we going?"

"A small detour."

"Oh?"

He laughed at her skepticism. "I know a quiet place where you'll still be able to see the bonfire."

They stepped through a patch of long, hay-like grass. "There aren't any snakes in here, are there?"

"Might be. You'd better stay real close to me."

She clasped his hand tighter and quickened her pace. But a heartbeat later, she realized she'd just fallen for the oldest line in the trickster's textbook.

"Very funny."

Vance chuckled.

In spite of herself, she grinned. She enjoyed seeing this lighthearted side of Vance, and she credited his jovial friends for loosening him up during the football game.

They reached the clearing, and, just as Vance said, the view overlooked the bonfire.

He sat down and leaned against the trunk of a massive oak tree.

"Are you sure there aren't any snakes hiding around here? I've been spooked ever since Tom's septic-tank story."

He tugged on her hand. "Any snakes are probably more afraid of you than you are of them, so relax."

She eased herself into a sitting position beside him and took in her surroundings: a perfect view of the bonfire below, the moon overhead, and a gentle breeze tousling the treetops. Talk about romantic!

"Something tells me you've been on this hilltop numerous times before," she teased.

"Yeah, but not in about ten years."

He set his arm around her shoulders, and Meg couldn't help snuggling against him. As nice as it felt, something weighed on her mind.

"Will you tell me about Angie?"

The sudden jerk of Vance's body told her that the question surprised him. "What do you want to know about her?"

"I don't know. Whatever you feel comfortable sharing."

Vance seemed to be thinking it over.

"Grams told me you two met in college."

"That's right."

"Love at first sight?"

"Definitely. Hit me like lightning."

"That's sweet." Meg smiled. "How long were you two together before getting married?"

"Not long. Angie was a decisive, take-charge sort of woman. Looking at her, you'd never know it. On the outside, she appeared very delicate and unassuming."

"Like Cammy."

"Yep." Vance laughed. "And I think Angie and her mother had our wedding planned out before I even got around to proposing."

"Did that bother you?"

"No. I'm pretty laid back, so Angie was good for me that way. Kept me on my toes and motivated."

"How long were you married before Cammy was born?"

"About a year. We were so excited. Didn't matter that we were stone broke and working our way through school. We just knew that somehow the Lord would provide for our needs and Cammy's. He did."

Meg pulled some long grass and wrapped it around her forefinger. "I'm sure the car accident—and losing Angie—has been devastating for you."

"That's putting it mildly." Vance pulled his arm away and straightened a bit.

Meg knew she'd hit a nerve. But she also knew that they needed to talk about this, to get it all out in the open, if their relationship was going to progress. So she kept silent, waiting patiently for him to either continue or change the subject.

"Angie was my reason for living. I had built my whole world around her. When she died, I felt like I'd lost my very soul. I didn't know what to do or where to turn for help. But, at the same time, I couldn't really dwell on myself. My daughter needed me. And so did my father. All this was going on while he was dying of cancer."

Meg's heart ached for Vance. She slipped her hand into his. He grasped it, entwining her fingers between his.

"My sister tried to be there for both my mother and me, but she had just gone through a divorce and was dealing with her son's learning disabilities. It was a rough time for her, too. Liz and Charlie were, and are, a huge help to me. My friends, too. And my pastor, my church family. They're all good about keeping in touch, being available if we need anything." Vance paused.

"Then, a little more than a year ago, I began feeling empty, depressed. And one night, it was like the Lord tapped me on the shoulder and reminded me that He'd been there for me all along. I just needed to turn to Him and ask for His guidance, provision, and healing. Make Him Lord of my life. I made that decision, and at that point, I turned the corner from living in complete despair to—" He took a second to find the right words. "—to being able to laugh again and find joy in raising my daughter."

"That's beautiful, Vance. The way God gave you hope."

"He did. And now, finally, I feel ready to go on with my life."

Meg leaned her head against his shoulder. She had never felt closer to him as she did in this moment. The feeling surprised her.

"Well, enough about me. What about you? Like it here in Kentucky so far?"

"Yeah, I like it a lot."

"Think you'll stay?"

"It's my every intention."

Vance shifted and put his arm around Meg again. "Mind if I ask what brought you here in the first place? A public school in Chicago has got to pay more than a little charter school in Stanford."

"Money isn't everything."

"True enough." He momentarily paused. "I got a settlement after the accident, but it was a bittersweet financial gain. I bought a handicap van and my Sport Trac. Both have come in handy, but neither brought me an ounce of happiness. But there I go again, talking about me."

"I like talking about you."

He gave her a nudge. "You were telling me why you decided to move to Kentucky."

"I was tutoring in one of south Chicago's roughest schools, and the job was going nowhere. I was also living with a guy, and our relationship wasn't going anywhere, either." She turned and tried to gauge Vance's reaction under the ivory streamers of moonlight. "By the way, I'm not exactly advertising this information. I won't deny it if someone asks, but I think a lot of people would love to point righteous fingers and say I'm no good because I was 'living in sin.'"

"I'll keep it under wraps."

Meg sensed understanding, not condemnation, in his voice. However, as she explained how her job, her relationship with Dillon, and ultimately her entire existence all unraveled, she began feeling ashamed of shacking up with Dillon in the first place.

"I know it wasn't—wasn't right."

"We all make mistakes, Meg."

"I know. Nobody's perfect. But I have to admit that living with Dillon was about the worst mistake I ever made."

"Why? Because it didn't work out?"

Meg shook her head. "No, because it wasn't real between us. There was nothing that bound us together. There was no—" She groped for the right word.

"Foundation?"

"Yes. That's a good way to say it. Ours was a relationship built on unstable ground, and it all came tumbling down—right on top of me."

"Ouch." She could practically hear him wincing. "So now you're searching for Mr. Right?"

"Actually, I'm not searching. I'm starting over here in Miracle, and the rest is in God's hands. Providence." Meg's gaze traveled to the starlit sky. "You know, I didn't used to believe in that, but I do now. The fact that I'm here in Kentucky, teaching school; that my dad and I have made amends, and I'm developing relationships with Donna, Kelly, and Ryan—all that is nothing short of one miracle after another." She smiled, amazed. "Even seeing you in Wal-Mart a week ago was what I'd have to call. . .*destiny*."

"You think?"

"Uh-huh."

"Well, I'd have to agree because. . .here we are." Vance hugged her around the shoulders a little tighter.

"Here we are."

An impregnated silence seemed to hover over them.

A second later Vance cleared his throat. "So, um, forgive my being nosy, but I just have to ask—any chance of you and that guy reconciling?"

"Me and Dillon?" She wagged her head with confidence. "Not a single one."

Vance moved closer. "Maybe he just made a mistake." His lips were suddenly close to her ear, sending little shivers of delight around her neck and down her arms. "What if he came crawling back to you, begging your forgiveness, and asking you to marry him?"

"I'd tell him to drop dead."

"Whoa!" He chuckled at her facetious remark and leaned back hard against the oak.

"Okay, maybe I wouldn't say it quite like that—"

Vance continued to laugh.

Meg sat by, smiling.

Then his tone took on a more somber note. "Are you still hurt from the breakup?"

"Honestly? No, I'm not. I'm relieved. So very relieved. Words can't begin to describe it." Meg couldn't have felt more sure of her reply. "What about you and Nicole? Any reconciliation in the works?"

"None." He paused as if in thought. "And you want to know the God's honest truth?"

"Let's hear it." Meg scooted sideways a few inches so she could see him better.

"In the few months that I was seeing Nicole, she and I never talked the way you and I are talking now."

"Seriously?"

"Seriously. I never felt prompted to share anything deeply personal about myself with her."

"I'm flattered." His admission truly did make Meg feel special. "But you and Nicole had to talk about *something*, right?"

"Sure, but it was superficial stuff, like our kids, jobs, Nicole's exhusband, the vacation she always dreamed of taking, the new car she wanted to buy—" Vance seemed to halt in mid-muse. "And speaking of—"

He leaned over and placed a sound but all-too-quick kiss on Meg's lips. She barely had time to respond before he stood and reached for her hand.

Disappointment and surprise surged through her.

"We'd better get back." He pulled her to her feet.

"You mean because people might talk?"

"No." Beneath the glow of the moon, he smiled into her eyes. "Because I just remembered that I gave Boz the keys to my Sport Trac so he could fetch Tara's jacket. It'd be like him to pull a prank and steal my wheels, leaving us to hitchhike back to town."

Chapter Twenty

Loretta felt her jaw drop when Meggie stepped out onto the screened porch. "You look positively stunning, hon."

"Thanks, Grams."

"Mmm-mmm." She smiled and couldn't help the maternal inspection of the calf-length black dress with spaghetti straps. It accentuated Meggie's feminine figure in a flattering yet modest way. "If Vance isn't smitten with you now, he will be."

She blushed at the compliment. "And to think I found this dress at the Goodwill store and paid only five dollars."

Loretta pulled her reading glasses off her nose. "Only five dollars?"

Meg nodded. "It still had the department store tags on it. Brand new."

"Well, I'll be." Loretta grinned. "What a blessing."

"I'll say." She strode forward.

"So, um, you like Vance Bayer, huh?" Loretta closed the *Reader's Digest* in her lap and remembered how she glimpsed the two of them sharing quite the passionate kiss last night after Vance walked Meggie to the door. Nothing obscene, just thoroughly romantic in a way that made Loretta miss Jeb. He'd been a passionate man, too.

"I like him very much." Meggie sat down and crossed her legs. "After the game, he told me about the car accident that killed his wife and injured Cammy."

Loretta closed her eyes and shook her head. "Such a tragedy."

"For sure." Pensiveness shadowed her face. "But he told me about all the good that came out of it, too. I never would have thought it."

"Satan meant it for evil, but God meant it for good."

225

Meg nodded. "Vance said Cammy's spinal cord wasn't severed. I wonder if she'll really walk one day."

"Never know."

"She wants to—she makes mention of walking at least once during every school day." Moments later, Meggie shrugged as if dismissing the matter for the time being. "Anyway, it was nice to get to know Vance better last night."

Loretta smiled. "I've always liked him, even though he gave his parents a run for their money."

"Yes, I heard a number of tales last night. Vance and I had to laugh, because we were such opposites in high school."

"Amazing how God can even up the score, isn't it?"

"Definitely." Meggie smoothed her dress over her knee, and Loretta noticed her bare wrists. She saw the plain silver balls in her earlobes, too.

"Hon, I have a sterling and diamond bracelet with matching earrings—I think they'd complete your outfit." Loretta stood. "Your grandfather gave them to me on my sixtieth birthday, and I think I've worn 'em only a couple of times. Let me fetch the set and you can tell me if you'd like to borrow it tonight."

Meg stood also. "I don't think I've ever worn real diamonds before."

Loretta teasingly began to sing a few bars of "Diamonds Are a Girl's Best Friend" while making her way through the house and into her bedroom. "A kiss on the hand may be quite continental. . ."

Meggie followed her, laughing. "You're too much, Grams."

Reaching her bureau, Loretta opened the top drawer and removed the velvet-encased box.

"They're beautiful! Are you sure I can wear them? What if I lose them?"

"Well, if you do, you do. And, yes, I want you to wear them."

"I'm just chaperoning a homecoming dance. It's not like this is my wedding day or anything."

"I know, but it's a special time just the same. Besides, I think your grandpa would like it that you wore this jewelry."

Loretta helped Meggie fasten the bracelet onto her slender wrist. Then Meggie removed her earrings and replaced them with the diamond studs.

She inspected herself in the mirror. "Well, I guess it's no more sparkle than some women would wear to an elegant dinner party or upscale restaurant."

"You like it?"

"Love it."

"You'll add sophistication to that homecoming dance." Loretta felt immensely proud of her granddaughter, who was so caring, smart, and beautiful. "Maybe the kids will be less inclined to spike the punch."

Meggie smiled. "Fat chance. But luckily Vance knows what to watch for since he's pulled every prank a teenage male can possibly think up."

Loretta had to laugh. "And then some, I'm sure."

* * * * *

Meg drove to the Bayers' so Cammy could approve of her dress. She was becoming very fond of that little girl. Meg admired her intelligence and spunk and noticed that the other teachers did, too. Even Kent Baldwin. Cammy gave one hundred percent to most of her subjects, and phys ed was no exception. She spurred her classmates on and generated excitement; even the kids whom Kent referred to as the "pee wees," she cajoled into participating in relay races. They figured that if Cammy played along despite her disability, they could play in spite of their smaller-than-average sizes, un-coordination, or un-athleticism. Cammy had also helped her team win most of the rowing contests, as her arms were stronger than most eight-year-olds from maneuvering herself around in her wheelchair. She'd become a much sought after team player. Meg was proud of her.

She pulled into the Bayers' driveway, parking over to the side, next to the handicap van as Vance requested. He said they'd drive to the high school in his Explorer Sport Trac tonight.

She walked to the front door and was greeted by a female who looked to be in her fifties. Her short hair was prematurely silver and her eyes, a startling blue. Meg knew at once the woman was Cammy's grandmother.

"I'm Liz Moffet." She opened the door. "You must be Meg."

"Yes. Hello. Nice to meet you." Meg stepped into the house.

"Cammy's been telling me all about you."

"She loves school."

"Sounds to me like she loves her teacher." The smile in Liz's voice sounded genuine, and Meg was touched by the compliment.

"Please, come in." Liz motioned her to step farther into the house.

Meg glanced around the living room. It had a country theme, blues and creams, with a quaint border pasted on the walls near the ceiling. Then her gaze fell on Cammy, who was propped up with pillows at one end of the sofa. In her lap was a colorful cardboard folder.

"Hi, Miss Jorgenson!"

"Hi, yourself."

"You look pretty."

"Thank you." Meg felt a bit embarrassed to have promised to show Cammy her dress. At the time, she didn't know Vance's in-laws would be present.

"I like your dress almost as much as that pretty Mary Poppins dress."

"It'd be lovely on you." Meg sat down on the other end of the sapphire-colored sofa and noticed the teeny cream hearts in the woven fabric. "So what have you got in your lap?" She pointed to the folder.

"American Girl paper dolls." Cammy's face brightened. "Gramma and Grampa got 'em for me. And they bought me my very own American Girl doll, too. She has blue eyes and short black hair like mine."

"And like mine, too—the way it used to be, that is." Liz patted her hair and took a seat in a worn brown armchair that appeared out of place in the room. "My daughter, Angela, had the same coloring."

"I assumed so, since Cammy doesn't resemble Vance in that regard."

"No, she doesn't. She's the spitting image of Angie."

"That's good, right?" Puzzlement crept across Cammy's face.

"It's very good." Liz beamed at her granddaughter before turning her attention back to Meg. "Vance tells us you're from Chicago."

"That's right."

"And you're living with your grandmother for the time being?"

"Right again. My parents divorced when I was just three, so I never got close to my dad's side of the family. Teaching here in Stanford is giving me that opportunity, and so far I'm extremely happy with my job at Fairview."

"Well, isn't that nice?" Liz crossed her legs and seemed pleased by Meg's reply. "Most twenty-something people I know don't want a single thing to do with their parents or grandparents. It's refreshing to meet a young, single woman who does."

"Thanks, but I have to admit going through that 'I don't want anything to do with my family' stage. I guess I just needed to find out who I was as a person first, without my mom or anybody else trying to tell me."

"I understand completely."

"Who am I as a person?" Cammy asked.

Meg chuckled and put her hand on the child's blanket-covered legs. "As you grow up, you'll discover the answer to that question."

"But I want to know now." She tipped her head and frowned.

Liz's smile grew. "Okay, then, you tell us. Who are you as a person, Cammy Bayer?"

For a moment, she seemed confused, but then she prattled off her name, address, phone number, her dad's name, Vance Elliot Bayer, his work phone number, and his cell phone number. Then she proceeded to list the names of her grandparents, the ones "in heaven" and the ones still "on earth." She knew her Gramma Liz and Grampa Charlie's phone number, too.

Meg tried in vain to conceal a laugh.

"Well, I think that, as a person, you're quite a little computer chip." Liz chuckled. "And you've got lots of memory."

"I'm smart. Right, Miss Jorgenson?"

"You're extremely smart, Cammy."

"Too smart for your own good." This retort from Vance.

Meg swiveled and found him standing in the archway that led into a hallway. Her pulse quickened at the sight of him in black trousers and a pale green dress shirt with coordinating necktie. She thought the hue of his shirt complemented his hazel eyes—eyes that stared back into hers.

She smiled.

He smiled.

Liz cleared her throat. "If you two want to run along, Cammy and I'll be fine."

Vance seemed to have difficulty forcing his gaze away from Meg so he could focus on his mother-in-law. He glanced around the room. "Where's Charlie?"

"Oh, he went to the store for some snacks to go with our movies." She waved her hand at him. "He'll be back anytime."

Vance hesitated, as if thinking it over, and then glanced at his wristwatch before looking back at Meg. "You all set?"

"Absolutely."

"All right, then, I'll just say good night to my little girl."

Meg stood just as Vance made his way toward Cammy. As he brushed past her, she caught the piquant scent of his cologne.

"Be good," he told Cammy.

"I will." She smiled up at him as he placed a kiss on her forehead. "Bye, Miss Jorgenson."

"See you later." She looked at Liz. "It was nice to meet you."

"Same here. Have a good time tonight."

"I'm sure we will," Vance said, following Meg out the front door. Together they walked to his truck and climbed inside.

"Cammy didn't complain once this evening about our going out again and leaving her home." He placed the key in the ignition and started the engine. "I think it helped that you came over to say hello. Awfully kind of you to drive out of your way."

"It wasn't any trouble."

Vance pulled his Sport Trac out of the driveway and turned up the road. "I know Cammy wants you to come over again and, next time, stay for supper. She plans on cooking up some mac and cheese for you."

"Mac and cheese is one of my favorites. I'd be happy to come over for supper one night." Meg actually hoped she'd be invited to Vance's home on a regular basis. "I'm just sorry it didn't work out for me to come over earlier like we discussed. Kelly wanted me to help her dress for the dance tonight, and, of course, my dad and Grams were snapping pictures galore."

"Hmmm, well, maybe I should've come get you like a true gentleman."

"It's not *our* homecoming dance. We're just chaperones. Remember?"

"It's still a date, so to speak, for us." He stopped at an intersection before turning left. Then he chanced a look at her. "Isn't it?"

His uncertainty was somehow both touching and amusing. "Yes, it's a date." She thought about how they'd be surrounded by jocks and giggling girls all night. "And it'll be one we won't soon forget, I'm sure."

He seemed to catch her drift and chuckled. "How 'bout we drive over to Danville after the dance and get something to eat?"

"That's an idea." Meg smiled, pleased that this night wouldn't end for them at ten o'clock when the dance was over. She suddenly felt that they were destined to have fun.

However, it wasn't long before Meg questioned her presumption. After entering the decorated gymnasium, she and Vance were immediately called to duty, Vance to hall monitoring and Meg behind the makeshift concession stand where kids could purchase soft drinks and popcorn.

Monotonous country music blared from speakers situated in all four corners of the gym. The polished floor was empty except for an occasional student cutting across to the other side of the gym, and Meg had to admit the songs weren't anything that made her want to dance.

About an hour into the event, the DJ apparently noticed the yawns coming from the sidelines and began to play a medley of oldies from the seventies, eighties, and nineties.

The floor began to fill up with couples, but Meg noticed that whenever a slower set was played, the majority of kids dispersed back to their tables and chairs.

Vance made his way over to the concession stand. "How's business?"

"Not bad. Are you having fun?"

"I don't know if I'd call it 'fun,' exactly." Beneath his mustache, a smile worked its way across his mouth. "I caught a couple of kids trying to sneak out of the building for a smoke, but that's been the highlight of my night so far."

"Well, thanks for being such a good sport." She set a Diet Coke
on the counter of the portable stand. "On the house."

He popped open the can. "Thanks."

While Vance took a swig, Meg couldn't help tuning in to the up-
tempo tune the DJ began playing. She remembered the song from when
she was about thirteen years old. Mom listened to the radio constantly in
the car and at home.

"It makes me feel ancient that this song is considered an oldie."

Vance laughed. "I know what you mean."

Meg leaned her elbows on the counter and stared out over the gym.
She spotted Kelly and her boyfriend. Both had smiles on their faces and
appeared to be having a good time.

A few students ambled over to the concession stand and purchased
sodas and popcorn. They walked away with their food and drinks just as
Celine Dion began singing, "My Heart Will Go On."

"Yo! Ol' Lady Jorgenson!"

Hearing her last name, Meg spun around to see Ryan standing
several feet away. He waved at her with his free hand; the other was
draped around his girlfriend's shoulders.

"Who do you think you're calling *old*?"

Ryan laughed good-naturedly. "I think you and Mr. Bayer—"
He said Vance's name with feigned formality. "—need to show us your
moves on the dance floor. More blast from the past."

Meg looked at Vance. "Wait till I get my hands on him."

Vance chuckled.

Ryan's friends joined in the goading. Before long, half the gym
was chanting and clapping. Meg wanted to strangle her brother on
the spot.

But Vance didn't seem the least bit riled. He straightened and held
out his hand. "How 'bout if we show these kids a thing or two?"

Meg felt so stunned by the offer that she set her hand inside of his without thinking it through.

He led her around the tiny concession stand and out to the middle of the gym. The students surrounded them with applause, and Meg felt her face flame with embarrassment.

Vance's right arm encircled her waist and pulled her close. "I'm no Fred Astaire." Amusement glittered in his hazel eyes.

"Now you tell me." She placed her left arm around his shoulder.

They swayed side to side with the melody, and Meg enjoyed the feeling of being held in Vance's arms. It felt nice, like getting a hug just when you needed one.

She stepped in closer, her temple resting against the side of his face. He gave her a nudge. "Look."

Meg glanced to her right and saw the scores of kids filing onto the dance floor.

"Seems we started something."

She gazed up into his eyes, sensing that Vance wasn't referring just to the teens. "Yes, it seems like we did."

Chapter Twenty-one
....

"So what did you do next, after the dance?" Leah asked from where she sat on the corner of Meg's desk. "Hello?"

"What?" Meg turned from the classroom window, where she'd watched Vance drive out of the school's parking lot. He'd just picked up Cammy, and Meg hoped to see them both later in the evening. "I'm sorry. What did you say?"

Her good-natured friend replied with one of her easy smiles. "I know it's Monday, but you can't have had that rough of a day. I saw you at recess this afternoon, and you seemed to have it all together." A twinkle entered her eyes. "Guess your mind's on other things."

"It is—and I apologize." For the last forty-eight hours, Meg's head had been in a fantastic fog, and she'd been having trouble concentrating. All she could think about, it seemed, was Vance.

Leah waved a hand at her. "Apology not necessary." She strode forward, wearing a fitted olive skirt and white blouse. "I just wondered what you and Vance did after the dance on Saturday night."

"Oh, well, we talked about getting a bite to eat, but instead we opted for coffee at the Hubble House. We ended up sitting there talking until about two in the morning."

"Good thing it's a twenty-four-hour place."

"I'll say. I still can't believe how much Vance and I had to say to each other."

"Seems you two have connected on numerous levels."

"Seems so." Just thinking about Vance made her insides all fluttery, and Meg felt blessed—yes, blessed!—to have finally met a guy who seemed to want the same things out of life that she did.

"Well, I had a date on Saturday night, too." Leah sashayed around half the room. "With Kent."

"Who? Kent?" Meg didn't think she'd heard correctly. "As in the phys ed teacher here at Fairview?"

"The one and only."

"A date?" Meg shook her head, confused. "What happened to Dave the marine?"

Leah visibly relaxed and scooted her backside onto Meg's desk. She gazed at Meg from across the room. "I finally got your attention."

"Undivided." Meg sat down in Bradley Rogers' desk. "I'm all ears."

"Okay, well, I got an e-mail from Dave on Friday, saying he's got leave over Thanksgiving and he's—" Leah wrapped her thin arms around her midsection, as if her stomach cramped with the very thought. "—he's coming to meet me in person. I'm so nervous and excited that I can barely eat a crumb. I've been dying to tell you, but I know you've had homecoming and Vance crowding your thoughts."

"Leah, I'm so sorry. I should have been there for you this weekend."

"No, no—it's all right. I'm just saying that I wanted to tell you, but because you were busy, I wound up spilling the news to Kent. He's been super nice and understanding. His minor in college was nutritional science, or something like that, so he took me out to dinner on Saturday night. He sort of coached me on the kinds of foods I should eat so my nerves won't be frayed and I won't lose more weight."

Astonishment shook her and Meg wondered if she'd misjudged Kent all this time. "Is it working? His coaching, I mean?"

"I ate on Saturday night and enjoyed each mouthful. Kent kept chuckling over each bite I took. But, see, I wasn't nervous around him because he's just a friend, while Dave is—well, he's the guy I think I'm in love with. It's just too bad I can't think of Dave as just a friend, but I seem to have psychologically and emotionally passed that point."

"Love sneaks up on a person, doesn't it?."

Leah bobbed her head in agreement. "I can't even tell you when it happened. It just did."

"One of the many mysteries in life." Meg thought it might be happening to her—falling in love with Vance—and the idea frightened her a little. What if things between them didn't work out? She didn't want to leave Miracle in order to escape a failed love affair.

That's what Mom always did.

And essentially, that's what Meg had done when she fled from Chicago. Of course, her dead-end job situation had been a huge factor in her leaving, too. And if things between her and Vance went sour, she'd have to see him every day, because she had every intention of keeping *this* job.

Was she willing to stick it out, despite the outcome of her relationship with Vance? Maybe she should slow her feelings down a little.

"Meg?"

"Hmmm?" She refocused on Leah.

"So what do you say?"

Meg cringed, hating to admit she missed the question. "You want to know what I think about—?"

"Coming over to my house for dinner tonight?"

"Oh." Meg considered the offer. Vance's in-laws were still in town; they planned to leave early tomorrow morning. Vance said he'd call her if he could make time to see her between visiting with them and readying Cammy for bed. But he said that wouldn't be until about nine o'clock or ten o'clock tonight. Grams had her quilting get-together. She hadn't heard from either Kelly or Ryan—and when she saw Ryan next, she didn't know whether she'd thank him or sock him in the arm for his little prank on Saturday night.

"Meg?"

"I'm sorry, Leah. Sure, dinner at your place will be great."

A smile brightened her friend's features. "Super. I'll tell Mama to set another place at the table."

* * * * *

"Daddy, I'm all done!" Cammy squeezed the water out of the washcloth and set the bar of soap in its plastic dish on the side of the tub. "Come and get me."

"Coming, punkin."

Cammy looked at the comb and scissors that Gramma Liz had placed by the sink and cringed. Every time Gramma came, she liked to cut off Cammy's curls. Cammy usually didn't care, but now she did.

She didn't want a haircut. No way.

Daddy came into the bathroom, wrapped Cammy in a large, soft blue towel, and lifted her out of the tub. Carrying her to her bedroom, he set her down, and while he took the towel back into the bathroom, Cammy slipped her nightie over her head.

He returned a few minutes later.

"Daddy, are you and Miss Jorgenson boyfriend and girlfriend?"

"Looks like it. If we're not, we're heading that way."

"Whoo-hoo!" She raised her arms, fists clenched, the way cheerleaders do. "I can't wait to tell Sasha."

He put his hands on his hips. "Well, just be careful what you say. Miss Jorgenson is still your teacher, and some kids might think that you're getting special treatment because she and I are seeing each other."

"But, Daddy, I always get special treatment."

He chuckled. "Guess you do."

Cammy saw Gramma standing in the doorway. "Ready to get beautiful?" She held the scissors in her hand.

Cammy shook her head. "I don't want my hair cut. I changed my mind."

Daddy gave her a curious look. "Punkin, your gramma always trims up your hair when she comes to visit."

"But I want to grow it long now. Like Miss Jorgenson's hair."

A slow grin curved Daddy's mouth.

But Gramma shook her head. "Miss Jorgenson has straight hair, and it looks nice long. But you have curls that'll soon get out of control if you don't keep it short. Your mama's hair was just the same way, and I used to cut hers, too."

"I know, but I want my hair long."

Daddy set his hands on his hips. "Cammy, I can't deal with long hair in the morning. It's hard enough getting the two of us packed up and out of the house on time as it is."

"You won't have to deal with it, Daddy. I can take care of my own hair. I'll keep it brushed and when it's long I know how to put it in a ponytail. And today, after school, Miss Jorgenson showed me how the clip in back of her hair worked. She just gathers her hair and clips it. It's really easy."

Daddy pushed out his mouth in a way that let Cammy know he was thinking about letting her have her way.

"This is nonsense," Gramma said. "Your hair isn't like Miss Jorgensons'; it's like your mama's. It's got to stay short or pretty soon you'll look like a shaggy dog."

"I don't care! I like dogs!"

"Cammy Ann Bayer, you'll mind your manners when you speak to your gramma." Daddy gave her a stern look.

Cammy lowered her chin and glanced from him to Gramma

Liz. "Sorry."

Gramma turned to Daddy. "Vance, the child needs to wear her hair short for so many reasons. I've been through this with Angie. She'd whine and cry about wanting long hair when she was a little girl, but in the end the only practical way to manage all those curls is to keep them short."

Cammy watched Daddy think it over. When he looked over at her, she mouthed the word "pleeeeze," and, just as she hoped, he gave in.

"All right. Grow it long. I don't care."

"Cammy, don't you want to be like your mama?" Gramma Liz tipped her head. She looked sort of sad.

In that second, Cammy felt a little confused. She wanted to always remember Mommy, but it was getting harder and harder. Cammy couldn't even squeeze her eyes close and hear Mommy's voice anymore. She heard Miss Jorgenson's. She was the best teacher Cammy ever had. Miss Jorgenson told her things in a way she understood. She wasn't just a regular grown-up. She was special. And pretty. And Daddy seemed lots happier now that he finally listened and asked Miss Jorgenson out.

Daddy looked at Gramma and raised his shoulders up and down.

Gramma Liz blew out a long breath. "Well, I pray each day for God to heal our hearts and help us move on, put the accident and Angie's death behind us." She set down the scissors and smiled at Daddy. But she still looked sort of sad. "I can't complain when God answers my prayers, now, can I?"

Gramma came over and hugged Cammy. "You're growing up too fast, know that? But I'll always love you, whether your hair is short like your mama's was when she was little, or long the way you want it."

Daddy pointed his finger at Cammy. "But I'm not dealing with unruly hair in the morning. Understand?"

"Yes, Daddy." Happiness bubbled up inside her. "I promise I'll take care of it all by myself."

"I'm going to hold you to that, because if it gets to be a problem, I'll take you over to Aunt Debbie's friend who cuts hair. She might not do as good a job as Gramma Liz."

"He's right about that." Gramma laughed.

Daddy smiled.

And Cammy couldn't remember feeling so happy in a long, long time.

* * * * *

Meg sat down at the Lawtons' cozy kitchen table with Leah, her folks— and Kent Baldwin. She hadn't any idea Kent was coming to dinner, too, but then again she hadn't been paying very close attention at the time of Leah's invitation.

"So how's school going for y'all so far?" Seth Lawton lifted the bowl of mashed potatoes and helped himself to a man-sized serving.

"Going well for me." Meg sent Leah's father a smile. She'd met him numerous times at church. He worked in construction and both he and his wife, Leah's mother, had gone to high school with Mom and Dad.

"School's going good for me, too." Leah grinned.

"Me, three." Kent chuckled and selected a thick piece of golden fried chicken, setting it onto his plate.

"Kent's so good with the kids," Leah added.

Meg couldn't argue. Her students had only glowing remarks about their phys ed teacher.

"I love my job." Kent filled half his plate with tossed salad.

Meg wondered about his own children. Had he been granted visitation rights yet, as he'd hoped? "Have you moved into your new condo?"

"I close this week. I can start moving in on the weekend."

"Congratulations."

"Thanks." He shifted in his chair and his arm bumped hers.

Meg could have sworn he did it on purpose.

"If you need help moving, I could round up some of the men from church." Seth forked some chicken into his mouth.

"Thank you, but that's not necessary. I've hired movers."

Rose Lawton dabbed her mouth with her napkin. "Tell us about yourself, Mr. Baldwin."

"Please. It's Kent."

Rose nodded. Like her daughter, she had nut brown hair and a sweet disposition. "All right then, Kent. What's your background?"

"Well, let's see—where do I start?"

Meg fought the urge to roll her eyes as Kent began what sounded like his life's story. He was born and raised outside of Minneapolis. His father owned a large, successful manufacturing company. Kent attended prestigious private schools, he did fairly well academically, and he excelled in sports.

Meg watched Leah as he spoke and suddenly figured out Kent's secret to getting her to eat. He talked so much about himself that she forgot all about her nerves and, instead, enjoyed her dinner.

The next moment, Meg chided herself for being so cynical about him.

"How come you and your wife divorced?" Seth's forehead creased with concern.

"I take full responsibility. It was my fault my marriage failed." Kent wiped his mouth with a paper napkin. "I made some very unwise choices."

"That can happen to anyone." Rose sent him a sympathetic nod.

"Well, I s'pose all that matters is that you're on the right path now."

"I think so." Kent flashed a smile.

"But it just seems to me that people these days have no sense of right and wrong." Seth cleared his throat. "Nothing personal, Kent. I was more thinking of this marine fella that's been corresponding with Leah over the

ANDREA BOESHAAR

Internet. For all we know about him, he's got a wife and family somewheres."

"No offense taken."

"Daddy, we've been through all this."

Meg had to grin at the way Leah, like most Southern females, no matter how old, still referred to her father as "daddy."

"Dave has no reason to lie to me."

"How can you know for sure?"

"Know any cops in Stanford?" Kent put a forkful of salad into his mouth.

"I do." Seth narrowed his brown-eyed gaze at his guest. "In fact, I personally know Mayor Miracle." His gaze slid to his daughter. "The mayor's single. Why can't you get to know a nice, upstanding man like him?"

"Oh, Daddy." Frustration pinched Leah's features.

"Look, why not have him or one of the policemen you know run a background check on Dave? If the police have the time, it'd be a simple thing to do."

"Great thinking, Kent." Seth's wide face split into a grin.

Leah practically threw down her fork. "Daddy, I forbid it. That's like—snooping or something."

"Actually, Leah, it's a good idea." Meg wondered why she didn't think of it herself. "Most employers run background checks. It's very common. And it wouldn't hurt to make sure Dave doesn't have a violent or criminal past."

A pained expression shadowed Leah's face. "I guess it'd be a good thing to do, it's just that—oh, I don't know. It seems so underhanded."

Kent draped one thick arm around Leah's shoulders. "You've got to protect yourself in this day and age."

She looked up into his face and conceded with a slight nod.

Meg sat back, surprised and impressed by Kent's benevolence.

She honestly didn't think he had the capability to think beyond himself. And the fact that he was sitting here, dining with Leah's parents when he was hardly the typical family man, was equally amazing.

Maybe Grams and Leah were right when they guessed that deep inside, Kent was a lonely guy.

Meg decided to work on altering her opinion of him.

After dinner and a delicious dessert of baked apples and coffee, they moved to the living room and chatted some more.

Finally, Kent announced that it was time for him to leave. Glancing at her wristwatch, Meg realized it was after nine o'clock and she hadn't heard from Vance. She wondered if she should stop by on her way home.

"Let me grab my purse, Meg." Leah stood to exit the living room. "I'll drive you back to school so you can fetch your car."

"Thanks." Meg rose from the sofa and stretched. She'd ridden home with Leah, mainly so they wouldn't have to end the conversation about Dave that they'd been engrossed in when they walked out of school. It had been one of those impulsive, girly decisions that wound up ending in inconvenience. But, what's done was done. "Excellent dinner, Rose."

"You're always welcome here, Meg. Anytime." Leah's mother turned to Kent. "You are, too. I hope you'll come back sometime soon."

"Thank you." He added a gracious bow to his reply and Rose actually blushed.

"And, Leah. Don't worry about driving Meg back to school. I'm happy to do it. I'm going that way anyhow. Makes no sense for you to go out of your way."

"Oh." Leah's gaze bounced between him and Meg. "Yeah, that'd work out. What do you think, Meg?"

"Sure." It made sense.

Shaking off an instinctive feeling of uneasiness, she said her thank yous and good-byes, then followed Kent outside to his Corvette convertible. He'd pulled the top back earlier, and the night air was mild, the sky clear.

"Beautiful night." He opened the passenger side door for Meg.

Except he didn't stand completely out of her way, so that she unintentionally brushed by him as she climbed inside.

Warning bells clamored, but she ignored them, telling herself to give him the benefit of the doubt.

He climbed in behind the wheel, closed the car door, and started the engine.

"I need to get right home." She hoped he'd understand that she wasn't interested in taking any detours back to school.

"Sure."

He backed out of the Lawtons' driveway, and soon they were zooming down the two-lane highway.

"Ever ride in a 1972 Corvette before?" He was shouting above the rushing sound of the warm Kentucky wind.

"No, never."

"What do you think?"

She thought about it and had to admit it felt recklessly exhilarating.

"Relax, Meg, I'm not going to bite."

She pushed out a smile, wondering if she really appeared as uptight as she felt.

"I get the feeling you're afraid of me. How'd that happen?"

"I don't know." Meg couldn't really say.

"I'm harmless."

"We'll see." She emphasized each word, then grinned.

He laughed.

Minutes later he pulled into Fairview's parking lot and halted with an impressive squeal of his tires beside her car.

"You know? That was fun."

Kent turned sideways, facing her. He placed his arm around the back of her leather seat. "Let's be friends, all right? Seriously. I could use some camaraderie. My ex-wife is slaughtering me emotionally and financially."

Meg grimaced, imagining the ugliness.

"She's keeping the kids away from me. It's eating me up inside. I might have been a lousy husband, but I was always a good father."

She heard him swallow hard and felt her heart constrict with sympathy. "I'm sorry you're going through such a difficult time. It's got to be painful."

"It is." He moved his right arm, touched her cheek briefly, then held out his hand. "Friends?"

She considered the offer, then looked into his face. She couldn't fully make out his expression with the darkness around them, but she took him at his word.

"Okay. Friends." She slipped her palm into his.

In one, smooth move, he brought her fingertips to his lips.

Meg pulled her hand away. "And if you try that again, I'm going to pop you one—*friend*."

Kent laughed, sounding genuinely amused. "Meg, you are one refreshing female."

She felt mildly complimented as she got out of the car and walked around to the drivers' side of her Civic.

"*Arrivederci.*" Kent revved his engine.

She laughed, suddenly finding him humorous instead of dangerous. Talk about macho!

Meg sent him a wry grin. "G'night, Kent."

Chapter Twenty-two
....

The winding, narrow road leading to Miracle wasn't a favorite drive for Meg in the dark, especially the section that spanned the steep ravine, so she ditched the idea of stopping by Vance's house and went straight home. She had hoped to hear from him, but the phone never rang. She wondered how he was passing the time, and then it occurred to her that she'd never dated anyone with kids. And although Cammy was hardly helpless, she did require more attention than most children. Vance had his hands full. Little wonder he had any social life at all. At least he had his priorities in order, and that was one of the things she admired about him. He was a family-oriented guy. And of course, Cammy's grandparents were still in town.

Meg pondered the situation after correcting her student's math quizzes. She wondered what she could do to meet Vance halfway in the future—or even help him out. Suddenly, she stuffed the graded quizzes into the large black bag she lugged to and from school and made her way downstairs.

"Grams, I've got an idea and I want to bounce it off of you." She entered the living room, where her grandmother sat and stitched a piece of quilting.

"Bounce away, hon."

"I'm thinking of making a casserole or something that I can take over to the Bayers' for supper tomorrow evening. I want to invite myself over for dinner." She couldn't suppress a sheepish grin. "But I'll at least supply the food so Vance won't have to go to any trouble. What do you think?"

Grams set down her sewing and peered at Meg from over her glasses. "Why, I think that's a thoughtful thing to do. But I'm happy to cook for y'all if you want me to. I'll fry up some pork chops and make some dirty rice, turn it over into a glass baking dish that you can stick into Vance's oven and warm up." She thought it over for a couple of seconds. "What's more, I'll drop it off at Fairview tomorrow on the way to my missionary convention planning meeting at church."

"Really? That would be awesome." Meg took a seat on the old plaid sofa. "But I really don't want to take advantage of your generosity."

"What else do I have to do around here if you don't take advantage of my generosity?"

Meg saw the teasing glint in Grams' blue eyes.

"My sons never call me. Neither do my grandsons."

Meg stifled a giggle. She'd witnessed this good-natured rant in the past.

"Just wait until Christmastime when I forget to buy presents."

"Grams, you're going to get another clock from Dad and my uncles if you're not careful."

"Are you planning on tattling on me?"

"Heck, no."

"Then how're they ever going to find out that I fuss about them not calling me?"

"Guess you've got a point there." Meg kept smiling.

Grams stood. "Well, now, I'd better take those pork chops out of the freezer so they're thawed by tomorrow."

Meg followed her out of the living room. "Will you show me how to make dirty rice?"

"Course I will."

Grams pulled out a worn and stained cookbook. Its pages were yellowed and some of the print had been rubbed away.

"We can make up a batch tonight. It's really better the second day."

Meg rubbed her palms together. "Let's go for it."

The next day when Vance dropped off Cammy at school, he was apologetic for not calling.

"It got late and with my in-laws leaving today—"

"Not to worry, Vance. I understand." Meg smiled at Cammy, who, as usual, was staring up at her with an adoring expression on her impish face.

"Meg, um—"

She turned back to Vance and caught the incline of his head. He wanted to speak to her in private.

"We'll be right back, punkin."

"Okay, Daddy."

Meg followed him to the coatroom.

"I'm sorry. I thought about giving you a call at least a dozen times and then got distracted by one thing or another."

"I really do understand, Vance."

"Some women don't." He searched her face, her eyes, as if gauging her reaction.

"Our relationship is still new, but you'll learn soon enough that I'm not like 'some women.'"

"I know that already."

His scrutiny made her feel like she might melt like an ice cube right there on the edge of the classroom.

"Maybe I can get my neighbor to sit with Cammy for a while tonight."

"I have a better idea. I'll bring dinner over for you, Cammy, and me."

"No, Meg, I don't want you going out of your way and buying dinner—"

"I don't intend to." She smiled. "Grams offered to make pork chops and dirty rice for us. She's dropping it off later."

Vance looked touched. "Awfully nice of her."

"Remember, Grams loves to feed people."

He laughed. "Yes, that's right. She does."

Some children ran into the classroom by way of the coatroom and called greetings to Meg.

"Listen, I'd better let you go. I need to get to work anyhow, but the dinner plan sounds good to me. I know Cammy will be thrilled you're coming over tonight."

"Good. I'll look forward to it."

"Me, too."

Meg felt the affectionate squeeze Vance gave her elbow as they made their way back into the main part of the classroom. Then he kissed the top of Cammy's head. "Have a good day, punkin."

"I will, Daddy."

"Meg." He inclined his head in that reserved manner that she found so charming.

"Have a good day, Vance."

He gave her a quick wink as he walked out the door, and Meg's heart felt light, her energy level high, as she faced her busy day.

* * * * *

"Dude, if the talk is true, you sure know how to pick 'em."

Vance slid a glance in Boz's direction and scowled. "It's not true." Sitting at the picnic table on the side of Hank's Small Engine Repair, he took a bite of the bologna sandwich he'd thrown together this morning.

"Well, Jeff said he saw her last night in the school parking lot. He and some of the guys were shooting hoops. He saw her with that musclehead gym teacher, kissing in his Corvette."

"I think Jeff just wants your fifty bucks," Vance said, recalling some of the guys' stupid bet they made on Labor Day.

"What do you plan on doing about it?" Boz guzzled his cola.

"Nothing." Vance eyed his red-headed friend. "Look, I learned a lot about Meg this weekend, and she's even coming over for dinner tonight."

"And maybe she's playing the field. But, if she is, you should know. Right?"

"If she is, she has a right to. We're not committed to each other at this point."

Boz fell silent long enough for Vance to finish eating his sandwich.

"My mama was friends with Meg's mother back in the day. They were in high school. Mama said she was a nice girl until after Meg was born, and then it seemed she went crazy or something. She started going to bars and getting drunk, and things escalated from there. She had lots of men, Vance. What if Meg's the same way?"

"She's not." Vance's confident reply belied the nugget of doubt lodged in his throat. Then the words he told his own daughter last night boomeranged around and hit him square between the eyes. *You'll always have a little piece of your mama in you.* But Vance had meant it in a positive way, and surely Meg's mother had some redeeming qualities. Perhaps those were what Meg inherited, because she certainly wasn't some sort of hussy. She'd made her share of mistakes, but she admitted it and seemed determined not to repeat the past.

"Look, man, I don't want you to get hurt or anything."

"I appreciate it, Boz."

"I mean, Nicole's a piece of work. The last thing you need is another loony female in your life."

"Meg's not that; she's not altar-bound like Nicole." Vance still couldn't believe he'd been a victim of such deceitful feminine wiles, whether they were consciously or unconsciously executed. And, as far as he knew, Nicole was still dating that college professor of hers—even though it was just a month ago that she cornered Vance and said she loved him.

He raked a hand through his hair. Loony, all right. A guy couldn't keep up with a woman like Nicole. He wished the professor lots of luck.

"I agree with you about Meg." Boz rolled his soda can between his palms. "Tara and I like her. I actually didn't want to say anything negative, but Jeff told me what he saw, and, well, I'm your best friend."

"I know."

The hearsay hung over Vance for the rest of the afternoon like a suspicious dark cloud over a picnic. He figured the only way to alleviate it was to confront it head on.

So, later the night, after Cammy was snug in bed, Vance decided to bring up the subject while he and Meg sat together on the covered porch that stretched along the front of his house.

"There's a rumor flying around that you Kent Baldwin were—" He cleared his throat, deciding there was no other way to say it, but to spit it out. "Making out in his car in the school parking lot last night."

"What?" She sat forward and twisted around to face him. The double wicker rocker creaked in agony. "That's a lie." She paused and her insistent expression waned. "Well, I was in his car, but only because he gave me a ride back to the school parking lot after we had dinner at Leah's house. Honestly, Vance, there was no 'making out.' Nothing of the sort."

"I believe you." He did, too. "But, you know, Meg, you're a free agent. You can see whomever you want." As much as it ran contrary to his feelings, the thought had crossed his mind more than several times this afternoon. After all, she'd only been here a couple of months.

"I'm aware of that fact, and it's nice to know you're not some possessive freak."

He grinned at the tart reply.

"I'll be truthful, Vance, it'd be so easy for me to—to fall for you. I feel like I'm teetering on the brink." Meg relaxed in the rocker again. "At the same time, I want to teach in Stanford, live in Miracle forever. That's why

I refuse to do anything that might, well, destroy our faith in God and others' faith in us." She paused. "I guess what I'm saying is, I don't want to do anything either one of us might regret later."

"Nor do I." He hadn't expected such candidness, but he appreciated it. And it was still further proof that she would never be deceptive.

"I want to take things slow, leave it in God's hands." Meg's voice sounded soft, but sure. "That way I can face my family and sit in church with my head held high—because I've done nothing wrong."

She snuggled in beside him, and he caught the delicate, floral scent emanating from her silky hair.

"What do you think, Vance?"

"Um, yeah, taking it slow is good. Safe, you know—for both of us." He felt so distracted by her that he barely knew what he was saying.

"Exactly." She rested her head on his shoulder, and a few minutes of silence passed. "What a gorgeous night."

"Yeah."

"I enjoy your company."

"I enjoy yours, too, Meg. I look forward to seeing you every day."

"You're different from any guy I've ever known. You're *real*."

He couldn't help teasing her. "You in the habit of dating plastic men?"

Meg laughed. "You know what I mean."

She tried to tickle his midsection, but Vance caught her wrist before she could do any damage.

"I know what you mean." He recalled how she'd confided in him, telling him how she'd been hurt and betrayed in the past.

All humor left him. "I'll never break your heart, Meg. I swear."

"I know." She leaned against him and placed a kiss on his jaw.

Then her foot brushed against his blue-jean-clad leg, and his head spun like a top. Vance was no fool; he knew exactly what was happening to him. That brink she mentioned—he thought he might have just fallen over the edge.

Chapter Twenty-three
....

"Imagine that. It's the first week of November." Loretta sat at her kitchen table, sipping her morning coffee. Tom sat across from her, crunching on gingersnap cookies. "Three weeks until Meggie's birthday. And then Thanksgiving." She narrowed her gaze at him. "I don't suppose it's too soon to start planning now."

"Aw, Retta, don't blame me for getting you all sidetracked. September was a mite early for planning. You got to admit that."

"I'll admit to no such thing." She lifted her pen and jotted down a few names on the pad of paper beside her porcelain coffee cup. She'd been hinting around and felt confident that Meggie would enjoy a surprise birthday gathering with some of her new friends, such as Leah Lawton, Eddie, Boz, and his wife, Tara. Of course, Vance would be invited, too. "Maybe the Friday night before the Thanksgiving holiday would be a good time to have Meg's party."

Tom shrugged. "Good as any, I reckon."

Loretta ignored his apathy.

"Meggie and Vance Bayer are quite the talk of the town, aren't they?" Tom slurped his coffee.

"They are." Loretta was happy for the two young people. They both deserved some happiness after all they'd been through.

"She's over there at his house ever' evening after school, and he's over here with that little girl of his on Sunday afternoons. That is, when they're not over at Paul's place."

She smiled, feeling almost as pleased that Meg had become close to her family and was getting to know her cousins, uncles, and aunts. It was more than Loretta ever hoped and prayed for.

"If she marries Vance, she'd be an instant mama. What does Meg think about that?"

Loretta raised her chin. "I don't think she's intimidated one bit, Tom." She tipped her head, regarding her wrinkly faced friend. "Why do you ask?"

"Just wondering. It's a big undertaking, marrying a man with a handicapped little girl."

"Big undertaking for you or me, maybe, but not for Meg. She's a teacher and she loves children. And they take to her."

"Like cotton candy." Tom grinned.

Loretta smiled at the analogy and stood. "Want a warm up?" She knew he did, so without waiting for reply, she refilled his coffee mug along with her own.

"Speaking of kids." She reclaimed her seat at the kitchen table. "Did you see Cammy with those twins last weekend? Gracious me, but I never saw those boys acting like such clowns."

"Showin' off for the little girl." Tom smirked.

"Cammy laughed so hard."

"Sure did." A pensive expression clouded his weathered face. "A person forgets she's handicapped sometimes."

"True. It's such a shame she's bound to that wheelchair."

"Might be the Good Lord knew it was the only way a body'd keep up with her." Tom took another guzzle of his brew. "Sort of evens the odds."

* * * * *

"Meg, are you sure you don't mind?"

Crossing her arms, she stared back at Vance. "For the tenth time, I don't mind. Now, go play cards with your buddies. You need a night out with the guys."

"Yeah, Daddy, go."

Vance looked a little hurt as his gaze flicked from Meg to Cammy, who lay on the couch.

"Eager to get rid of your ol' man, huh?"

"Yep. Meg said we could paint our toenails tonight while you're gone."

Meg stared at the ceiling, feigning innocence.

"*Meg* said that, did she?"

When she looked back at him, he arched a brow.

"I told Cammy it was all right if she called me by my first name when we're not at school. I know we didn't discuss the matter." Meg usually tried to be careful not to tread on Vance's role as Cammy's father, but she'd grown to love the little girl and occasionally she forgot herself. "I hope it's okay with you."

"Of course it's okay with me." His gaze searched her face before he smiled. "It's really your decision and comfort level. I mean, Cammy might slip at school."

"I've heard worse slips. Trust me."

"Yeah, Daddy, you shoulda heard what Joey Milton said when he flunked his science test."

"If it's bad, don't repeat it."

"It's bad, so I won't."

Meg sucked in her lower lip to keep from grinning. The swear had even taken her aback. His parents had been notified and even the principal had gotten involved.

Vance's gaze returned to her. "Maybe I should carry Cammy into bed before I leave."

"We'll manage." Meg often assisted her in the bathroom at school, and she'd tucked Cammy into bed a number of times in the weeks past. "Now, go. You've got till midnight, Prince Charming." On tiptoes, she kissed his check. "Go."

From her perch on the sofa, Cammy giggled.

Vance crossed the room and placed a kiss on his daughter's forehead. "Be good."

Cammy heaved an exasperated sigh. "Daddy, will you just hurry and leave so me and Meg can paint our toenails?"

"Meg and I." The teacher in Meg never seemed completely off duty.

"Meg and I." Cammy stared up into Vance's face, giving him a sweet smile.

"All right. All right. I'm leaving."

Meg followed him on to the porch. She suddenly felt like they were playing house. She was the mommy and Vance was the daddy. . .

She felt an innate stirring in her soul. Playing house with Vance forever appealed to her. It appealed to her a lot.

"I'll probably only sit in for one hand."

"Enjoy yourself, Vance. You deserve it." Meg had seen firsthand how, after laboring over small engine parts, grease, and grime all day, he came home and mowed the lawn, tossed loads of wash into the machine, made supper, did dishes, helped Cammy with homework, prompted her to wash up, exercised with her, and finally tucked her into bed. The poor guy got very little downtime, and even though his insurance would likely cover the expense, he refused to hire a home health aid. While she admired his determination to care for his daughter, Meg found herself feeling somewhat neglected when Vance didn't get a chance to call. She'd learned to overcome it by insinuating herself into the Bayers' everyday routine.

Vance, of course, denied it was any kind of "insinuation." Time after time, he thanked her for "being there." He'd just never known how to ask, or he didn't think he'd had a right to.

"You know—" His brows drew together in obvious bemusement. "I can't recall the last time I went off to play cards with friends and felt totally at ease about leaving Cammy, except for maybe when her grandparents come for a visit."

"You're wasting ti-ime."

"Right." He leaned forward and placed a kiss on her lips. A moment later, Meg found herself wrapped in his arms. As always, her limbs went weak and she marveled that he could have such an effect on her. "Maybe I'll stay home."

Somehow she found the will to push him away. He needed a night out with his buddies. "Good-bye."

Re-entering the house, Meg closed the door, leaned against it, and smiled at Cammy.

"I never thought you'd get rid of him." She put her hand over her mouth and giggled.

Meg laughed, too, noticing the teasing glint in the child's blue eyes.

"Will you put that happy red polish on my toes?"

"Happy red?"

"Yeah, like the kind you wore to the Owenses' Labor Day picnic."

Meg found her black school bag and fished around for the bottles of polish she'd dropped in there this morning. She'd known for a couple of days that Vance had been invited over to Boz's tonight, and when Cammy mentioned she wanted to polish her nails. . .

"This one?" Meg held up the bottle, then set it in the little girl's outstretched hand.

"Yeah!" Cammy sat forward. "This is it! It's the color I've begged and begged my daddy for, but he said he wasn't about to pay three dollars for nail polish, and I didn't like any of the ninety-nine-cent ones. But this is just perfect."

"Well, if you don't like it once it's on, we can take it off and use a different color." Meg retrieved the polish remover and cotton balls from her bag, too.

"Oh, I'll like it just fine."

Meg took care as she placed Cammy's foot in her lap. She felt the child's gaze as she began the procedure. "I never painted someone else's toenails before."

"Me neither."

Meg grinned.

She finished with one foot, and while the polish dried, they turned on the TV and watched about ten minutes of a program before Meg started on the other foot.

"Hold still, will you?" A glob of "happy red" now colored the tops of two toes because Cammy had wiggled.

Wiggled?

Meg slowly turned, feeling herself gape. *She wiggled!*

"I'm sorry, Miss Jorgenson—I mean, Meg. But it tickled."

"You can feel me painting your toenails?"

"Uh-huh." Cammy bobbed her dark head.

Confusion welled up in Meg. How could that be? An involuntary movement? But Cammy said she felt something. Had she really?

Met let several minutes pass before she surreptitiously tickled the sole of Cammy's foot. She watched for a reaction, even a hint of a reaction.

Nothing.

With a dab of polish remover on a cotton ball, she removed the wayward crimson streaks, realizing how very little she knew about spinal cord injuries and neuroscience in general.

* * * * *

"Are you still doing research?"

Meg glanced up from the screen of her notebook computer and smiled at Leah. Since she didn't have an Internet connection at Grams' house, she'd been here at school since eight this morning, even though it was Saturday. She'd told Leah to meet her here at Fairview and then they'd do their shopping and have lunch as planned. "I'm just waiting for this Web site to load. Hey, did you know that there's a program at the University of Kentucky Children's Hospital for kids with SCIs—spinal cord injuries? Pediatric neurosurgeons are using these experimental wireless devices that they strap onto their patients' legs. They send controlled bursts of electricity to the muscles, and many of their patients learn to walk again!"

"No kidding." Leah looked amazed.

"One neurologist said that a lot of SCI patients get written off by their doctors and told nothing more can be done for them. From what Vance has told me, it sounds like that's how it is with Cammy. But these medical devices have given a lot of people hope. The only drawback is that the equipment is expensive, and most insurance companies don't cover the cost."

"Have you mentioned these devices to Vance?"

"Not yet." Meg scanned the Web site she'd logged onto, then decided it wasn't what she wanted. She exited out of it and shut down her computer. "He's let me know in certain ways that the subject isn't really open for discussion. I mean, he answers my questions, and he'll talk freely about Cammy's injuries, but when I broach the subject of new technology or getting second opinions about her condition, he clams up tight."

"Sounds like it's still painful for him."

"To a degree, yes, and yet—" Meg paused, wondering whether it was appropriate to share her observations. Then she decided that, if anything, *she* needed to talk about them. "When Vance's wife was killed and Cammy paralyzed, it was so traumatic for him that I think now he balks at any kind of change. For instance, I put away some dishes in the wrong cupboard and he corrected me and showed me where they go.

He was really sweet about it, but when I pointed out that it might be more convenient if the dishes were placed in a different spot, he refused to even consider the idea."

"Set in his ways?"

"It's more than that." Meg walked around her desk and leaned against it. She stuck her hands in her blue jeans pockets and regarded Leah. Her friend sat just a few feet away, wearing faded jeans and an oversized sweatshirt. "I sometimes wonder if he expects a woman who will pick up where Angie left off, and I'm not willing to assume that role. I want my own, unique role in Vance's life. Cammy's, too. I've told him that, but I don't think my words sank in."

"So what are you going to do?"

"Not sure. Both Vance and Cammy have managed to find special places in my heart in a very short time. I can't imagine my life without either of them, and yet I can't live my life in the shadow of Angie."

"Pray, Meg. Just pray. Only God can set a guy straight when it comes to his thinking."

"I hope you're right, Leah, because I have been praying. A lot." She stepped back around her desk and locked up her computer in its large bottom drawer. As she snatched her purse, she determined to focus on the day ahead. "Ready to shop till you drop?"

"Ready."

Meg locked up her classroom and then she and Leah ambled out to the parking lot. The sun shone down from between dusty-looking clouds, and the air hung thick with humidity.

"Guess it's going to storm later."

Meg pulled out her car keys. "I heard the same thing this morning on the radio." She pointed to her Civic. "Let's take my car."

"Okay, I'll drive next time."

Meg unlocked the doors with her keychain and they climbed in.

"Heard anything from your mom lately?"

"Heard from her this morning, in fact." Meg couldn't constrain a laugh as she pulled the seatbelt across her chest. "Mom e-mailed me and said she thinks I'm having a nervous breakdown because I enjoy living in Miracle and actually look forward to the women's weekly Bible study. Mom wrote that she raised me to be a 'free thinker,' and it hurts her that I'm allowing myself to be brainwashed."

"How'd you reply?"

"I wrote back, saying that if this is a nervous breakdown and I'm being brainwashed, then bring it on, because I've never felt happier in my life."

Leah smiled. "I love hearing you say that. It encourages those of us who have chosen to stay in our hometown. After all, your mama isn't the only one who has left this area feeling bitter and oppressed, looking for something more out there."

Meg started her car. "I don't know if my mother was ever bitter and oppressed. Sounds like Dad tried to give her the world on a silver platter. For myself, I learned Mom's approach to life doesn't work."

"God's way does."

"God's way does." It still surprised Meg to hear herself admit it.

She pulled out of Fairview's parking lot and passed Kent's Corvette.

"Look over there."

Meg directed her gaze out the window to where Leah pointed at Kent and a group of middle-school-aged boys, kicking a black and white ball across the grass.

"He's got his soccer team together." Leah sounded awed. "Good for him."

"Yep. Kent stopped by my classroom this morning. I must have mentioned I was going to be here, although I don't remember doing so. But he brought me a cup of Starbucks coffee."

"How thoughtful." Leah turned a smile on her. "Don't you think?"

"For sure." Meg couldn't recall the last time she'd had a cup of the strong, rich brew. It'd been a nice surprise, and she'd enjoyed the coffee as she surfed the Internet.

"Kent's changed a lot, I think." Leah's voice sounded quiet and thoughtful.

"Well, I don't know about 'a lot.' But he's changed—and for the better."

"He loves kids."

"He's great with Cammy." Meg had to admit it. "And when I mentioned that experimental surgery at the University of Kentucky Children's Hospital, he wanted to know more about it. I wrote down the Web site for him."

"He misses his own children."

"I know." Meg's heart actually ached for the guy.

She slowed as she drove by the field. Kent spotted her car and waved.

"Let's shop in Danville." Leah settled back into the passenger seat. "They've got some stores that we don't have here."

"Okay."

"I practically need a whole new wardrobe before Dave arrives." She blew out a nervous-sounding breath. "He'll be here two weeks from Wednesday. Dad and I are picking him up at the Bluegrass Airport."

"I know. You'll be fine. Relax, Leah." Meg didn't add that Dave was scheduled to fly in on her birthday. She hadn't told Vance or Cammy and hadn't reminded Grams and Dad or Ryan and Kelly. If felt odd to promote her own birthday, and she didn't want anyone going out of their way just because she'd told them. She hoped Grams or Dad would plan something special, but if not, Meg would be happy to spend a quiet evening with Vance and Cammy. Their company would be gift enough for her.

"Dave's background check came out squeaky-clean."

Meg glanced at Leah. "You told me. What a relief, huh?"

"You can say that again."

While it was all repeat information, Meg didn't mind listening. Leah had been there for her. She'd lent an ear while Meg vented about Mom and Dad and Vance. Now it was her turn to listen to Leah.

"I hope I'm not getting on your nerves. I tend to say things over and over and over. I drive my dad and brothers nuts."

"Leah, you're one of my dearest friends." Without taking her eyes off the road, Meg stretched out her hand and Leah smacked her palm. "And friends encourage each other."

Leah caught her hand and gave it a sisterly squeeze. "I've needed a good friend. I've prayed for a long time for one like you. Someone I could match wits with, someone who wouldn't mind coming over to watch a movie with while eating super-buttery popcorn. Most single women I know like to drive into the next county to frequent bars and nightclubs, but I'm totally not comfortable in those places."

"Me neither. Not anymore, anyway." Meg couldn't even imagine herself at a club these days. "But I've never been much of a party girl."

"Me neither—obviously."

They shared a smile.

"But, seriously, before you came to town I felt—lonely. Like some homely loser whose only thrill was corresponding with troops overseas."

"Don't put yourself down. That's a viable mission."

"Yes, but I guess what I'm trying to say is, if for nothing else, Meg Jorgenson—" Leah's voice was thick with emotion. "—you came to Miracle just for me."

Chapter Twenty-four

Vance showered away the day's grease and gunk, toweled off, and changed into clean clothes. Towel-drying his hair, he entered the dining room where Cammy sat at the table, working on her homework.

"What time's Meg coming over?" He couldn't believe he forgot to ask.

"About now."

Vance half-grinned at the distracted reply. "Did she say anything about bringing supper? Maybe I should throw something together."

Cammy lifted her gaze. "She's bringing supper."

"Good. I'm starved."

"Me, too."

Vance felt a smidge of guilt, because he'd begun to anticipate Meg making supper every night. She insisted she enjoyed bringing over meals; it was part of her passion for "feeding people," after all.

Vance thought he could get used to having Meg around full-time. He thought about her all day long, to the point of distraction. He looked forward to seeing her briefly in the mornings. Her sunny smile made his day. He relished spending time with her in the evenings, and maybe it was wrong, but sometimes he couldn't wait until Cammy went to bed so he could have Meg all to himself.

Cammy peered up at him. "Daddy, are you and Meg going to get married?"

"Maybe."

"Why maybe? Don't you love her?'"

Vance pulled out one of the dining room chairs and sat down. Did he love Meg? He thought about her all the time. He missed her when their schedules conflicted and he didn't see her in the evening. He relished their conversations, their easy banter, and the sound of Meg's laugh. And when he took her in his arms and kissed her, all his troubles seemed to vanish. But there was a small part of him that felt a pinch of guilt for finding happiness with Meg, even though he had felt ready to get on with his life for some time now. In some weird way, he felt unfaithful to Angie.

"Daddy?"

Vance shook off his musings and looked at Cammy. She stared back at him, obviously waiting for her answer.

"Sure, I love Meg, but we'll have to make sure before we can talk about weddings. Meg's only been in Kentucky three months. We need to give things more of a chance."

"Oh." Cammy nodded like she understood. "Well, I can't tell you that Meg loves you, cuz she said she wants to tell you herself."

"I see." Vance hid his grin and rubbed his hand across the chest of his red T-shirt. It was a purely innocent blunder on Cammy's part. But why did he feel both apprehensive and overjoyed by her slip of the lip?

Well, he'd let God work it out in His time.

But speaking of slips of the lips. . .

"Hey, you didn't give away the birthday secret, did you? About Meg's party next week?"

"Oh, no, Daddy. I'm pretending I don't know anything about it and I make myself forget while I'm at school."

"All right. That's good. Because Mrs. Jorgenson wants it to be a surprise for Meg."

"I know." Cammy put her hand over her mouth and giggled. "She'll be surprised, Daddy."

Vance nodded and raked a hand through his damp hair. Sounded like the set-up might work. Kids got off at noon on Meg's birthday, the

Wednesday before the Thanksgiving holiday, but teachers had to stay until four o'clock. Vance took a vacation day to help prepare for the party. Boz and his wife and their kids were coming. Leah and her dad had to pick up her marine friend, but then they'd join the party later. Meg's dad and stepmom, sister and brother had been invited, too. And, of course, Tom Haynes. It'd be a nice little get-together—if Meg didn't figure things out first.

A knock sounded at the front door, followed by Meg's entry.

"Anyone home? Anyone hungry?"

"That's a double affirmative." Vance turned and saw Meg struggling to carry the burden filling her arms. He rushed to assist her. "Why didn't you call? I would have met you in the driveway."

"Oh, yeah, I guess I could have done that." She laughed, stooping down and sliding a baking dish onto the kitchen counter. "I'm so used to being on my own, doing things myself."

"Get over it." Vance tossed her a teasing grin.

She smiled at the quip, but too soon a somber expression pulled at her brows. She stepped beside him and touched his forearm. "After Cammy goes to bed, I need to talk with you about something important."

"All right." The intense look on her face made Vance wary. "Can you give me a hint so I don't have to fret for the next three hours?"

"It's about some information I requested. It came in the mail today."

"What kind of information?"

"That's what I have to speak to you about." Meg smiled. Next, she stood on her tiptoes and kissed him. It warmed Vance's insides, and his arms instinctively encircled her waist. "Nothing to worry about." She leaned back, peering up at him. "Would you like to see what's for dinner?"

"Maybe in a few minutes." He stared into her face, memorizing each freckle smattered across her cheeks and nose. "You're beautiful, you know that?" He bent to place a kiss on her full, pink lips, when—

"Are we ever going to eat?" Cammy voiced her impatience.

She'd rolled her wheelchair into the kitchen and now sat grinning at the two of them.

"Of course we're going to eat. I'll dish up the plates right now." Meg sent Vance a look filled with both remorse and embarrassment.

He just smiled and scrutinized his daughter's expression. It seemed to be saying, "What do you need to make sure of? You love her. Just marry her, you big silly!"

* * * * *

Once Meg was certain that Cammy had fallen asleep in bed, she grabbed the brown paper packet from the University of Kentucky Children's Hospital and plopped herself down beside Vance on the sofa.

"This is what I wanted to show you. It's information about these new experimental wireless devices that are being used to help SCI patients walk."

Meg saw a flick of interest enter his gaze before he took the colorful brochures from her and started leafing through them.

"The initial consultation is free."

He examined the material. "The other alternative discussed in this brochure is surgery. Cammy's had enough surgeries in her young life."

"I realize that, but I wanted you to consider the wireless devices."

He flipped through the information too fast to have read it. Finally, he shook his head. "This won't help Cammy."

"How can you be so sure?"

"Because doctors have said she'll never walk again."

"Doctors here in Stanford, at Logan Hospital."

"The physicians here are just as skilled and capable as the ones at UK Children's Hospital."

"I'm sure they are, but things in the medical field have changed greatly in the last three years. New and better technology has been developed."

"I take Cammy to see her doctor and a physical therapist every three months. Nothing has changed with her condition."

"Getting another opinion, Vance, might be a wise thing to do. In any case, it can't hurt."

He seemed to turn himself off at that point, erect a wall, and block her out, just like he did when she suggested putting the dishes in a different cupboard or the knives in a different drawer.

But Meg wasn't ready to give up. "You told me Cammy's spinal cord wasn't severed, just bruised."

"Her back was broken."

"Several vertebrae, right?"

"Right."

"Well, Vance, something's changing with her; she told me it tickled when I polished her toenails. And Kent Baldwin said she moved her leg while in the rowing machine before he lifted her out. She remembers how to walk, and those muscles have nerves that remember, too. I'm no doctor, but it seems to me that these new medical devices might enable Cammy to use her legs again. Maybe even walk." Meg set her hand on Vance's shoulder. "What's wrong with at least getting a free consultation?"

Long, tense moments passed, then Vance looked her way. "If I agree to do this, you know Cammy will get her hopes up. And what if it doesn't work? Why should I shatter my daughter's dreams of walking again? Part of being a kid is having idealistic views about the future. Why should I destroy them by taking her to doctors who'll just say the same thing the doctors here in Stanford have said?"

"Because there is a good chance they might say something different." Meg didn't want to argue with him. "Just think it over, all right?"

He let the literature balance on his left leg, and Meg noticed the stubborn set to his jaw.

"Kent agreed that Cammy might be a good candidate for the devices."

"Kent?" Vance whipped his gaze at her. "Who asked him?"

Meg detected a note of jealousy in his voice, even though Vance struggled to keep his tone calm and even. "He's Cammy's phys ed teacher, and he's got a background in PT."

Vance gathered up the material. "Let's drop this subject, okay?"

"Won't you at least think it over?"

Without a word, he stood. Meg did the same and followed him into the kitchen. She watched with a mix of hurt and surprise as he threw the info packet into the garbage.

"Vance?"

"This discussion is over."

She crossed her arms. "Why are you being so hard-headed? It's a free consultation. You won't even consider it?"

"Time to mind your own business, Meg." Vance brushed by her and left the kitchen.

She felt like she'd just been slapped. Immediate tears welled in her eyes. "I thought you and Cammy were my business." She'd spoken the words so softly, she felt sure Vance hadn't heard.

But she'd heard his message loud and clear. *Mind your own business.* His words cut deep.

She flicked her gaze around the kitchen, the baking dish and saucepan in the sink along with plates, silverware, glasses, and coffee mugs. She always cleaned up the supper dishes. Vance usually offered to help. Tonight, however, she wasn't going to clean up his kitchen. He could do it himself. She wasn't some sort of hireling, but that's how he'd just made her feel. *Mind your own business.*

She was good enough to prepare a meal for him, but not worthy enough to have her ideas and opinions considered.

Meg glanced at the cupboards and then her gaze moved upward to the kitchen's pretty little border. Those four words also told Meg that she'd never completely have Vance's heart.

Having just part of it wouldn't be enough for her.

She walked through the dining room and collected her purse. She slung its skinny leather strap over her shoulder. Vance sat statue-still, staring at a television commercial for deodorant soap. Couldn't he even look at her? He might try apologizing. That'd be a start to a healthy discussion.

Nothing.

Without a word, Meg left his house, got in her car, and drove back to Miracle. Vance didn't even make an attempt to stop her from leaving.

* * * * *

Vance hated the way Meg left. He hated himself for not begging her to stay. She'd only been trying to help. She loved Cammy—and hadn't he been hoping and praying to meet someone who'd love his little girl like she was her own?

Sitting forward on the couch, Vance put his head in his hands and thought over their conversation. While the free consultation idea might sound good to Meg and that musclehead Kent Baldwin, it ran contrary to the very grain of Vance's soul. Medical procedures involved risk. What would happen if he'd lose Cammy? In the span of three short years he'd lost Angie and both his parents. There was only so much losing a man could take.

As for those wacky medical devices, he wasn't interested. They sounded like some newfangled gadget on a TV infomercial, and he certainly wasn't about to allow his daughter to be some kind of experiment.

Vance's fault was that he didn't bother sharing his feelings with Meg. But he'd been afraid he'd sound weak-minded, wimpy—uneducated. Maybe she'd understand. Maybe she wouldn't. But one thing was sure: Meg hadn't deserved the harsh way in which he'd reacted.

Oh, God, I let my insecurities take over my common sense, and I hurt Meg.

He stood, ambled into the kitchen, and faced the mess. He didn't mind cleaning it up. As for Meg, he'd let the situation cool off tonight and look at things with a level head tomorrow. He'd apologize first thing in the morning. Knowing Meg, she'd be quick to forgive him.

* * * * *

After school, Cammy watched Miss Jorgenson—Meg—as she erased the white board. All the other kids had left, and Daddy would come to pick her up soon. She knew something wasn't right between him and Meg. Daddy acted crabby all weekend, and Meg wasn't smiling and talking to him a lot. She didn't come over on Friday or Saturday, and after church Daddy didn't drive them to the Jorgensons' for Sunday dinner. She didn't come over yesterday, either.

What happened?

"Miss Jorgenson?" Cammy didn't use her first name since they were still at school. "Are you coming over tonight?"

She turned and Cammy thought she looked a little sad. "No, not tonight."

"Are you ever?"

She looked down, then towards the door, and finally back at Cammy. "I don't know."

"Don't you and my daddy love each other anymore?"

"My feelings haven't changed, Cammy."

Uh-oh, Daddy must have done something wrong, wrong, wrong!

But, even if he had, Cammy knew deep inside that he still loved Meg.

"Sometimes people say things they don't mean. Like once a fifth grade boy called me 'the retarded girl in the wheelchair.' He didn't mean it. He just didn't know that I'm not retarded."

"I know, Cammy. I'm aware that people say things they don't mean. I've done it myself."

"If my daddy said something wrong, he can apologize."

"He already has."

"Don't you forgive him?"

"Well, yes. But, as I've told your dad, our misunderstanding, or whatever it is, goes beyond mere words." She shook her head. "I'm sorry, honey, but I can't discuss anymore of this with you."

"But I miss you."

Meg swallowed hard and placed her fingertips on her lips, like she was trying to keep her feelings locked in.

"Please come over. I'll cook. You already know how I make macaroni and cheese."

"The best I've tasted. But, no, I can't come over."

Cammy felt scared inside, thinking Meg wouldn't be Daddy's girlfriend anymore. Then they wouldn't get married and Meg wouldn't be Cammy's new mommy. She'd already imagined what their wedding would be like and how they'd be a happy family together.

And what about her surprise birthday party tomorrow?

"Please, Meg. I mean, Miss Jorgenson."

Before she could answer, Daddy walked through the door. Meg got all nervous and started straightening papers on her desk. "Better pack up, Cammy." She didn't even look up when she spoke.

"Yes, Miss Jorgenson." Cammy looked at Daddy. He placed a kiss on the side of her head.

"Did you have a good day, punkin?"

"No." She stuck out her lower lip and folded her arms real tight. She was mad at both of them.

"We had a fine day." Meg gave her warning, as if Cammy fibbed. But she wasn't fibbing. "How was your day, Vance?"

Meg was pretending to be happy. Cammy could tell.

Daddy put his hands on his hips but didn't say anything right away. He just stared at Meg.

Then, finally, he said something. "You about ready to talk to me now?"

"Sure, if you're ready to choke down your pride."

"Choke it down, Daddy. Hurry!"

A little smile curved Meg's mouth as she lifted her big black school bag and slung its thick straps over her shoulder. "Good night." She headed for the door.

"Wait, Meg, don't go. Please don't go." Each word hurt as it left Cammy's lips. They felt like they were being ripped from her heart. She started crying. "Please don't go. . ."

Daddy knelt beside her wheelchair and set his large hand on Cammy's shoulder. "Shh, punkin."

"Daddy, don't let her go. Please don't let her."

He glanced over his shoulder, and Cammy looked through her tears toward the door.

But Meg was already gone.

Chapter Twenty-five
....

Some birthday.

Meg stood at the back of her empty classroom, watching the rain streaming down the windows. What a lousy day. The worst birthday ever. Mom would probably make a correlation between the dismal weather and birthday and call it "bad karma," but Meg wouldn't know; her mother hadn't called or e-mailed. Meg kept checking her messages. Dad hadn't tried to reach her, either. And this morning Grams didn't so much as utter a single "happy birthday" as she poured their coffee.

Meg felt forgotten. Worse, she still felt wounded by what happened between her and Vance.

Turning from the windows, Meg's gaze fell on Cammy's seat. She hadn't been in school this morning, and when Meg checked with the office, she was told that Vance phoned in the absence saying Cammy had a doctor's appointment.

Had she been so distraught last night that she'd had to see a physician and miss school? Meg couldn't bear the thought. She shouldn't have made such a hasty exit yesterday while Cammy was in tears, but she'd been upset herself, and Vance had done nothing to comfort either one of them.

And now, it appeared, he wasn't returning her calls.

Fine. She'd just keep trying to reach him.

She walked around her desk and plucked her cell phone from her purse, which she'd tucked inside her larger school bag. For the fourth time today, she pressed in Vance's phone number and, once more, got his voice messaging system. Again, she left a message.

Then she pushed the END key and dropped her phone back inside her bag, unconcerned that it missed her purse and landed among her papers and other school supplies.

Seconds later, Kent walked in. "Still here? It's after four."

"I'm just getting ready to leave." She felt his stare as she zipped her bag.

"Why such a heavy frown?" Kent strode farther into the room and perched himself on the edge of Meg's desk.

"I'm worried about Cammy."

"Cammy?" Concern marred his blond brows. "What's going on?"

"I don't know. That's just it. She wasn't in school today. The office noted a doctor's appointment. I don't believe it was pre-scheduled, and I can't get a hold of Vance."

"Hmm. Well, I'm sure it's nothing."

"No, Kent, it's *something*." Meg felt her throat constrict with day-long suppressed emotion, but she did her best to gulp it down.

"Meg? What is it? You can tell me. We're friends."

She thought she could use a friend right now. "Remember that University of Kentucky Children's Hospital Web site?"

Kent nodded. "I remember it well."

"I requested information and gave it to Vance, but he wouldn't even consider the idea of taking Cammy in for a free eval. And then—" She waved a hand in the air, wishing she could dismiss the whole thing from existence. "Well, there's that issue, along with some others, which Vance and I can't seem to agree on. There's a rift between us, Cammy noticed the distance, and last night she got really upset. Unfortunately, I was too upset myself to be of any consolation."

"Why, Meg, you make it sound as if it's over between you and Vance."

"You mean our relationship?" She tossed her hands in the air. "Who knows? I feel so confused. I also feel terrible, thinking I might have had a hand in emotionally bruising Cammy."

"Bruises heal, and Cammy is a resilient little girl."

Meg couldn't argue, but the remark didn't make her feel any better. She abhorred the thought of Cammy getting bruised in any way, shape, or form.

Several moments of silenced lapsed.

"Something else bothering you?"

She lifted one shoulder in a half-shrug. "Well, yes, if you must know, it's my birthday and no one remembered." It sounded childish to her own ears, but the whole caboodle made for one heap of misery.

"Your birthday?" Kent brought his cleft chin back in surprise. "Why didn't you say so?"

"Because I didn't want anyone to make a fuss—except, the people I care about should have known. Does that make sense?"

"Sort of." Kent arched one brow. "Meg, I think you need a night out. Let's drive into Lexington. We'll have dinner, champagne."

"Kent, I—"

He lifted a hand as if anticipating her refusal. "Nothing romantic. It'll just be two friends enjoying a night out, celebrating a birthday." His smile appeared both easy and sincere. "Besides, I could use some fun myself. I've been working overtime here at school trying to organize the boys' soccer team, and my plans for Thanksgiving fell through." His tone took a rueful dip. "I had hoped to fly back to Minnesota and see my kids, but that didn't work out. My ex-wife is bent on revenge, and she's keeping my children from me. Needless to say, it makes for a lonely holiday."

Meg usually wasn't a sucker for a sob story, but for whatever reason, this one plucked a sympathetic chord with her. Perhaps because she felt so hurt herself.

"All right, let's go out."

Kent's countenance brightened. "Great."

"As friends."

"Purely platonic." He stood. "We'll take my car. Ready to go?"

"Ready."

Meg followed him out of the classroom, turning off the lights and locking the door behind her. In the parking lot she stopped by her Civic. After extracting her small purse, she tossed her school bag into the backseat.

Leah hailed them from across the lot. "See y'all later."

Meg waved and watched her climb into the four-door sedan. Her father sat behind the wheel, ready to drive them to the airport to meet Dave.

"Good luck tonight."

Leah waved back.

Meg had to smile. She could practically feel her friend's exuberance.

"Let's go, Meg." Kent tugged on her elbow. "I don't enjoy standing out in the rain."

"Me neither."

Together they scurried to his Corvette and climbed inside. As he started the engine, Kent began to sing. "'Kentucky rain keeps falling dow-ow-own.'"

Meg smiled. "Not bad, but you're no Elvis."

"Alas, the story of my life."

"Right."

Her smile grew as he accelerated out of the parking lot, and she thought maybe this wouldn't be such a rotten birthday after all.

* * * * *

Every clock in Loretta's house suddenly announced the time: nine p.m. She stopped her pacing of the kitchen floor long enough to glance at Tom. "I can't imagine where Meg could be." She'd only said that a million times since six thirty, when Meg was supposed to have arrived.

But she was nowhere to be found. The guests arrived, waited, ate at Loretta's insistence, and then left. Only Vance, Tom—and Meg's mother, Tricia—remained.

Tricia!

Loretta stared through the patio doors to the screen porch, where her former daughter-in-law inhaled deeply of her cigarette. What a stink her arrival caused. Imagine flying all the way from Arizona for Meg's birthday and not telling a living soul you're coming!

"Guess the surprise is on us, eh?"

Loretta glanced back at Tom. Once again he'd read her thoughts. "I'm getting worried. Do you think Meg got wind of her mama's coming to Miracle and took off someplace?"

Tom leaned his back up against the counter. "Meg wouldn't run. She's not afraid of her mother, although, I gotta say, the woman is a formidable creature."

They both looked out onto the porch once more and then at each other.

Vance entered the kitchen. "I tried Meg again. Don't know why she's not answering her cell."

"I'm worried." Loretta couldn't help repeating herself.

"We're all worried, Retta." Tom rubbed his whiskery jaw. He, indeed, appeared as troubled as she felt.

Tricia slid open the patio doors and stepped into kitchen. She was dressed in faded blue jeans that might as well have been painted on, and a brown-beaded, long-sleeved shirt that hugged the rest of her slim body. In Loretta's opinion, she resembled the likes of a teenager with that burgundy-colored hair hanging past her shoulders and those bangs in her eyes. Who'd guess, unless they looked real close into her face and saw the lines of time, that the woman was pushing fifty?

"I called Meg. Still no answer." She glared at Loretta, Tom, and Vance. "I want to know where my baby is."

"We'd tell you if we had a clue." Loretta pulled out a chair and lowered her weary frame into it.

"She probably got bored silly and realized I've been right all along: It was a mistake for her to move out here. Meg's got a lot of living to do. No offense, but a girl gets stifled here in Miracle."

"On the contrary." Loretta squared her shoulders. "Meg is perfectly happy here, Tricia. She's got a good job, friends. . ."

"Oh, yeah? Then where is she?"

Loretta just couldn't imagine.

"And just so you know, I plan to do everything in my power to convince Meg to go home with me. The plane ticket is her birthday present. She'll jump at the chance to leave. You just watch. I didn't go through all the trouble of leaving this little nothing town and showing her the wonders and opportunities in the world just so she could come back and fall in love with some—*hillbilly.*"

From out of the corner of her eye, Loretta saw Vance shift his stance. Loretta grimaced, thinking Tricia always did know how to chop a man to pieces with that razor-sharp tongue of hers.

A knock sounded at the front door, and before Loretta could stand to her feet, Vance had answered it. Leah Lawton and a man in army fatigues stepped into the house.

"Hi, everyone. This is Sergeant Dave Spears."

He smiled a greeting before setting down a large, brightly wrapped gift on the coffee table, right next to the twenty-seven fat red roses that Vance had purchased for Meg.

Leah made the introductions and, in turn, Loretta introduced Tricia. Poor Leah looked so shocked, a body could've knocked her over with a feather.

"Meg's mom? Wow. Nice to meet you." Recovering, she glanced around the room. "So, where's the birthday girl anyway? Is the party over already?"

"Party never started." Vance kneaded the back of his neck. "Meg never showed."

"What? But I saw her after school. She and Kent left in his car. I just assumed he was distracting her for an hour or two until it was time for the party."

"Kent?" Loretta pushed her brows together in consternation. "Kent Baldwin? Why, I didn't think to invite him. Meg's not particularly fond of the man."

"Oh, boy, then I spoke out of turn." Leah grimaced. "I mentioned the party to Kent days ago. I mean, we're all friends. I just took it for granted that—" Her gaze slid to Vance. Glimpsing his smoldering expression, as Loretta did also, she swallowed the rest of her explanation.

"So let me get this straight." Vance's tone sounded soft, restrained. "Baldwin knew about the party, and Meg left Fairview with him. But they never showed up here." He nodded. "Hmm. I'm beginning to get the picture."

"Now, Vance, Meg wouldn't choose going somewhere with him over a party with us." Loretta couldn't imagine it.

"But Meg didn't know about the surprise party." He crossed his arms and leaned against the corner of the wall.

"You're right. She didn't. We've all been so careful not to breathe a word about it—"

"Even Cammy didn't spill the beans, which is pretty amazing." In spite of the situation, he grinned.

Loretta lowered herself onto the sofa. Tom stoked the glowing embers in the fireplace and then sat down beside her.

Leah found a place in the armchair, while Dave claimed a seat on the large, square ottoman.

"Listen, I have no idea what you're all talking about or *who* you're talking about." Tricia lifted her purse off the end table and tossed her head. "And I'm far too tired to figure it out. I'm going back to the Holiday Inn Express in Danville. When Meg shows up, I expect a phone call."

Tricia stomped out of the house.

The room felt silent.

Inching forward, Tom cleared his throat. "So, Sergeant Dave, what do you think of Kentucky so far?"

* * * * *

After an enjoyable meal at an upscale Italian restaurant, Meg and Kent walked back to his place. The rain had stopped hours ago, so they had decided to leave Kent's Corvette parked at the condo and walk to the restaurant. He'd wanted to shower and change clothes before dinner, and Meg thought it was a reasonable enough request. While she waited, she roamed his new digs, smiling at the colorful metal bunk beds he'd erected for his kids in the second bedroom and admiring the grand piano in the living room. Next, she'd settled into the plush white sofa and paged through a finance magazine while trying not to think about Vance or worry about Cammy.

Kent took her hand now as they crossed the lot of the Fayette Center, a large shopping and restaurant complex, but she pulled out of his grasp. She'd been thwarting his advances all night, and it was starting to get old.

"Did you enjoy your meal?"

"Yes. It was excellent."

"And the champagne?"

Meg arched a brow. Kent had consumed almost the entire bottle by himself. Still, he'd gone out of his way to make Meg's birthday special, and she appreciated it.

But she'd still rather be with Vance right now.

They jogged across the wide, busy avenue, heading for the

condominium complex in which Kent lived. It was conveniently located across the street from the mall. Taking in her brightly lit surroundings, Meg noted a coffee shop down the block and a twenty-four-hour restaurant on the corner.

"I see you no longer have to pass the *tar store* when you want your morning java."

"Darntootin' I don't."

She grinned at his retort.

Within minutes, they stood at Kent's front entrance. He fumbled with his keys and Meg realized he was intoxicated. Next she wondered just how drunk he was and how long it would take until it wore off enough for him to drive her home.

He unlocked the door, allowing her to step into his condo first.

"How about a nightcap?" He moved toward the portable bar at one end of the expertly decorated room.

"How about some coffee?" She eyed him, watching his every move. He wasn't swaggering or slurring his speech. Maybe he hadn't consumed as much alcohol as Meg thought.

But despite her suggestion, Kent poured himself a brandy.

"I need to get home."

"Let's allow our food to digest a while first."

"Half hour. Tops."

"Okay."

Meg sat on the couch and pulled one leg beneath her.

"Did you have fun tonight?" He lowered himself down beside her.

"I had a very nice time. Thanks for dinner."

"Happy birthday." He leaned over and kissed her, but Meg turned in time so his lips touched her cheek.

"Will you quit already?"

He chuckled.

"Friends, remember?"

"That was a *friendly* kiss."

She couldn't help a laugh as she rolled her eyes. "You're pathetic, you know that?"

"And you have a beautiful smile."

She regarded him with skepticism. "Thanks."

He downed the brandy, then set his empty glass on the table. He lazed back, and within seconds Meg found herself wrapped in his arms. One hand moved down her back, the other roved upward. "You're a lovely woman."

His mouth sought hers, but Meg managed to slide out of his embrace. She stood, feeling a little breathless from the rush of defenses.

Now she was angry. "You jerk. You promised you'd keep your hands to yourself."

"I did no such thing."

"Maybe not with those exact words." She pointed an accusatory finger at him. "But we agreed this wasn't a date. We went out as *friends*."

Kent pushed to his feet and stepped toward her, unbuttoning his white collared shirt. "I've wanted you from the day I met you."

She shook her head. "Back off."

He held his arms out in a helpless gesture. "What's wrong with two friends enjoying each other?"

"It's not real, that's what's wrong. I don't know about you, but I want forever, not a succession of one-night stands."

"Who's to say it won't be 'real' between us? Let's find out." He came nearer, and Meg took a step backward. She didn't feel frightened, just extremely irritated.

And betrayed.

"You know what you're problem is? You're not a promise-keeper, Kent." She suddenly remembered how he'd vowed to speak to Vance

about the new rowing machines at school, but forgot. Cammy had
been so disappointed. It was only much later that Kent finally got around
to discussing the matter. "You only think about your own immediate
gratification and never stop to think about the future and how your
selfish actions might impact others."

"You're wrong. I'm thinking about you right now."

"No. You're thinking about you."

Meg felt a strange sort of déjà vu envelop her. Hadn't she had this
conversation before, but in a different context? With her mother. Years ago.

Meg shook her head. "I want to leave. Now."

Kent regarded her for half a minute as if deciding his next course
of action. Finally, he shrugged. "Sorry, but I can't take you home." His
voice was just above a whisper. "You're going to have to spend the night
with me regardless."

"What?" She blinked in disbelief.

He raked a hand through his blond hair. "I drank too much to get
behind the wheel of my car. I can't afford another DUI. I'll lose my
license. I'll lose my job. And then I'll never get my kids back."

She understood, even respected, the fact he refused to drive while
under the influence. But she noticed that it was still all about him.

"Come on, Meg." He set his hands on his hips. "Why do you think I
insisted we walk to the restaurant and back? It was just a given you'd stay."

"Stupid me. Here I thought you wanted to walk because the rain
stopped and it's a gorgeous, brisk November night."

His broad shoulders rolled with a laugh. He glanced at the white
carpet, then at her once more. Stepping around the couch, he reached
out and allowed his finger to trace her cheek before Meg moved to a
safer distance.

His arm fell to his side. "You're serious about all this 'real' nonsense,
and promises, and the gorgeous, brisk November night, aren't you?"

"Dead serious. Laugh at me all you want to, I don't give a rip." She didn't, either. Her mind was fixed on figuring out how on earth she'd get home from Lexington.

"I'm not laughing, Meg. Not at you, anyway. Your ideals are both commendable and refreshing." His gaze honed in on her. "I can honestly say I've never met anyone quite like you. You're the real deal, that's for sure. Vance Bayer's a lucky guy."

Vance. No, she couldn't call him. He had Cammy to think about and could hardly drop whatever he was doing now, at midnight, and make the forty-five-minute drive to come and get her.

"Years from now, he'll never have to lie awake at night, wondering if you'd been faithful."

"That's sort of the idea behind a *real* and committed relationship, Kent." Meg's temples began to throb. She couldn't call Leah, either. Dave was in town, staying in the Lawtons' guest room, and Leah's folks would never understand if their daughter had to take off suddenly and pick up her friend who'd made a series of unwise choices and stranded herself in the drunken gym teacher's condo in Lexington.

Meg suddenly realized she was in the worst possible situation a woman could ever find herself facing. She hadn't sensed any danger. She had felt that Kent was harmless, that she could adequately defend herself if necessary. But what if he had been more determined? The outcome might have been disastrous.

She instantly regretted letting her guard slip and giving Kent a chance. Hadn't she sensed all along that he was untrustworthy? She should have obeyed her instincts about him.

He left the room and returned minutes later with one of his T-shirts. It had the words *Minnesota Vikings* printed across the front. He handed it to her, then pointed toward his kids' never-before-used bedroom. "You can sleep there, but if you change your mind—"

"I won't."

"Didn't think so."

"And I'm not staying over, Kent." She tossed back his shirt and began digging through her small purse for her cell phone. She'd have to call Grams. If nothing else, Grams would help her think of a respectable solution. After all, she couldn't very well ride into Stanford in Kent's Corvette at eight in the morning on Thanksgiving Day when her car had been parked in Fairview's lot all night long. Someone, somewhere was sure to see it, and she could only imagine the gossip that would follow.

Now, where was that phone?

She dumped her purse's contents out onto the narrow, glass-top table behind Kent's sofa and rummaged through the items. It was only then that she remembered: She'd dropped the phone into her school bag—which was in the backseat of her car.

Shoot!

Kent had ambled down the short hallway and into his bedroom.

"Hey, can I use your phone?"

"Sure. My cell's in here. Come and get it."

"Yeah, in your dreams, buddy."

He chuckled.

She clenched her jaw, seeing nothing amusing about the situation. She felt suddenly trapped, her back against the wall. Lolling her head back, she stared up at the stark, white ceiling.

Then she closed her eyes. *Lord, what do I do now?*

Chapter Twenty-six

Vance finished his umpteenth cup of coffee, feeling glad he'd arranged for Cammy to stay with Debbie tonight. At first his little girl had been disappointed about missing Meg's surprise birthday party, but after Vance explained that he planned to settle the differences between him and Meg tonight, she was quick to agree to spend the night at her aunt's.

Vance combed his fingers through his hair. Things just couldn't go on this way, Meg not speaking to him, giving him the cold shoulder. He was half out of his mind. He loved her, and he planned to tell her so. He'd also share the news of what happened with Cammy at her consultation today. That'd be the icebreaker.

Now if she'd just come home.

Suddenly every clock in the Jorgenson home sounded, giving Vance more of a jolt than the coffee he'd just drunk. His gaze flew to the mantel clock. Midnight.

"I'm sure Meg will be here any minute now."

Vance nodded at Mrs. Jorgenson while quelling the skepticism that threatened deep inside of him. He trusted Meg completely, but he trusted that macho gym teacher about as far as he could throw him. Which he'd enjoy doing right about now. "I hope you don't mind my hanging around until Meg gets here."

"Of course I don't." She pressed her lips together as she worked her needle and thread in and out of the quilted fabric on her lap. "I'm just sorry tonight was such a catastrophe."

That it was. Vance couldn't argue.

He stood and walked to the kitchen, where he poured himself another cup of coffee. Then he meandered onto the screen porch. The air had a chill to it. He brought the ceramic mug to his lips and tried not to speculate as to what was going on inside Meg's head when she climbed into Baldwin's sports car. He only hoped and prayed she was all right.

He stayed outside until he'd finished drinking his brew. He couldn't handle an ounce more or he'd stay awake until Sunday. As he slid open the patio doors and entered the kitchen, the phone rang. His heart jumped, and he quickened his steps into the living room where Mrs. Jorgenson had lifted the telephone receiver to her ear.

"Meg, where are you?"

Vance's entire body tensed. He held his breath. Wasn't she coming home?

"Oh, my. I see. . .you forgot your cell phone. . ."

Vance rolled his eyes. That explained a lot.

"Oh, yes, you did the right thing. It's not too late to call. . ." Her blue eyes flicked to Vance. "We'll come and get you right away. It's no trouble."

He understood the collective "we."

"Where is she?" He whispered the question.

Mrs. Jorgenson lifted a forefinger as if telling him to be patient. "Now, let me get this straight, hon. You're at the Denny's, across from the Fayette Mall. . ."

Vance felt his gaze widen in surprise. He knew where the mall was located. He'd find the restaurant easy enough. But what was she doing way over there?

"Stay put and stay safe. We'll be there as soon as we can." Mrs. Jorgenson hung up and turned to Vance. "Seems she went out to dinner with Kent and he drank too much—can't drive her home."

Vance's world reeled as he imagined what might have happened if the guy had gotten behind the wheel of his sports car. Losing Meg in another senseless drunk driving tragedy? Unthinkable.

"To Kent's credit, he refused to get behind the wheel in his state, and Meg, of course, refused to spend the night at his place. So she's in need of a ride home."

Vance extracted his keys from his jeans pocket. "I'm on my way."

* * * * *

Meg sipped her coffee, trying to quell the jackhammer in her head. It seemed that all the tension of the last week, combined with tonight's fiasco, converged to result in one fine headache.

She massaged her temples while keeping watch out the window for either Grams' or Tom's car. When Grams had said, "we'll be there," Meg presumed Tom would be with her. At least, Meg hoped that was the case; she disliked the thought of Grams driving all this way by herself in the dark.

What a mess this whole night turned out to be.

She took another sip of coffee and looked at the door in time to see Vance walk in. She felt herself stiffen. What was he doing here? Where was Cammy? Was she in the hospital?

Before Meg could slide out of the green vinyl booth, he scooted in beside her.

"Is Cammy all right?"

He appeared puzzled by the question. "She's fine. She's with my sister tonight."

"She's not sick? The school office said she had a doctor's appointment. I've been worried all day."

Vance's featured relaxed. "We'll talk about Cammy's doctor's visit later." He considered her, searching her face while rubbing his thumb and fingers along the sides of his beard. "But first, would you mind telling me just what you were thinking tonight when you left Fairview with Kent Baldwin?"

"What do you mean? It was—well, it was my birthday and since it didn't appear I had anything to do, and no one to spend it with, he offered to take me out to celebrate."

"Hmm."

"Nothing happened, Vance. We're just friends." She paused. "Were. We *were* friends. The guy's a total jerk." Meg massaged her temples. "Got any aspirin?"

"Might be a bottle out in the truck. Don't tell me you're nursing a hangover already."

"Not even close." She took another drink of coffee. "So how is it that you came to pick me up, anyway?"

"I'm a little hurt you called your grandma first and not me."

"I thought Cammy was sick, and I knew you couldn't just up and leave her."

"Well, that's true, but—" Vance shifted and draped one arm around her shoulders. "I'd try to move heaven and earth for you, Meg."

She could see in his eyes that he meant every word. An instant later, she regretted the circumstances that kept them apart for the last several days. Placing her hands on either side of his face, she kissed him long and deep.

"Happy birthday."

"Thanks, but it's been a rotten day."

"Well, it didn't have to be. It just so happens that your grandmother had a surprise party all planned with food and cake and a houseful of folks. Only problem was, the birthday girl never showed up."

Meg felt her heart drop. "No way."

Vance nodded.

"I didn't think anyone remembered."

"Oh, we remembered. All your friends were there, including Leah and Dave." Vance smiled. "Seems like a nice guy."

Meg felt completely crestfallen.

"Your dad, stepmom, brother, and sister came, too, but they left just as soon as your mother arrived. Most folks did, actually."

"What?" Meg blinked and her heart missed a beat. "My mother? She's in town? Grams invited her?"

"No, she crashed the party, and I can honestly say, Meg, that you and your mama are as different as the night is to the day. I saw it firsthand. Everyone did."

But Meg was still recovering from her shock. "Mom's in town."

Vance hugged her around the shoulders. "You'll never have to worry about anyone comparing you to her again."

Meg felt grateful for that much. "Things really do happen for a reason, don't they?" Word would get around, and everyone would soon know that Meg Jorgenson wasn't about to follow in her mother's footsteps.

"Well, it seems your mother's bought you a plane ticket home as a birthday gift."

"Home? But I am home!"

Vance removed his arm and regarded Meg with a pointed gaze. "She said she doesn't want you falling in love with some Kentucky hillbilly."

"Too late." Meg couldn't help teasing him.

Vance smiled.

"I do love you, Vance." Meg slipped her hand into his. "I never realized it more than I did tonight. We've got something very special between us. Something rare and precious. Something *real*."

Softness entered his hazel eyes, and his expression turned somber. "You're right. We do. And—" He gave her hand a squeeze. "I love you more than I can say, Meg." Leaning forward, he pressed a kiss on her lips.

"You really love me?"

"Can't you tell?"

"I'll never replace Angie."

"You don't have to." Vance lowered his gaze for a moment and seemed to gather his thoughts. "I realized that what's between us, Meg, can become every bit as wonderful and powerful as my relationship with Angie was, and yet it's different, because you and Angie are different people. And that's okay."

Meg smiled. "You just gave me the most perfect birthday present ever."

"Well, that's not all I have for you." Vance grinned, and there was a twinkle in his eyes. He threw a couple of bucks onto the table. "Come on, let's get out of here." He pulled her from the booth. "I want to tell you all about Cammy's doctor's appointment on the way home. Talk about a *miracle.*"

* * * * *

With the turkey stuffed and seasoned, Loretta slid the roasting pan into the oven. No telling what the day would bring, what with Tricia being in town.

She stifled a yawn. Meg and Vance had literally stayed awake all night, sitting in the living room and talking. From her bedroom, Loretta had heard bits and pieces, although she tried not to eavesdrop. But a body couldn't help it in this small house.

She smiled and closed the oven door. They loved each other. Why, the fact was plain as day and had been for some time. And Meggie said she had no intentions of going anywhere with her mother. Said that this morning when Loretta made a pot of coffee. Miracle was her home.

The back door creaked open and then banged shut. Tom ambled into the kitchen.

"G'morning, Retta." He eyed her with a frown of concern adding yet another crinkle to his face. "You look tired. Didn't you sleep well?"

She wiped her hands on her apron. "I slept in short intervals." She smiled. "Vance and Meggie decided to make up for lost time and chattered the night away. They did their best to be quiet, but every so often I'd hear a laugh or footsteps in the hallway, and I'd wake up." Loretta poured Tom a cup of coffee. "But that's all right. I really didn't mind one single bit."

"And you're still thinking of a big Thanksgiving Day meal?"

"Well, yes, but later. Paul and Ryan are hunting, and Lord only knows what'll happen with Tricia. Meggie met her for breakfast this morning. I hope she's got her wits about her. That girl's been up all night, and that mother of hers has tricks up her sleeve."

Tom took a noisy slurp before folding his lanky frame into one of the kitchen chairs. "So you think she'll convince Meg to leave town like she said?"

"Not a chance. But it's possible Meg will invite her here for Thanksgiving dinner. She didn't want her mother to spend the holiday alone, so when she mentioned asking her mother over, I told her there's room at the table. And stop scowling at me, you ol' goat. What else could I say?"

Tom seemed to think it over while sucking down more of his coffee. "Well, maybe Tricia won't come."

"Maybe. But if she does, then Paul and Donna won't show. But Ryan and Kelly promised to come. They're not intimidated by Tricia and they love Meg. Speaking of loving Meg, Vance and Cammy will be here. So will Vance's sister and her boyfriend. And last night Leah and Dave said they'd come by later for pie. Leah's folks are stopping by, too."

Tom laughed.

"What's so funny?" Loretta placed her hands on her hips. She raised a stern brow. "Stop your sniveling."

"I can't help it." His bony shoulders shook with each chortle. "One way or the other, Retta, you'll have this house all filled up with folks, just like you wanted. One way or the other."

* * * * *

Just a few breakfast stragglers milled around the lobby of the hotel in which Mom was staying. She hadn't wanted to go out to eat, even though Meg offered to treat. Mom just wanted coffee, so Meg helped herself to the continental fare.

Meg sipped from her glass of orange juice and looked across the table at her mother. "It's Thanksgiving Day. I told Grams I'd invite you to dinner. She said it's fine. Can't you forget your animosity long enough to at least enjoy the holiday? Just this once?"

"Why's it so important to you?" Mom cleared the morning cragginess from her throat. "It's really just another day. Holidays were never a big deal for us."

"I know." Meg took to studying her glass of juice. "Maybe that's why they're important to me now." She glanced back at her mother. "I've really gotten into the whole family thing."

"It's a phase." A knowing look entered her blue-green eyes. "I went through it, too, but it'll pass. Just remember: family ties are the ones that bind and gag."

"I beg to differ."

"Beg all you want. It's true." Mom sipped from her coffee cup. "And if you marry that guy I met last night, you'll regret it."

"Vance?"

"Whatever."

"Mom, I love him, and he's got the sweetest, brightest daughter. She's eight years old." Meg thought of what Vance told her last night.

The news still thrilled her.

There had been a cancellation, and Vance got Cammy in to see a doctor for a consultation at the University of Kentucky Children's Hospital yesterday. More tests needed to be run, but the preliminary report was that surgery wouldn't be needed and that Cammy was a prime candidate for treatment with Neuromuscular Electrical Stimulation Systems. "Mom, listen to this. Cammy was injured in a car accident a few years ago, but now—"

"I don't want to hear about it, and if you think for one minute that I'll want to be a grandmother, you're crazy."

Meg didn't think she understood. "I want to tell you about this exciting news about Cammy. She might walk again."

"Oh, Meg, you don't want to take on someone else's problems. A guy with a kid who can't walk?" Mom shook her head. "Marry him and you'll be sorry." She brushed her maroon hair away from her eyes.

"No, I won't." Meg couldn't quite believe her mother's cold-hearted reaction.

"You'll suffocate in a small town. Just like I did."

Meg shook her head to the contrary. "I'm happy here. In fact, I wish I would have been open-minded enough to get to know Dad and his other family—" She halted. "No, make that *my family*—years ago. They're fun-loving, sweet, decent people."

"Well, there's gratitude for you." Mom sat back hard in her chair. "What am I? Chopped liver?"

"No, of course not, but—"

"But?" She lifted her brows.

"But." Meg squared her shoulders. "You're searching for something that's not really out there." Seeing her mother's look of confusion, she clarified. "Mom, it's like you're digging for gold in a litter box."

"Oh? And you think you've struck it rich here in Hicksville?"

"Yes, I do, because I've found people here who love me in the purest sense of the word. They're not just out to get something from me in return. They care about what happens to me, and now I can be a better person and give right back to them. And to my community."

"They've brainwashed you." Mom looked aghast. "These nuts have brainwashed you."

Meg couldn't hold back the tiny smirk pulling at her mouth. "If you believe that, then I suppose you won't want to hear that I attend Bible studies and go to church. And that *I like it.*"

The living color drained from Mom's face. "This is worse than I thought." She pushed back her chair, stood, and walked to the stainless breakfast counter.

Meg watched her, feeling a sense of remorse for slinging this information at her. But she knew from experience that nothing short of shock got through to her mother.

"Okay, listen." Mom made her way back to the table. "I want to buy you a plane ticket to Arizona. As a birthday gift."

"I don't want it. I'm staying here."

"Maybe getting away for a while would be a good thing. You know, you can think, get your head together."

"It's as together as it's going to get, but thanks anyway. I appreciate the offer."

The muscles around Mom's lips tightened with anger.

Meg didn't want to fight with her. "Mom, it's Thanksgiving. Can we just let bygones be bygones and enjoy the day together? We don't have to spend it at Grams' house if you don't want to. We can find something else to do."

Mom's hardened expression didn't change. "Forget it. And just know this, Meg: no daughter of mine will live in Miracle, Kentucky, or anywhere near it. I worked hard to get us out of here. If you stay, you're committing an unpardonable sin against me, my very person, and I'll never forgive you." She grabbed her purse and stormed from the lobby.

For several long moments, Meg couldn't breathe. She felt crushed by the weight of her mother's ultimatum. And, yet, there wasn't anything to deliberate. Meg had made her choice a long, long time ago.

Chapter Twenty-seven

Two weeks later, an unusual cold snap moved through Central Kentucky and snowflakes wafted on the frosty, Friday afternoon air. Loretta bent to place the folded "heart and soul" Queenie under the Christmas tree. Wrapped in white tissue paper with a fat, pink satin bow, it made for an inviting gift. She'd watch Meggie open it on Christmas Eve when the rest of the family came for dinner after the five o'clock Christmas service. Loretta was just glad she'd finished Meg's quilt, and with time to spare, too.

"You all set, Retta?"

She swung around when Tom entered the room. "Yes, I am."

"I gotta taste for that country fried steak the Depot Restaurant serves up."

"Sounds good to me." She fetched her coat from out of the closet.

"Heard from Meg?"

"Saw her this morning. She thought maybe we'd see her, Vance, and Cammy tonight at supper."

"Good, good." Tom gave a thoughtful nod. "They sure make a fine couple—Meg and Vance, I mean."

"Yes, they do."

"Think Vance'll pop the question soon?"

"I suspect so."

The clocks all went off, marking the half hour.

"Time's a-wasting. We'd best go if you want to get a seat. You know how crowded the Depot gets on Friday nights."

"You're right." Loretta turned back to Tom. He stood there, all dressed up in a multi-colored sweater that hung over black denim trousers. He looked real nice, and she appreciated his effort.

She smiled and stepped closer to him. "Did I ever tell you that you're my best friend?"

"Don't have to. I already know."

She put her hands on either side of his wrinkly face and planted a kiss square on his mouth.

Tom turned as red as a beet.

Laughter bubbled up inside her as she walked to the door.

"Retta?" His voice took on a sudden somberness. "Some folks in town wonder how come you and me don't get married."

She paused to think it over before pivoting to face him again. "Maybe it's because you never asked me."

"Well, I would." He rubbed his jaw, looking uncomfortable. "But marriage is an awful big step."

"Yes, it is, and you're much too young to get tied down."

He snorted at the quip but looked none-too-amused.

"I'm sorry, Tom. Seriously, when the time comes where you feel good and ready, why, then, you just go ahead and propose to me like a regular gentleman."

"Maybe I will."

Loretta thought he looked troubled. She hoped he hadn't felt obligated to bring up the subject of marriage. She truly was happy with things just the way they were.

"Of course, if you should decide to propose to me, there's no guarantee I'll say yes."

He drew his brows together, obviously surprised.

"Now, let's go eat before I faint from hunger."

"Don't boss me, Retta."

"Oh, hush, you ol' cantankerous thing!" She batted a hand at him before donning her winter coat.

Relief washed over his features, as though everything in his world had righted itself.

They walked outside and climbed into his car.

"Just look at those snow flurries, swirling in the air. So pretty." Loretta pulled on her gloves.

Tom started up the engine and smiled at her. "Feels sorta like Christmas already, don't it?"

* * * * *

Meg tried to absorb the sights around her. Blue, red, green, yellow, and white lights blinked on the decorated Christmas tree that filled an entire corner of Grams' living room. Both wrapped and unwrapped presents were scattered about, and friends and family members seemed to fill up the rest of the space. As a girl, Meg used to avoid such get-togethers whenever visiting Dad, and she'd hid herself away somewhere with a book. Now, she thrived on them.

Meg shifted, getting comfy on the sofa. Beside her, Cammy sat opening a gift from Kelly.

"Red high heels with pointy toes!" The child's blue eyes lit up as she inspected the shoes. "Wow!"

Meg laughed and eyed her sister, who wore an amused grin of her own.

"They're too big for you right now. They're for when you can walk again."

A happy smile curved Cammy's pink lips.

"Maybe they'll fit by the time you go to your first homecoming dance."

"Yeah!"

Kelly stood from where she sat on the floor and hugged Cammy.

Sitting on the other side of Meg, Vance cleared his throat.

Kelly gave him a sheepish look. "That is, if your dad allows you to go to homecoming, of course."

"I don't know. I've seen how y'all behave at those homecoming dances." Meg ribbed him with her elbow.

Vance laughed. "Okay, well, good thing there's time to think about that one."

"Thank you, Kelly." Cammy put the lid on the shoebox and handed it to Meg, who added it to the child's ever-growing pile of gifts near the coffee table.

"Wow! Look what I got!"

"Me, too!"

Meg smiled at her twin cousins, who waved handheld video games in their palms.

"Thanks, Uncle Paul." Both redheaded boys spoke in unison.

"Can I see your games?" Cammy craned her neck around Kelly.

"How about after you finish here? You've got more of your own gifts to open." Meg handed her another one.

Cammy's expression lit with excitement as she tore into another present. "This is the best Christmas ever. I never got so many presents before in my whole life."

Meg had to admit the little darling was certainly making a haul. American Girl clothes for the doll her grandma Liz had given her; Hannah Montana books and CD; a board game from Dad and Donna; and all kinds of clips and barrettes for her hair from Leah.

Cammy remembered her manners and thanked everyone for their generosity.

Then came the very special gift from Grams.

"You sewed this just for me?" Cammy gaped as she ran her hand over the beautiful Queenie with all kinds of shoes printed in the fabric. "Thank you, thank you, thank you, Mrs. Jorgenson!"

"You're very welcome, honey."

Meg opened her own gift from Grams, too, and fingered the expertly stitched, multicolored quilt. She unfolded it to get a better view of the pattern. Every other square was either a heart or a cross, except for the four middle squares, which spelled out the word "LOVE" in a diamond shape.

"Oh, Grams, this is lovely."

"And it's you: all heart 'n soul." Grams' eyes lit with sincerity.

Meg held the Queenie to her chest. "I'll treasure it for the rest of my life. Thank you."

The doorbell rang, and when Leah entered, both Meg and Vance stood. They left Cammy in the company of Kelly, who, over the past months, had unofficially adopted her as a little sister.

"Merry Christmas!" Meg wrapped her arms around her friend, then helped her out of her coat and hung it in the closet.

Leah's cheeks were pink from a nip in the December wind. "Look what Dave bought me." She held out her narrow wrist and showed off the silver bangle. "He had it sent to me from overseas. Wasn't that thoughtful?"

"He's an okay guy." Vance gave her a thumbs-up, and Leah's face turned fuchsia.

Meg stood by smiling. Everyone liked Dave, and Leah's father didn't have any more reservations about the man.

"Come on in, Leah. Would you like some eggnog?"

At Leah's nod, Meg led the way into the dining room, where an array of foods, from thick slices of country ham and angel biscuits to bourbon balls, had been set out on the table for all to enjoy.

Vance poured eggnog into a short glass and handed it to Leah. "Yep, I think any guy who gives a woman jewelry at Christmastime oughta to be commended."

"Oh, I commended him." Leah laughed and took a sip. "The best I could by e-mail, anyway."

Wearing a grin, Vance lifted a decorated tray filled with candy canes. There were thirteen of them, and each came with a note card, tied with a red ribbon, on which passages of Scripture detailing the Christmas story had been printed. "Time to pass these out." He nodded toward the living room. "Come on."

Meg and Leah followed. He handed out the candy while Dad got everyone's attention.

"These here aren't just regular candy canes." He smiled at the kids and turned the cane upside down. "Now it's a J for Jesus, and y'all know it's His birth we're celebrating on Christmas. And see these red stripes on the candy? The Bible says that by His stripes we are healed. Jesus died and rose again and everyone who believes in Him will join Him in heaven one day. Now ain't that happy news?"

The children nodded.

"So when you eat this candy cane, you remember that, now." He shifted his stance and gazed around the room. "Let's commence reading the Christmas story. Some of you were lucky enough to get a candy cane with a number on it, eight through twenty." He turned to Grams. "I believe you go first, Mama."

" 'The Gospel of Luke, chapter two verse eight: And there were in the same country shepherds abiding in the field, keeping watch over their flock by night.'"

One by one, people read from their cards.

Cammy was the last one to read. "And the shepherds returned, glorifying and praising God for all the things that they had heard and seen, as it was told unto them."

A moment's pause, as everyone's hearts seemed touched by what they'd heard.

Then Dad spoke up again. "Well, now, there's supposed to be one more." He glanced around the room until his gaze found Meg. "Meggie, I believe it was on your candy cane."

She shook her head, holding up her cane, noting nothing of significance.

"Oh, my bad. I gave her the wrong one." Vance reached into his shirt pocket and pulled out another red and white candy cane.

She took the proffered candy but didn't see anything special about this one, either—until Vance let go of the white ribbon. There, dangling from a loop in the bow, was a diamond engagement ring.

Hoops of laughter, giggles, and cheers suddenly filled the room. Cammy clapped her hands. Leah smiled with tears in her eyes.

Meg felt like the wind had been knocked out of her. She couldn't breathe. Her face flamed with embarrassment and her heart swelled with joy.

Vance got down on one knee. "Marry me?"

"Yes." She could barely eke out the word, but she didn't even have to think about the answer.

He laughed and stood, then enfolded her in his arms. Meg just wanted to hide in his embrace. How utterly embarrassing.

"Meg, you are, like, so fun to tease." Ryan's voice rose above the din. "You walk right into everything. It's great."

"Aren't you surprised, Meg?" Cammy's face was flushed from all the excitement.

"Oh, I'm surprised, all right." She stepped back. "I guess I'm not used to hanging out with such pranksters." She shot a glance at Vance.

"This is no prank, Meg." With one arm still looped around her shoulders, he half-hugged her to him. "I want you to be my wife."

"I knew it! I knew it! I knew it!" Cammy was cheering from the couch. "Me and Jesus had it planned all along."

Vance stared at his daughter and raised a brow.

"Speaking of pranksters." Grams gave each of her three sons a pointed stare. "I was always the target of one joke or another."

At that precise moment, her clock collection rang and sang, and everyone laughed all over again.

Sometime later, when the activity in the house died down, Meg and Vance walked Leah outside to her car. The cold air felt refreshing as it filled Meg's lungs.

"Oh, I almost forgot!" Leah began to dig in her purse. "Kent told me to give you something."

"Kent?" Meg crossed her arms. She hadn't been on speaking terms with him since her birthday.

"He left yesterday. You know he resigned from Fairview, right?"

"No, I didn't." Meg was stunned to hear the news. "He left? Right in the middle of the school year? The kids are going to be so sad."

"I know. But—" Leah pulled out an envelope and handed it to Meg. "Kent got a better job offer in Orlando and somehow got out of his contract here."

"So he moved to Florida?" Standing next to Meg, Vance leaned one arm on Leah's car and set his other hand on his hip. "That's a long ways from Minnesota. I thought he had kids up there."

"He does, but he can't get visitation rights and he's never been happy in Kentucky. Besides, all the hills around here were hard on his Corvette."

Meg rolled her eyes.

Leah pulled her coat more tightly around her neck. "If you ask me, he's running from God, but he won't get far. The world is only so big."

"I imagine he's running from something." Meg couldn't seem to help the facetious remark.

She heard Vance's soft chuckle.

"It's too bad, you know. I mean, Kent was always nice to me." Leah sighed. "I never did understand why Dave told me to stay away from him after he met Kent."

"I do." Meg didn't elaborate, as Leah already knew what happened. Instead, she turned the envelope in her hand, inspecting it beneath the far-reaching glow of the yard light. It was business-sized, so it couldn't be a Christmas card, unless it was one of those homemade holiday newsletters.

"Leah, let's get you into your car before we all catch a chill." Vance moved to open her door.

"Good idea."

"Wimps. It's like forty degrees out here. That would be a heat wave this time of year in Chicago."

"It's practically freezing to us Southerners." Leah laughed. "Merry Christmas—and congratulations to both of you." She hugged them both before climbing in and starting up the vehicle's engine.

Meg and Vance waved as she drove off.

"Here, you can read this." Meg handed the envelope to Vance as they made their way back into the house.

In the kitchen, Vance tore into it and read the letter inside. Meg peeked at it and saw the missive was typed out on Baldwin Manufacturing letterhead.

Vance finished and refolded the letter. He looked at Meg and she glimpsed the baffled frown that creased his brows.

"Apparently Kent told his father about Cammy and the electronic medical devices that doctors want to use as part of her new therapy. His father decided she was a worthy cause, and his company donated a healthy sum to the UK Children's Hospital in Cammy's name." Vance shook his head. "Part of me doesn't want to accept it, even though it's a generous gift. The settlement I got years ago will see to Cammy's needs."

"Guess it's up to you, Vance." Meg didn't know what to make of it.

"The letter's addressed to you."

He handed it to her and she skimmed the contents.

"Sounds like it's a done deal." Meg glanced up at him. "That is, the hospital already has the money. This is just notification that it was sent on behalf of Cammy."

Vance squeezed his eyes shut for a second, scratched the back of his head, then shrugged. "I don't know, Meg. Guess it's a nice write-off for Baldwin Manufacturing, but it sure makes me have to swallow down a chunk of my pride. I'm wondering if that was the intention."

"No." Meg honestly didn't think so. She suspected it was a half-baked attempt at an apology, but perhaps his motive wasn't that dubious. "Kent was fond of Cammy, just as he was fond of all the kids at school. Maybe he wanted to help her achieve her dreams, and this is the way he chose to do it."

"Hmm."

Meg slipped her arms around his waist and peered up into his bearded face. "I say we ask Cammy to write a thank-you note to Baldwin Manufacturing and stop speculating about the reason behind the donation."

"All right. I'll go along with that. After all, 'every good and perfect gift comes from above' anyway."

* * * * *

Vance watched with mild trepidation as pediatric neurologist Jason McDonald fitted Cammy with the new medical device designed to help her walk. He knew he shouldn't feel so nervous, but he couldn't seem to help it.

As if she sensed his apprehension, Meg slipped her hand into his.

"This system has been approved by the FDA and is perfectly safe. As for how successful it will be, well, that's up to how hard Cammy works and how much her family's willing to cheer her on."

"I'm a hard worker." Cammy watched the doctor's every move.

"And we're dedicated." Vance gave Meg's hand an affectionate squeeze, then caught his daughter's eye and sent her a wink.

She smiled back. "I can't wait. I can't wait." She moved the upper half of her body so she bounced on the exam room's table.

"Hold still, young lady." The tall, long-limbed physician smiled kindly at Cammy before he adhered two large white pads onto her skin, just above both knees. Then he looked over at Vance and Meg. "Since her nerve endings are still intact, this device should actually enable her body to repair its own nervous system."

"That's totally amazing."

Vance smiled at Meg's reply. He didn't know what he would have done without her these last few weeks. Her positive attitude had never waned, even though he himself had felt doubtful at times. He'd worried that Cammy would end up disappointed and discouraged.

But now they'd arrived at the moment of truth.

"Are you almost done? Can I try to walk now?" Cammy's blue eyes were round and eager.

"As soon as I make a few adjustments. This may take a while. Be patient." Dr. McDonald glanced at her and grinned. He held a dial in his hand. Coated wires ran from it to the patches on Cammy's knees. "I suggest you save your energy for when the physical therapist comes in to help you get on your feet."

"Yes, sir."

Vance hid his amusement. Though Cammy had stopped her wiggling, he could tell she was bursting at the seams with excitement.

After several long minutes, the doctor trained Vance and Meg on the usage of the medical device, and then he summoned two medical assistants and the physical therapist into the room. Cammy was given stainless cane-like supports to grip with each hand, and a safety harness was secured around her waist. All the while, Dr. McDonald explained procedures and processes to Vance and Meg.

Lord, it's by Your grace that my little girl walks. He'd uttered this prayer a thousand times. *Thank You for the wisdom You've lent these doctors—and all the medical staff.*

"I want to walk down the aisle when Daddy and Meg get married." Cammy was like a champion race horse, chomping at the bit.

"We'll do our best to see that you do." Dr. McDonald smiled. "Just relax."

Before long Cammy was on her feet. More adjustments were made. And then—

Vance watched in awe as her right foot inched forward.

Then her left foot inched forward.

Sheer joy spread across Cammy's face. "I'm walking! I'm walking! I'm walking!"

Epilogue

....

"Vance, hurry up. I'm feeling a little carsick with this blindfold on." Meg clutched her rounded mid-section as the van went up and down the hilly road and rounded a bend. She had to keep swallowing hard so she didn't lose the grilled hamburger and potato salad she'd eaten at the Owens' Labor Day picnic.

It was hard to believe a year had flown by since she first met Vance and Cammy.

"We're almost there." She felt Vance reach over and take hold of her upper arm. "Hang in there, all right?"

"I'll make no promises."

He chuckled in reply.

"Hurry, Daddy, I can't wait to see the surprise."

"Just a minute more, punkin."

It seemed like more than "a minute" before Vance rolled the vehicle to a stop. "Don't look just yet. Keep your eyes covered. Both of you."

Meg heard him get out. "What do you think it is, Cammy?"

"I think he bought me a pony and you a horse!"

"You think?"

"Yep."

Meg envisioned herself, six months pregnant and riding horseback. She laughed. "I don't think I could mount a horse right even if we found a crane to hoist me into the saddle."

Vance opened their doors and helped Meg from the van before lowering Cammy to the ground. Although she could walk now—and was getting better at it each day—there were still plenty more times she required the use of her wheelchair.

Vance looped Meg's arm around his elbow and pushed Cammy's chair over bumpy ground. As they stepped forward, Meg felt long grass tickling her ankles and legs.

"Where are you leading us, Vance?"

"Just a few more feet and you can look."

"There's no snakes around here, are there?"

"Tons of 'em."

Meg felt herself stiffen.

Cammy giggled. "He's just teasing, Mommy."

"Hmm." If not for the blindfold, Meg would be giving Vance one of her sharp glances right about now.

"Okay. Count to ten and then you can both take off your blindfolds."

Meg and Cammy began counting. "One, two, three, four, five, six, seven, eight, nine, TEN!"

Meg peeled off the folded bandana that Vance had tied around her eyes before they left the Owens' farm. She blinked until her eyes focused. Cammy did the same. Together they stared out over grassy pasture that was surrounded by steep, wooded hills.

Vance stood in the middle of it with his arms opened wide. "What do you think?"

"It's pretty countryside."

"Where's my pony, Daddy?"

"Well—" He cantered across the pasture. "Once we build the stable, we'll keep him in here."

"Yay!"

Meg frowned, puzzled. A stable?

"The house will be here." Again Vance jogged across the field.

"The house?" Meg felt her knees growing weaker. They'd talked about building a house, but she thought it was only a fantasy.